MADAME
BUROVA

RUTH HOGAN

TWO
ROADS

First published in Great Britain in 2021 by Two Roads
An Imprint of John Murray Press
An Hachette UK company

1

Copyright © Ruth Hogan 2021

A CIP catalogue record for this title is
available from the British Library

Hardback ISBN 978 1 529 37331 8
Trade Paperback ISBN 978 1 529 37332 5
eBook ISBN 978 1 529 37334 9
Audio Digital Download ISBN 978 1 529 37335 6

Typeset in Stone Serif by Hewer Text UK Ltd, Edinburgh
Printed and bound in Great Britain by Clays Ltd, Elcograf S.p.A.

John Murray policy is to use papers that are natural, renewable
and recyclable products and made from wood grown in sustainable
forests. The logging and manufacturing processes are expected to
conform to the environmental regulations of the country of origin.

Two Roads
Carmelite House
50 Victoria Embankment
London EC4Y 0DZ

www.tworoadsbooks.com

MADAME
BUROVA

To Jean and Peter Hogan
Mum and Dad
I love you

Never tell a secret, never tell a lie
If you break a promise you will surely die
Say your prayers at bedtime, God forgive your sin
Then when you get to heaven the angels let you in

The Promise

Madame Burova was a woman who knew where the bodies were buried. She had spent a lifetime keeping other people's secrets and her silence had come at a price. Some revelations – forbidden affairs and minor indiscretions – had been easy enough to bear. Like feathers on the wind. But others, dark and disturbing, had pricked her conscience and been a burden on her soul. She had seen the lovers and the liars, the angels and the devils, the dreamers and the fools. Her cards had unmasked them all and her cards never lied. Madame Burova knew the killer, the victim and the murder weapon.

Outside, the warm, late-summer twilight was smudged with soft thumbprints of light from the illuminations strung along the promenade. High season was coming to an end, but for now the screams and squeals of excitement from the funfair still carried on the wind; soprano notes duetting with the baritone of the waves booming onto the beach and rattling the pebbles as they slunk back into the sea. Madame Burova – Tarot Reader, Palmist and Clairvoyant – proclaimed the painted sign on the front of the booth where she had been dukkering, as her Romany mother always called it, for over fifty years. Today had been her swan-song. Madame Burova was retiring: reluctantly, sadly, but inevitably. Her mind was still sharp and her gift as infallible as ever. But she was weary of other people's lives – their questions, their problems and their secrets. She needed rest and a little piece of life for herself while she still had the chance. She sat down in a chair beside a small round gypsy table covered with a velvet cloth, where her crystal ball stood next to a silver-framed photograph of her long-dead, beloved borzoi, Grisha. The rings on her fingers flashed and sparkled as she picked up two brown envelopes. She had been entrusted as their guardian and had kept their secrets safe and silent for all these years. She turned them over in her hands. The hands that had held countless others and read the future in their palms. The envelopes held a secret that had troubled Madame Burova more than most, and now the time had come for her to open them and fulfil a promise made long ago.

1

1972

Imelda Burova checked her appearance in the bedroom mirror and was satisfied. So was Rod Stewart. '*You wear it well*', he sang, his voice rasping out from the small radio sitting on her dressing table. The dress, a green velvet midi with a fitted bodice and balloon sleeves, was Biba and had been bought especially for today on her last trip to London with her mother, Shunty-Mae. *Today* was Imelda's first day as proprietress of the family's dukkering booth on the promenade. Shunty-Mae had taken it over from her own mother, and it was there that she had taught Imelda to read palms and tarot cards, and to fathom the past and future from the depths of a crystal ball. Various Romany aunts and cousins had helped out for a summer season here and there, but the booth belonged to Shunty-Mae and now she was handing it over to her only daughter. Today, Imelda became Madame Burova – Tarot Reader, Palmist and Clairvoyant. She drew back the curtains to let the early-morning sunlight stream in. Shunty-Mae was in the back garden by the open door of her caravan, smoking a cigarette and cursing. Now in her early seventies, she was still an

1

extraordinarily striking woman with sea-green eyes and only whispers of silver in her long black hair. She had left her travelling life behind when she married Imelda's father, Alexei, but had flatly refused to give up her traditional gypsy vardo and insisted on keeping it in the garden. Whenever she and Alexei rowed, she stormed off to the vardo and often slept there.

Imelda could hear the clatter of pots and pans, and her father whistling in the kitchen downstairs as he prepared to cook breakfast. He had a fiery temper that was easily a match for Shunty-Mae's passionate outbursts, but whereas his anger was quickly spent and soon forgotten, his wife's could sometimes smoulder like hot coals and flare again at the slightest provocation. Alexei was a successful tailor with his own shop, but a gorger, a non-Romany, and Shunty-Mae's family had objected vehemently and vocally when their courtship was discovered. The pair had eventually eloped, and faced with a fait accompli the Romany relatives grudgingly accepted the marriage. Their love for one another was immutable, but their life together a volatile alliance of disparate cultures and traditions.

There was a groan from beneath the rumpled covers of Imelda's bed and a long, pointed nose appeared.

'Get up, you lazy hound!'

Two soulful brown eyes and a pair of furry, floppy ears emerged, followed by a wriggling body on gangly legs with a crazily wagging tail. Imelda had found the puppy a few weeks ago, scavenging in the bins along the promenade. He was painfully thin, and his feet were sore and bleeding. But his sorrowful gaze was irresistible, and Imelda was instantly smitten. She took him home. Shunty-Mae had not been happy, but Alexei had been delighted.

'He's a borzoi!' he had declared. 'A fellow Russian!'

'It's a dog,' Shunty-Mae had objected. 'It's probably got fleas.'

Imelda rarely crossed her mother, but when Shunty-Mae had told her to get rid of the puppy, she had been adamant.

'If he goes – I go with him!'

Shunty-Mae had eventually yielded, fearful of losing her daughter and knowing that this was a battle she would not win. But she attempted to dignify her capitulation by disguising it as oblivion. She simply refused to acknowledge Grisha's existence and completely ignored him. Shunty-Mae had given birth to four sons before her longed-for and only daughter eventually arrived, and it was clear from the start that Imelda had inherited her mother's independent spirit and stubborn streak. The first word she had spoken was 'no'.

Imelda hurried downstairs followed closely by the now wide-awake puppy who skittered into the kitchen and immediately sat down at the feet of Alexei, who was frying eggs for Imelda's breakfast.

'You need a good meal inside you, Melda. It's a big day.'

Imelda poured herself a mug of tea and sat down at the table.

'Why's Mum in the vardo?'

Alexi served her two eggs on toast and smiled.

'I told her not to go to the booth today. To let you have your first day as the queen bee in peace.'

Grisha had squeezed underneath the table and was nudging Imelda's knee with his nose. She slipped him a small piece of toast.

'I take it she didn't welcome your advice, Papa?'

Alexei sat down opposite her and took a deep draught from his mug of tea.

'She said that I obviously thought she was an ugly, interfering old woman of no more use to anyone, and that next I'd be plotting to have her put in a home and then I'd run off with some gorger floozy.'

'I said *cheap* gorger floozy!'

Shunty-Mae was at the back door, listening. She walked over to her husband and looped her arms lovingly around his neck before planting a kiss on the top of his head.

'But now I forgive you. If you cook me some eggs.'

Imelda glanced up at the clock on the wall. It was eight o'clock and time for her to leave. She wanted to be at the booth early and savour every moment of her first day of sovereignty. She fed a final piece of toast to Grisha whilst her mother struggled valiantly not to notice, and then grabbed her bag, coat and puppy and swept off down the hallway. Madame Burova was on her way.

Jeanie peered into the mirror and wondered if she could get away with a bit more eyeshadow. For once, she decided not to push it. Her dad would be waiting downstairs to see her to the bus stop and she didn't want a row to spoil today. He preferred a more natural look to what he called Jeanie's full face of slap and he even thought that her skirts should be below the knee. She had eventually resorted to taking her lipstick and eyeliner with her and applying it on the school bus, and rolling up her skirts at the waistband after she'd left the house. Honestly – she was sixteen! But he treated her as though she was still a kid, even though today she about to become a working woman. She was already planning how to spend her first pay packet after she'd given her dad some rent money. He hadn't wanted her to pay him anything at all, but she was adamant. For as long as she could remember, it had just been the two of them. He had always looked after her and put her first and now she wanted to contribute. Maybe he might be able to buy himself something nice for a change. Top of Jeanie's list were some new nail polish and a Billie Holiday LP. She might not share her dad's views on fashion, but their taste in music was much more harmonious. Ray had raised his daughter on the greats: Etta James, Nina Simone, Ella Fitzgerald, and, of course, Billie Holiday. Jeanie scrabbled through her jewellery box, pulled out a simple gold band on a chain and fastened it around her neck. It had been her mum's wedding ring and she wanted to feel that her mum was with her today. For luck.

'Jeanie! What the bleedin' hell are you doing? Do you want to be late on your first day?'

'All right, all right! Keep your hair on, Ernie. What's left of it.'

What was left of her dad's hair was hidden under the peak cap of his uniform as he waited impatiently for his daughter at the foot of the stairs. Ray Rogers had been delivering milk for over ten years, and he loved his job.

But since Benny Hill had topped the charts with his song about the hapless milkman, Ernie, Jeanie had not been the only one to rib him mercilessly. He clipped her playfully around the ear as she galloped down the stairs and gave him a twirl.

'How do I look?'

Ray shook his head and smiled wistfully. She was the image of her mother at the age when she and Ray had begun courting. 'Where's my little girl gone? You look lovely. And very grown up. Your mum would've been proud of you.'

It was exactly what Jeanie needed to hear. Although she would never have admitted it, her excitement was matched by apprehension. It was her first day working as a clerk at a swanky private secretarial college in town – earning her own money and making her own way in the world. Jeanie had big dreams, and this was where they began. Ray gave her a tight hug and a peck on the cheek. 'Come along, sweetheart. I'll walk you to the bus stop.'

'Didn't you look in the mirror when you got dressed this morning?' Ruby Campbell raised her eyebrows at her eleven-year-old son before pulling him towards her by the lapels of his blazer and releasing him so that she could straighten his crooked tie.

'There. Don't you look smart? Randall – look at your boy.'

Her husband raised his eyes from the newspaper he was reading and grinned.

'He looks like a proper young man. And handsome too – just like his daddy.'

Their son was, in fact, a striking blend of his parents' genes. His blonde-haired, blue-eyed mother and Jamaican father had produced a beautiful child with eyes the colour of aquamarines. But his good looks had done him no favours with his classmates and as a new term in a new school threatened, Treasure was wary. He smiled obligingly at his dad, but Ruby saw the doubt in her son's eyes and the knot in her stomach that she had been trying to ignore since she woke that morning twisted and tightened just a fraction more. Treasure was a tough little boy – small and wiry, and fast as a hare. But Ruby knew that for him life was not always easy. She remembered the 'no blacks' signs in the windows of the flats that she and Randall had seen when they were hunting for their first home, and the casually cruel insults they had endured simply for being seen together and holding hands in public. Treasure wasn't black, but he wasn't white enough for some people either, and no man's land was never a safe or comfortable place to be. She watched him struggle with a few spoonfuls of cornflakes before pushing his bowl to one side. Ruby wished that there was something that she could say or do to protect him from the bullies and the bigots, but she knew that he would have to fight his own battles and forge his own armour with whatever resources he could muster. Growing up was hard for anyone, but for kids like Treasure it was always harder.

Randall folded up his newspaper and pushed back his chair from the table.

'What's in my lunch box today, darling wife?'

Ruby laughed. 'The same as usual: corned beef and tomato. The only thing you'll eat in your sandwiches.'

'Why should I have anything different when I found the perfect filling? Delicious, nutritious and fulfilling all my wishes!' Randall traded a loving kiss on his wife's cheek for his packed lunch and on his way out of the kitchen placed both hands on Treasure's shoulders and gave them a squeeze.

'Good luck, son. Have pride in yourself and you'll be fine.'

Half an hour later, Treasure stood outside his new school. His stomach churned and his heart beat so hard that he could hear its frantic rhythm pounding in his head. Swept along by the mob of noisy children streaming through the gates, he had never felt so alone.

Madame Burova stood in the doorway of her booth and closed her eyes. The sound of waves and swooping gulls and the chatter of passers-by washed over her. The late-afternoon sun warmed her face and a salty breeze ruffled her hair. Grisha stood beside her, his black nose twitching and his feet fidgeting – eager for a run. It had been a good day and the cash box was almost full. A coach party of Women's Institute ladies on a day trip had kept her busy for a couple of hours and passing trade had been brisk. When she nipped to the café next door at lunchtime to pick up a coffee and a cheese roll, she had pretended not to notice Shunty-Mae wandering along the promenade with studied nonchalance. She hoped that her mother had seen the queue of customers waiting patiently for readings outside the booth. The crowds were thinning now and the owners of shops and cafés were pulling down their shutters. Imelda fetched her coat and bag and clipped Grisha's lead to his collar before he dragged her outside, heading for the beach. She reined him back just long enough to close the door to her own little kingdom behind them and turn the key in the lock. It had been a good day.

2

1972

'I want you to tell her to stop hiding my baccy!'

Ernest Plumb was one of Imelda's regulars. He was a short, stocky man with a bellicose air, who trailed a pungent whiff of mothballs and pipe smoke in his wake. Since his wife, Joan, had died, he had come to see her every few weeks to continue the constant bickering that had been the mainstay of their forty-two-year marriage. Imelda had tried explaining to Ernest that spiritual readings weren't like telephone conversations. She couldn't simply dial dead people and have a chat at will. Joan was no more cooperative in death than she had been in life. She only came through when it suited her, but today she did have something to say and Imelda struggled to suppress a grin.

'Joan says that she'll stop hiding your stinking tobacco when you stop living like a filthy pig and wash the net curtains at the sitting-room window. And she wants you to stop smoking your pipe in the house. She says that's what your bloody shed is for.'

'It's not like he uses it for anything else,' Joan grumbled. Imelda could see her standing behind Ernest with her hands on her hips. 'He's no gardener – he wouldn't know a daff from a dandelion. And as for DIY – he's never so much as changed a light bulb. And he needn't think I didn't know about those mucky magazines he kept in there. *Health and Efficiency* my—'

'Perhaps if you just gave the curtains a quick wash and opened the window when you lit your pipe?' Imelda's suggested compromise was not well received by either party.

'Those nets need a damn good boil wash, and when I say outside, I mean outside!' Joan was not to be swayed.

'I won't be dictated to by a dead woman! It's my house and I'll smoke where I like.'

Imelda was pretty sure that he wouldn't. Not if he wanted a quiet life.

Once Ernest had paid and left (and promised to return in a couple of weeks), Grisha leapt from the blanket where he had been snoozing, hoping for a walk. Imelda opened the door a crack and peered out. It was raining heavily, and on the distant horizon the sky and sea were almost indistinguishable from one another. Grisha tentatively poked his nose outside, only to have it battered by a barrage of raindrops. He swiftly retreated to his blanket where he lay down with an exaggerated sigh. Imelda followed him and knelt beside him. He had been her constant companion since she had rescued him from a life on the streets, and never before had she loved a living creature so easily and utterly. She took his head in her hands and kissed his wet nose.

'Never mind, my boy. We'll go later. How about I fetch you a sausage roll from the café?'

Grisha gently wagged his tail. Maybe the rain wasn't such a bad thing after all.

———————————

Next door to Imelda's booth, the café was heaving with both regular customers and day-trippers taking shelter from the inclement weather. The holiday season was over now, but coach trips and tourists kept coming for most of the year. The café was owned and run by Ruby Campbell's sister and brother-in-law, Diamond and Jack, and Ruby was sitting at the counter drinking coffee and sharing the gossip from Larkins Holiday Park, where she worked as assistant to the newly appointed general manager.

'It seems like a daft time to appoint a new manager right at the end of the season,' said Jack as he drained some more chips from the fryer.

'The whole park's being given a revamp, and Marty has been brought in to oversee the work.'

'Ooh, it's Marty now is it? That's a bit familiar,' Diamond teased her sister.

Ruby was excited by the changes. The holiday camp had grown tired and shabby, and guest numbers had dwindled over the past few years. Marty had ambitious ideas, including plans for a whole new programme of entertainment. He had already booked a Wall of Death stunt motorcyclist for next season and had asked Ruby to help him seek out other new acts. She was both flattered and proud that she had been given more responsibility.

'I've found three sisters who do a mermaid act,' she told Diamond. 'They perform synchronised swimming to music in an aquarium and their costumes are gorgeous!'

Jack could barely contain himself. 'Shame there's not four of them. They could call themselves Diana Bass and The Sardines!'

Diamond threw a tea towel at him, but he wasn't finished yet. 'Maybe I should offer my services. My Tom Jones impersonation is legendary. Our Gareth says I could moonlight as a professional doppleganger,' he said, swivelling his hips.

'Your Tom Jones impersonation is only legendary for sounding nothing like him and our son is as tone deaf as you are,' countered his wife as she took two plates of eggs and chips from him and served them to one of the tables.

'There is someone in the family who can sing though.' Diamond returned with a stack of empty plates and passed them over the counter to Jack along with a chit for a new order of two bacon rolls and a pot of tea. 'Jeanie's got a lovely voice and she looks more like her mum every day.' Jeanie was their niece and the daughter of their late sister, Emerald. 'She's doing ever so well at her new job, according to her dad. Not sure how long she'll stick it though. She's a livewire, that one, and the secretarial college sounds a bit dull if you ask me.'

Ruby checked her watch and drained her coffee cup. Her lunch break was almost over. Diamond handed her a large slice of chocolate cake in a paper bag. 'Here. Take this to have with your afternoon tea.' She winked cheekily at her sister. 'You can share it with Marty.'

Ruby took the cake from Diamond, but she wasn't going to eat it. She would save it to give to Treasure when he came home from school. He hadn't said anything to her, but then he didn't need to. She was his mother. She knew that something was wrong.

The bell above the door rang and Jack waved at the young woman who rushed in from the rain.

'Now this is exactly who you need to keep your guests entertained at Larkins,' he told Ruby. 'Let me introduce you to the amazing Madame Burova – tarot reader, palmist and clairvoyant!'

3

1972

Jeanie propelled the post trolley along the polished wooden floor of the corridor, singing more loudly than she should have been. She had been warned about it several times before, but she couldn't seem to help herself. The acoustics in that part of the college building made the temptation too great. 'I've Got My Love to Keep Me Warm' was her current favourite and she twirled the trolley in a full circle as the corridor widened at a junction. A door opened and a stern-looking woman in a tweed suit peered crossly over her glasses at Jeanie.

'Miss Rogers! I believe that you are employed here to deliver the post, not second-rate renditions of cheap romantic ditties. Please conduct yourself with a little more decorum. My students are trying to work, and they will be able to concentrate considerably more easily if they are not subjected to your deplorable caterwauling.'

Jeanie exposed her teeth in an expression that was more akin to a snarl than a smile, but answered demurely. 'I'm truly sorry, Miss Sharp. I don't know what came over me. I suppose I'm just so happy in my work.' She picked up a pile of brown envelopes fastened together with an elastic band and handed them to Miss Sharp, who snatched them from her and then shut the classroom door in her face.

'Miserable old cow! How dare she call a Billie Holiday classic "cheap". Bloody caterwauling. I'll give her cater-wauling,' she howled loudly before rattling off with her trolley at perilous speed to continue her round of deliveries.

At lunchtime in the college refectory, Jeanie was finishing her cheese and tomato sandwich when a young woman, whom she recognised as one of the students, approached her table and asked if she could join her.

'I'm Vivienne,' she said, holding out her hand having set down a cup of coffee on the table.

'Jeanie. Take a pew. What can I do for you?'

Vivienne was slim, slight even, with long, blonde hair and grey eyes, but there was something determined in her manner and expression that belied her delicate physique. She sat down opposite Jeanie and shrugged off the cardigan that was elegantly draped around her shoulders.

'You have an amazing voice.'

Jeanie smiled. 'Ha! So, you're one of Miss Sharp's? My apologies for disrupting your shorthand lesson.'

Vivienne stirred her coffee. 'I hate shorthand, and I'm no fan of Miss Sharp either. She's a dried-up, bitter old spinster who hates us because we are young and have our whole lives ahead of us. All she's got to look forward to each night is Ovaltine and an empty bed.'

16

'If you hate shorthand, what on earth are you doing here? This *is* a secretarial college. Just in case you hadn't worked that out yet.'

'Escaping from my parents.' Vivienne took a packet of cigarettes from her handbag and offered one to Jeanie, who declined. She lit one for herself and blew out a long stream of smoke.

'Well, I suppose that's not strictly true as they're currently in America. I'm escaping from their plans for me.'

Jeanie leaned back in her chair to avoid the cigarette smoke that was wafting in her direction.

'And what are their plans?'

'To marry me off to some eligible young man from a good family. Someone who works in the City and plays in the country.'

Jeanie wrinkled her nose in disgust. 'God, that sounds a bit dire. So, what's your plan?'

'Not sure yet, but by persuading them to let me come here, I've bought myself some time to think of one before they get back.'

Vivienne flicked the ash from the end of her cigarette. 'What about you? What are you doing here?'

'Earning my keep until someone pays me to sing for a living.'

'Well with a voice like yours, I'm sure that won't take long.'

Jeanie was flattered, but also fascinated by her new friend. She was so sure of herself, so grown up, and yet she could only be a year or two older than Jeanie at the most. She felt a sudden need to impress her.

'I'm singing tonight – at Larkins. Come along if you like.'

'What's Larkins?'

'The holiday park. They're having a talent show – looking for new acts. Anyone who's good enough might get a permanent job there when the season starts.'

Vivienne delved into her handbag and retrieved her powder compact. She considered the invitation as she carefully reapplied her lipstick. For some reason, Jeanie was suddenly desperate for her to accept. Vivienne snapped the compact shut and dazzled Jeanie with the full beam of her smile.

'I'd love to.'

4

1972

'Well this is no good at all. You wouldn't be able to hear yourself think.'

Shunty-Mae was not at all in favour of Imelda giving readings at Larkins Holiday Park and she was making it her business to raise objections at every turn. The newly refurbished entertainment lounge was a large room with a stage at one end facing numerous rows of red and gold chairs, and a bar at the other. A rotating glitter ball hung from the ceiling, showering the room with a twinkling confetti of tiny lights, and gilded palm tree lamps stood in columns along the walls. At the foot of each palm tree was a pair of pink flamingos flanking an outsize martini glass containing a paper umbrella and a plastic cocktail cherry.

'It looks like a brothel!' she added.

Imelda laughed. 'And how would you know?'

Imelda hadn't yet agreed to do anything, but Ruby had invited her along to take a look. The recently appointed manager had asked Ruby to organise a talent show to audition new acts and when Shunty-Mae had heard about it, she had insisted on coming too.

'I wouldn't be doing readings in here,' Imelda reassured her mother as they took their seats amongst the packed audience. 'I'd have my own booth.'

Imelda never felt very comfortable in a crowd. The white noise of so many different voices, thoughts and energies often gave her a headache and she was glad when a man appeared on stage in a very dapper tuxedo and tapped the microphone to get proceedings underway.

'Good evening ladies and gentlemen, and thank you so much for coming. My name is Marty Mount and I'm the new manager of Larkins Holiday Park. We have a real treat for you this evening as we search for new stars to provide top-class entertainment for our lucky guests this coming season. So, sit back and enjoy, and don't be afraid to let us know what you think. And here to introduce the first act is my glamorous assistant, Ruby Campbell!'

Shunty-Mae rolled her eyes and whispered rather too loudly to Imelda, 'And doesn't he just think he's the cock of the walk?'

Ruby, dressed in a figure-hugging black frock, walked onto the stage a little self-consciously and took the microphone from Marty, who looked rather put out at the enthusiastic applause and whistling that greeted her appearance. She cleared her throat nervously before announcing the first performer.

'Please give a warm welcome to Magic Melvin and his Unbelievable Balls!'

Magic Melvin was a small, skinny man with a black moustache and a quiff that looked as though it had been painted to match his facial hair. He made his entrance on a unicycle, wobbling precariously as he pedalled furiously backwards and forwards to maintain his balance. And then he dismounted. Bizarrely, it turned out that the unicycle was simply his chosen mode of transport rather than part of his act. Once his feet were on solid ground, he produced three golf balls from his sleeves, proclaiming, 'As if by magic!' and began to juggle them accompanied by the theme tune to *Match of the Day*. Next, he pulled tennis balls from his trouser pockets and repeated the rather pedestrian performance. The audience was growing restive. Attempting to spice things up, Melvin threw the balls a little higher and hopped first on one leg and then the other. However, his increased exertions had an unfortunate effect on his hair, which rather than being dyed was, in fact, a hairpiece that clearly hadn't been satisfactorily secured and was now slipping backwards with every hop. The climax to Magic Melvin's act was an attempt to juggle footballs and for one ball to bounce on his head with each rotation. The attempt failed and Melvin and his hairpiece parted company. They were both rather unkindly but justifiably booed off stage.

'That bloke *has* got unbelievable balls if he calls that an act,' the man sitting behind Shunty-Mae and Imelda grumbled to his wife.

Up next was a comedian, who quickly had the audience in stitches, and Marty Mount rubbing his hands. Shunty-Mae, however, was not impressed with his risqué jokes, which she thought were a little too blue for her daughter's ears.

'What kind of a place is this?' she demanded.

'Well, what do you expect in a brothel?' Imelda replied with a grin.

The comedian was followed by Titus Marlow, a tall, imposing figure with alarming eyebrows. He wore a dark suit and an expression of barely concealed menace. Titus was a hypnotist and having coerced several 'volunteers' to join him on stage, he placed them in a trance and got them to embarrass themselves by singing, dancing, doing silly walks and sitting on one another's laps. The audience found their humiliation hilarious and Titus received a standing ovation.

The next act was a husband and wife and their performing doves. The beautiful white birds hopped obligingly from a series of perches onto various props including a miniature trapeze, a small seesaw and a brightly coloured roundabout. They flew on command to pluck coloured silk handkerchiefs from the hand of the husband, circle the stage and then land on the hand of the wife. Well – most of them did. There was one bird who looked a bit truculent from the start. He preferred preening his feathers to paying attention to the commands being given by his master and he performed each trick rather grudgingly. Imelda thought he seemed a bit bored. She was right. All at once, he decided to go solo. He flew high over the heads of the audience and landed on top of one of the palm trees where he sat pecking at the gilded leaves. The act was brought to a hasty conclusion and the remaining doves were returned to their cage. But the audience was clearly far more interested in how the renegade was going to be retrieved. The husband approached the base of the palm tree, accompanied by an agitated Marty, who was not at all happy that his expensive interior design feature was being used as a perch by one of the performers. The bird was eventually persuaded to fly down, but not before relieving himself from his lofty perch, depositing generous white splashes on the suits of both men standing beneath him. The audience was highly entertained and even Shunty-Mae was unable to supress a sanctimonious grin.

Ruby reappeared on stage to calm the commotion by announcing the next act. Sara-Jade Virtue was a fine-looking woman comfortably past her fortieth birthday, with a body as lithe as a teenager's. She wore black tights and a leotard sprinkled with sequins, and was swathed in a series of sheer, sparkling lengths of cloth. As she sashayed around the stage accompanied by some Egyptian music, she discarded each veil with a seductive swirl.

'A woman of her age should know better than to flaunt her body for all and sundry to gawp at,' hissed Shunty-Mae to Imelda. 'She's practically naked. This so-called holiday park is little better than Sodom and Gomorrah!'

But it was soon apparent that Ms Virtue was much more than an exotic dancer. She was also a contortionist of extraordinary skill. She lay down on her stomach facing the audience and raising her torso on her forearms, she swung her legs backwards over her head and folded her feet underneath her chin. In the same position, having untucked her feet, she used one to take a cigarette and place it between her lips, and the other to light it with a match, both handed to her by Ruby. The audience was transfixed. She then performed a series of manoeuvres so fluid and improbable that they seemed to defy the presence of any bones in her body whatsoever, save for her skull, and those in her hands and feet.

Her final flourish was to fold herself completely and inexplicably into a small suitcase and close the lid. The silence that followed stretched almost to the point where the audience became fearful for her fate, but then she burst from the case with a triumphant smile and rearranged her limbs into a more conventional configuration in time to take her bow.

The next act could only be an anti-climax. It was a man tap dancing with biscuit tins on his feet.

The final performer of the evening was a young woman called Jeanie Rogers whom Ruby proudly introduced as her niece. Jeanie looked very young, but as she took the microphone from Ruby, her confidence was unmistakable. She looked completely at home in the spotlight on stage. As soon as she began to sing, the audience was stunned into absolute silence. The voice they heard was that of a world-weary jazz diva, but it came from the mouth of a teenage girl. The disparity was mesmerising. '*I put a spell on you*,' Jeanie sang, and the audience was bewitched.

After the show, Imelda was keen to go home, but Shunty-Mae perversely insisted that they stay for one drink. It seemed that, despite her protestations, she was quite enjoying herself. At the bar, Imelda found herself standing next to Ruby and her niece.

'Madame Burova! I'm so glad you made it.'

'Imelda. Please call me Imelda. So am I. Your niece was the star of the show. You must be so proud of her. I have no need to read her cards to be sure that she will go very far indeed.'

Ruby was clearly delighted and gave the blushing Jeanie a hug.

'Jeanie, this is Madame Burova – Imelda. I'm trying to persuade her to come and give readings to the guests at Larkins.'

Jeanie smiled bashfully as she disentangled herself from her aunt's embrace.

'How fascinating.' An elegant young woman had appeared at Jeanie's side and was coolly observing Imelda with her pale grey eyes. Imelda met her gaze and felt just the slightest prickle of apprehension.

'Vivienne! You came! What did you think?' Jeanie was clearly very anxious to hear her friend's opinion.

'I thought you were wonderful, darling. Now what would you like to drink?'

'She's having an orange and lemonade,' said Ruby rather pointedly. 'Can I get you one?'

'No thanks,' Vivienne smiled, completely unfazed by Ruby's tone. 'I'll get my own.'

Imelda ordered and paid for two vodka and tonics and returned to the table where Shunty-Mae was happily people-watching. Shunty-Mae frowned as Vivienne took Jeanie's arm and led her away from the bar.

'That Jeanie has a God-given talent,' she said admiringly and took a large swig from her glass. 'But the other one – she's got the devil in her.'

5

Now

It was a new pencil case kind of day. Although it was many years since Billie had left school, that was how she always thought of a crisp, sunny day in September. She still remembered the shiny shoes that rubbed a little, stiff collars and cuffs, and the too-long sleeves of a blazer that was bought to grow into. On the first day of a school year, Billie's uniform was always pristine and she always had a new pencil case. Her mum had made sure of it.

23 Honeyhill Road was a small, neat terraced house with bright white net curtains at the windows. But beyond the nets the house was empty save for the memories that it held. The 'sold' sign outside had gone up earlier that week, and Billie was here to take a last look around her childhood home and bid a final farewell. The front door caught on a pile of junk mail as she pushed it open, and the air in the hallway was warm and still and slightly fusty. There was a rectangle of wallpaper where the pattern was still bright, unfaded by the sun. It had been preserved by her graduation photograph which had hung there in pride of place – one of the first things visitors saw when they came

into the house. She walked through into the kitchen where they had eaten so many family meals together. Hurried breakfasts of tea and toast before school for her, and the bus depot for her mum and dad, where they had both worked, met and fallen in love. She could still picture her mum standing at the counter making sandwiches for their packed lunches while she sang along to songs playing on the radio. She remembered picking fresh mint in the garden for all those Sunday dinners, and the smell of bread sauce simmering in a pan and turkey roasting in the oven on so many Christmas mornings. Billie unlocked the back door and followed the well-worn path down the narrow garden. The path on which she had drawn hopscotch squares with chalk, and the garden where she had played with Bubble and Squeak, her pet guinea pigs. The lawn was a little overgrown now, and the narrow flowerbed that bordered it was sprinkled with weeds. But soon, no doubt, it would be covered in decking and dotted with carefully chosen architectural plants in zinc containers. The couple who were moving in next month had shared with her their plans for a 'low-maintenance outdoor entertaining space'. Billie wandered back inside and glanced through the door to the lounge, where she had sat together with her mum and dad on the sofa watching TV and sharing boxes of chocolates and bags of crisps – their Saturday night treats. After her mum died and her dad became ill, she had come home to look after him and they had watched travel documentaries together. Just before he died, he told her that he felt as though he had travelled the world without leaving his armchair.

Upstairs, there were two bedrooms and a bathroom. The smaller room had been hers, and when she had moved back in just over a year ago, the posters from her teenage years were still Blu Tacked to the wall. George Michael wearing ripped jeans and a leather jacket, Rick Astley, Whitney Houston and Patrick Swayze. It was sad to think that they were all dead now apart from Rick, and he had been her least favourite anyway. In her parents' bedroom, the Laura Ashley wallpaper had been there since the 80s. Her mum had saved up and then splashed out on it. The paper had a cream background with tiny sprigs of blue flowers and her mum had loved the pattern. It hadn't been cheap, and they never had money to throw around, but she had seen it in a magazine at the hairdresser's and set her heart on it. Billie remembered that there hadn't been quite enough, but to save the expense of another roll, her dad had left a gap behind the chest of drawers. Her mum never knew.

It had been a happy house and they had been a close-knit family. Billie had always felt safe in the certainty of being loved. Even when her dad had died here, the memory of it wasn't sad. It had been his time to go, and he left peacefully, without pain, sleeping in his own bed. When she found him the next morning, he almost looked as though he was smiling. And now, on this new pencil case kind of day, there would be a fresh start for Billie. The house was sold, she had said her good-byes and now she could move on. But to what?

As Billie locked the front door for the last time and dropped the keys through the letterbox, Rita Barnet, the elderly neighbour, came out to speak to her.

'End of an era, Billie. That's what it is – the end of an era. I still remember the day when your mum and dad moved in, only a few weeks after us. They were good friends to me, especially after my Tony died. I'm not looking forward to the new lot moving in. They look a bit la-di-da to me.'

'They seem all right, Rita. You probably won't see that much of them. I think they both work in the City.'

Rita folded her arms and hugged them to her bony chest. 'What did I tell you – la-di-da.'

Driving back to her flat, Billie pondered for the umpteenth time what she might do next. It was exciting considering the possibilities, but also a little daunting to have so many choices. Since her divorce had been finalised the previous year and she had taken voluntary redundancy from her job as a university lecturer to look after her dad, her life had been somewhat in limbo. But now she was completely free. With her modest redundancy payment and her share of the proceeds from the marital home, she could even afford not to work for a while. There would be little left from the sale of Honeyhill Road as she had persuaded her parents to take advantage of an equity release scheme to supplement their meagre pensions, but even so, there was enough in her bank account to finance a modest sabbatical. Maybe she could go travelling – take a gap year. She grinned at the thought of backpacking around Australia in a pair of shorts and hiking boots. Glamping for a week in Dorset was probably more realistic – and definitely more comfortable at her age.

She parked her car outside the large, slightly run-down Edwardian house where her rented flat took up the entire second floor. The paint on the front door was flaking off in places, but the stained-glass panels were still intact and along with the original brass knocker and a rusty boot scraper in the porch, they gave the entrance an air of faded grandeur. In the shared lobby she collected the mail from her allocated metal post box and climbed the stairs to her front door. The flat was light and airy, and even had a small balcony where she was attempting to grow some herbs and a couple of pots of geraniums. The bare walls were punctuated with well-framed prints of paintings she loved and knew intimately from her years of teaching history of art, and various antiques and curiosities were displayed on side tables and in cabinets around the room. Unlike her university lectures, her collection was neither curated nor hung to demonstrate any meaningful narrative. It was simply a cacophony of clashing colours and contrasting styles that brought her daily joy. Skulking in a corner was a set of golf clubs, undisturbed and gathering dust since Billie had propped them there on the day that she had moved in. She kept meaning to sell them. She had learned to play to pacify Giles, her ex-husband. He had insisted that they try something new together in an attempt to resuscitate their ailing marriage. Giles had suggested golf, but Billie would have preferred salsa, so they tossed a coin. Golf won and Giles loved it, but it bored Billie to death and finally finished off their marriage. It was a mercy killing. Giles became secretary of the golf club and Billie became a free woman once again. Perhaps now it was time to sell the clubs and find a salsa class. In the galley kitchen she flicked the switch on the kettle and while she was waiting for the water to boil, she sifted through the post. Amongst the bills and junk mail was a brown envelope, which she knew from the postmark must be from their family solicitor. It was probably something to do with the sale of her parents' house. She poured boiling water over a teabag in her mug and then tore open the envelope. As she read what was written on the pages it contained, her whole world washed away like the chalked hopscotch squares of her childhood in a sudden downpour of rain.

6

Now

Billie left the building through the grand stone portico and wandered down the short flight of steps into bright sunlight. It was late October and the leaves on the trees in Brunswick Square were a fluttering tessellation of reds and golds in the brisk autumn breeze. Billie pulled her scarf up higher to cover her chin and the lobes of her ears and set off in the direction of St Pancras station. She was trying to recalibrate her place in the world. She had thought that a visit to the Foundling Museum might help. But it hadn't. The buttons, pennies and scraps of cloth left by desperate mothers as tokens by which they could identify their children, should they ever return to collect them, were heartbreaking to see. The humblest of objects, vessels for the most precious hopes, however remote they might have been. The final, fragile umbilical thread between mother and child.

Billie had no real idea what she had been looking for, but whatever it was, she hadn't found it in Brunswick Square.

The station welcomed her with the scent of fresh flowers and coffee. Beneath its gleaming canopy of glass and iron her spirits soared skywards as they always did towards the sunlit panes, and amidst the bustle of so many lives and so many journeys, she felt a sense of peace returning. This morning's visit to the museum had been a disappointment. She had felt no connection, no recognition. She made her way upstairs to the statue of John Betjeman. It was a ritual that her dad had started with her; every time they were in the station, they would visit it and rub Betjeman's rotund tummy for luck. Her dad had been an avid fan, not only of his poetry, but also of his work to preserve so many architectural treasures. St Pancras had been his favourite – the jewel in the crown, he called it. After its restoration, they used to come here just to marvel at its splendour. They sometimes had coffee and cakes and listened to the people playing the free pianos. Occasionally they would have a pint and a packet of crisps in The Betjeman pub, and on Billie's last birthday before her dad died, they had had lunch in The Booking Office as a special treat. He could have told her here. Here in their special place, bolstered by Betjeman and a pint or two of bitter, he could have shared the secret that had been kept for so many years. But he had remained silent. Until after his death. Her mum would never have spoken of it – too afraid to fracture their perfect family. And it was this that broke Billie's heart. Not the secret itself – shocking though it was – but the fact that her mum hadn't trusted Billie's love and loyalty enough to test it. That she could never now reassure her mum and dad that their family was as strong as it had always been, and that her love for them was unshakeable. But *something* had changed. Irrevocably. Inevitably now, there were questions to be asked even if the answers were never found. Her dad's letter, forwarded by their solicitor just after the house had been sold, related only the bare facts.

We adopted you when you were just three weeks old. You were a foundling and then you found your way to us. We couldn't have loved you more if you had been our own flesh and blood, and we never thought of you as anyone but our very own precious daughter. But when you grew up, I thought you had the right to know the truth. I wanted to tell you, but your mum was afraid that we would lose you, or at least a part of you. It would have killed her and so I kept quiet. And once your mum was gone it seemed like it was too late. Too much water under the bridge. But in the end, I couldn't meet my maker without making my peace with you. You have the right to know and you shouldn't have to find out from anyone else. Maybe I was a coward not telling you to your face, but my darling, darling Billie, I couldn't have taken it if you had been disappointed in us. Please know that we both loved you to the moon and back . . .

It was what they had always told her as a little girl when she went to bed. She believed it then and she believed it still. But now she knew she was a cuckoo who had been fortunate enough to land in a very comfortable nest. A mysterious genetic synthesis of two complete strangers. A question mark.

She rubbed Betjeman's cool bronze belly and followed his gaze upwards to where the sun flashed on glass and girders from the bright blue sky beyond. She was an orphan twice over. But she had also known the best love a mother and father could give, unlike the pitiful souls who had passed through the Foundling Hospital commemorated in Brunswick Square. She had no reason for self-pity, but she could murder a latte. Downstairs, clutching a paper cup in one hand and a muffin in the other, she found a seat close to one of the pianos, where an urbane-looking gentleman in his mid-sixties was just settling himself down to play. His hair and small moustache were dove-white and neatly groomed, and he wore a tweed suit, pink shirt and striped bow tie. His fingers were long and slender as he held them poised above the keys before straightening his back and nodding his head to signal the beginning of his performance. He began with 'Bring Me Sunshine', then 'Strangers in the Night', and by the time he had finished 'As Time Goes By', he had attracted quite a crowd. Billie finished her coffee and got up to find a bin, but the first notes of the next song pulled her back. 'Smile'. She couldn't help but. Her dad used to sing it to her when she was little and fell off her bike. He sang it to her mum on the rare occasions that they fell out and on rainy days to the passengers on his bus. 'Smile' was his cure for all ills and inevitably it had sent him on his way to whatever comes next at his funeral. Billie drew nearer to the piano, weaving her way through the crowd, until she was almost close enough to touch the man at the keys. But she had no need to – he knew she was there. As the final notes evaporated into the chilly air and the crowd drifted away, he turned and handed her a pristine white handkerchief. Although she was still smiling, her cheeks were wet with tears.

7

Now

The musician's name was Henry Hayward and he travelled to the station every Thursday to play the piano. Having been very happily married, he had suddenly found himself alone, and performing at St Pancras had at first been a welcome distraction but was now the highlight of his week.

'When Jocelyn died, I was completely bereft,' he told Billie, sipping the tea that she had bought him as recompense for the loan of his handkerchief.

'We did everything together, you see. It sounds a little fey, but we were truly soulmates. It was quite a shock to find myself flying solo again after twenty years with a co-pilot. I moped about for a bit feeling sorry for myself, but that wasn't what Jocelyn would have wanted. We were always having adventures together, so I decided to try a few on my own. The Pilates was perhaps a little *too* adventurous – I don't think I'm designed to be that bendy. The watercolour class was much more enjoyable, but sadly populated with several somewhat predatory widows, one of whom took rather a fancy to me and kept bringing me homemade fruit cakes and inviting me out to lunch. I can't abide fruit-cake – the mixed peel always gets stuck between my teeth. Eventually I decided to return to my first love – the piano. And here I am.'

Billie had already missed one train and was about to miss another, but she didn't care. Henry Hayward was worth it. He just made her smile.

'And what about you, young woman? What are you doing here in the blessed Betjeman's opus magnum? Arriving, departing or simply hanging around hoping to meet debonair musicians?'

Billie laughed but it caught like a fishbone in the back of her throat. Henry reached over and for the briefest of moments placed his hand over hers.

'Why the tears, my dear?' he asked with unbearable kindness.

She bit the inside of her lip hard enough to draw blood, determined not to cry again, but found herself unable to contain the barrage of emotions that had confounded her since the day she had read her dad's letter. She told Henry Hayward everything. A man that she had only just met – little more than a complete stranger. She told him all the things that she had tried to share with her friends but had so far failed, for reasons she had yet to fathom. She told Henry that she was a modern-day foundling. She had been to the Foundling Museum and found nothing that had helped.

Henry's response was unexpected.

'How exciting! You're a woman of mystery! It sounds as though you might be about to embark on an adventure of your own.'

There was not a trace of pity nor patronage in his voice, but he was anxious to reassure her that he was not insensitive to her feelings.

'I know it must have knocked the wind out of your sails, but now you have an opportunity to set a completely new course. Your childhood was happy, your parents loved you and you loved them. That was the past and none of that will change. But the important thing now is what will you do with your future?'

Henry checked his watch and drained the last of his tea.

'It's been a pleasure to meet you, Billie, but my piano awaits. Come and see me again. The tea will be my treat next time, but don't expect any fruit cake.'

By the time Billie caught the train home it was late afternoon, but she managed to find a carriage that was not too crowded. She wanted some peace and quiet. Time to sit and stare out of the window and think about her future – about whether she could face it without first addressing the questions about her past. Could she brush them under the carpet, or would they keep tripping her up? Did she want answers or need them? The first implied a choice, but the second did not and that was what worried Billie. What if she needed the answers but there were none to be had?

Just as the train was about to depart, a young woman talking loudly into her mobile phone jumped on and threw herself and her bag down opposite Billie.

'Yeah. I've just got on the train. Yeah, St Pancras. Yeah, babes, I'll be back in about half an hour. Can you pick me up from the station? Thanks babes. Can you bring me a can of Coke? I'm gagging for a drink. Thanks babes. What you doing now?'

Billie was tempted to suggest that 'babes' was probably about to grab a can of Coke and set off for the station to pick up Miss Mouth Almighty, but she resisted. The young woman tucked the phone between the side of her face and her shoulder and continued talking while rummaging through her bag. She eventually retrieved a bottle of nail polish. The carriage quickly filled with the pungent stench of ethyl acetate as she unscrewed the lid and began painting her nails a vibrant shade of purple, having first propped up her feet on the seat next to Billie. Billie looked around at the other passengers in the carriage to see if any of them were as irritated as she was. Several were pulling disapproving faces as the smell permeated the air, and a man across the aisle was quietly tutting at the sight of a pair of feet in scruffy trainers resting on a seat where some unsuspecting commuter would later sit. But nobody said anything. The young woman was either oblivious or simply unconcerned and continued her prattling and primping. Normally Billie would have kept quiet too. But Billie was recalibrating 'normal'. She took out her mobile and pretended to make a call in a very clear and slightly louder than necessary voice.

'Hi hun. Yep, I've just got on the train. Yep, St Pancras. I'll be back in about thirty mins. Can you pick me up from the station? Thanks hun. Can you bring me some ibuprofen? Thanks hun. No, I'm fine now, but I'm going to have a headache by the time I get off. Yep. Well, the woman sitting opposite me is painting her nails and you know how much nail polish stinks. Yep. The whole carriage reeks.'

The whole carriage was now listening to Billie's bogus conversation with interest, including the nail painter who had ended her own call in favour of eavesdropping on Billie's.

'Ha ha! What, take a picture and post it on Twitter under hashtag train etiquette? Yep, I know it's not very considerate behaviour, but to be honest, I don't think she'd be bothered. She's even got her mucky feet up on the seat where some poor soul who's paid a fortune for a ticket will have to sit.'

The nail painter was looking slightly annoyed, having lost concentration and smudged two nails.

'Are you talking about me?' she asked.

Billie continued speaking into her phone, 'Just a minute, hun, she's interrupting me now.'

Billie looked up. 'Excuse me, but this is a private conversation. You shouldn't be listening. Is there a problem?'

'Yeah. If you're slagging me off there is.'

'Well, please feel free to tell me if I've got anything wrong?'

The nail painter got off at the next station, and as she alighted, the man sitting across the aisle caught Billie's eye and smiled.

'Bravo!'

8

1972

The Larkins Holiday Park Christmas party was in full swing, and Imelda could hear music and the chatter of excited voices coming from the entertainment lounge along the corridor. She had set up her temporary booth just off the main reception area. With some curtains across the door, a few velvet drapes and cushions, some crystals, a couple of lamps and her gypsy table, the former store cupboard had been transformed, and Imelda had already given several readings. This was a trial run to help her decide if she was prepared to appear here on a regular basis. Shunty-Mae was still set against it, but Imelda was beginning to warm to the idea. The Christmas party had been organised by Ruby at Marty's request, to generate some income before the refurbished park opened its gates to the first residential guests in the new holiday season. Tickets had been sold to the public, promising an evening of music, dancing and a delicious finger buffet, but many of the newly appointed entertainment staff had also been invited. A chance to get to know one another, Marty had said. But he had also persuaded some of them to perform – for no fee, Ruby had noted. No such thing as a free finger buffet.

Imelda heard voices outside her booth and through a small gap in the curtains she recognised the young woman, Jeanie, who had sung so beautifully at the talent-spotting evening and her fair-haired friend Vivienne, the cool sophisticate.

'Ooh! Let's get our fortunes told. I can find out whether I'm going to be a star or end up back at the secretarial college pushing the mail trolley until I'm old and wrinkled like Miss Sharp, and smell of cat wee and Ovaltine.'

'Surely you don't believe in all that hocus-pocus? It's complete rubbish. Gypsy nonsense. They just make it up, you know – preying on poor, feeble-minded souls who don't know any better.'

Imelda swept back the curtains and was gratified to see a faint blush appear on Vivienne's cheeks.

'Can I help you ladies with anything?'

Jeanie was immediately flushed and flustered, but her friend regained her composure almost instantly.

'No offence intended, of course,' she reassured Imelda with a smile. 'It's just not my cup of tea leaves.'

'None taken.' Imelda lied. 'And of course, I understand. Not everyone is willing to trust the things they don't understand. But what about you, Jeanie? Would you like me to read your cards? Do you trust me?'

Jeanie glanced uncertainly at Vivienne, but then she nodded and followed Imelda into the booth. Vivienne was clearly a little irritated by her friend's small rebellion.

'I'll see you back at the bar then. I've spotted a handsome man who I'm sure would like to buy me a drink.'

Imelda motioned for Jeanie to take a seat at the gypsy table. She placed three sets of tarot cards in front of her and asked her to choose a pack. Imelda handed the chosen cards to Jeanie and asked her to shuffle them and then she took them back and laid down a Celtic Cross, card by card, on the table.

―――――――――――

Imelda packed away her cards and crystal ball and decided to look in on the party before heading home. She'd had a busy and successful evening and was beginning to think that Larkins might be very good for business. She had not been allowed to bring Grisha with her this evening, but that would have to change if Marty Mount wanted her to make regular appearances. The entertainment lounge was festooned in all its Christmas finery. The palm trees were hung with coloured tinsel and the flamingos were wearing Santa hats. Marty Mount was dressed as Father Christmas and was brandishing a sprig of mistletoe with a lascivious glint in his eyes. Too many Bacardi and Cokes had loosened his tongue and livened his hands, and female guests and staff alike were on the receiving end of his largely unwelcome attentions.

The finger buffet had just been served. Shunty-Mae had instructed Imelda not to partake. 'Why would you want to eat anything that everyone has been fingering?' she asked in a disgusted tone. 'You'll catch something terrible. And then don't expect any sympathy from me when you're retching your entrails up for days on end afterwards.' Imelda nibbled on a couple of vol-au-vents as she listened to Jeanie singing 'White Christmas', accompanied by a young man playing the piano. It was hardly surprising that she had been hired by Monty after the talent show, and she had told Imelda that she couldn't wait to hand in her notice at the secretarial college. Imelda couldn't help hoping that when she did, her friendship with Vivienne might fade, but sadly her cards had given no indication that it would.

'So, have you decided yet whether you'll be joining us for the new season?'

Ruby had just made a swift escape from Marty and was selecting a sandwich with seemingly little enthusiasm.

'I'm still thinking about it. But this evening's gone well. You've done a wonderful job with the party. Everyone seems to be enjoying themselves. Except, perhaps, you,' she added, noting Ruby's preoccupied manner.

Ruby smiled. 'I'm fine. I'm just feeling a bit guilty about my little boy, Treasure. I've been so busy here that I haven't been at home much lately, and with Christmas coming . . .' She shrugged as her words tailed off. 'He's probably fine – sitting watching TV with his dad, who will have let him stay up much later than he's usually allowed.'

Marty had found Ruby again and sidled up beside her, slipping his hand onto the small of her back and then sliding it lower. He dangled the mistletoe over her head and lunged his face towards hers, planting a wet kiss on her lips before she had a chance to turn away. If Imelda had had a drink in her hand, she would have tipped it over him, but instead she took Ruby by the arm saying that she needed to speak to her in private.

'We staff mustn't monopolise your time, Mr Mount,' she told him pointedly. 'I'm sure our paying guests are much more deserving of your attention.'

When the performance was over, Ruby went off to introduce the next act and Imelda made her way to the bar where Jeanie had found her friend. They were talking to a striking-looking man with chiselled cheekbones, lips that were almost too full and a deep scar on his chin. His eyes were the blue of a winter sky on a fine day. He was holding a pint of cider, and on the back of his hand was another scar – older, like a puckered silver spider. As Imelda approached, he held her in his steady gaze and smiled. A smile that would break hearts wherever he went and stirred emotions in Imelda that she would much rather have left to languish in peace. She ordered a whiskey and soda.

'This one's on me, if you'll allow it.'

The man passed some coins across the bar before she had a chance to answer. He offered her his hand. On his middle finger was a large silver ring in the form of a skull.

'I'm Cillian Byrne. Soon to be an employee here at Larkins along with the lovely Jeanie. She's been telling me you have the gift. That's a rare thing when it's genuine.'

Imelda wasn't sure if he was baiting her or not. She took his hand. It was rough and warm, and his grip was strong.

'Will you do me the honour of a reading sometime?' he asked her.

'It would be my pleasure.' Imelda loved a challenge.

Vivienne was evidently growing tired of being ignored. She placed an immaculately manicured hand on Cillian's arm and coyly waved her empty glass.

'A lady can get very thirsty around here,' she purred.

Cillian took her glass.

'Same again?'

'Yes please, darling.'

'Jeanie – what about you?'

'Can I have a Coke please?'

Vivienne turned to Imelda. 'Cillian rides the Wall of Death on his motorcycle. Doesn't that sound thrilling?'

Imelda wasn't surprised. Whatever he thought about her gift, it told her that his was for danger. He had a wild energy about him that pulled her in even though she knew it would be safer to keep her distance.

'He certainly seems like a man it would be interesting to get to know,' she replied.

Vivienne glanced across at Cillian who was chatting to Jeanie and the barman, and then leaned in closer to Imelda.

'Well, don't go getting ideas into your head about that,' she warned, fixing Imelda with an icy glare. 'He's spoken for. And just remember, gypsy lady, I'm a paying guest here – you're just staff.'

She switched her smile back on and sidled over to join Jeanie and Cillian, placing a proprietorial hand on the small of his back. Imelda recalled her vague apprehension when she had first seen Vivienne at the talent show, and Shunty-Mae's more explicit warning – 'She's got the devil in her.' Her cards had confirmed as much. The High Priestess inverted, the Ten of Pentacles and the Ten of Cups.

Shunty-Mae was never wrong, and neither were her cards.

The young man who had been playing the piano arrived at the bar, perched on the stool next to Imelda and set down a plate piled high with food from the buffet.

Imelda smiled. 'Hungry?'

'Starving!' he replied. 'I haven't eaten anything since breakfast. Too nervous about tonight's show. But now I could eat a horse. Except I couldn't. I'm vegetarian.' He added with a grin.

'I'm Madame Burova, tarot reader, palmist and clairvoyant – but call me Imelda. I'm going to give readings here at Larkins for the guests.' It seemed she had decided.

'Charlie Martin. Pianist,' the young man volunteered, brushing crumbs from his shirt front.

'Let me buy you a drink, Charlie Martin!' Cillian appeared beside them and handed Imelda her whiskey and soda. 'I'm Cillian Byrne. Wall of Death rider. Now, what'll you have?'

9

1972

Treasure lay shivering in his pyjamas. He was curled up on the floorboards in the darkness of his bedroom, listening to the dog scratching at the door to get in. It was bitter outside. Too cold to sleep in the garden. The poor thing didn't even have a kennel. Treasure's bed was cosy, and a hot water bottle was tucked under the covers where his feet should be. But he didn't want to be warm and comfortable while the dog was cold and miserable. The dog was a border collie; black and white with a black patch over one eye. She was skinny and her fur had worn away on her elbows where she was forced to lie down on the concrete in Jimmy Cox's back yard. Jimmy Cox was their neighbour. He was a pawnbroker and 'all-round nasty sonofabitch' according to Treasure's dad when he thought that Treasure wasn't listening. But Treasure was always listening. And tonight, all he could hear was the dog scratching and the occasional pitiful whimper. She wouldn't dare bark. If she did, Jimmy Cox would come to the door and silence her with his boot. She didn't even have a name. He just called her

Dog. Treasure had begged his mum and dad to ask Jimmy Cox if he could bring her home, or at least take her for walks. Ruby had tried, but Jimmy Cox had laughed in her face and told her to mind her own business. He obviously didn't care about her. Didn't want her. But Treasure was beginning to understand that there were some people in the world who got pleasure from inflicting fear and pain on others weaker than themselves. The bruises on his hip and shoulder were a painful reminder as he lay on the hard floor. He hadn't told his mum and dad about the name-calling and the bullying. The shame and humiliation of being pushed over onto the rough tarmac of the playground and laughed at as he fought desperately and failed to hold back the tears. He told them he had fallen. An accident. But he did what he could for the dog. Every day he would push food through a gap in the fence. He would save the sandwiches from his packed lunch and sneak sausages and bits of cheese from the fridge. Sometimes, he would poke his fingers through the gap and try to stroke her face. But she was very scared, even of Treasure, and he could feel her trembling. So, he gave her food and the only other thing he could. A name. He called her Star.

He was trying to stay awake until his mum got home. She had gone to work at Larkins tonight. There was a Christmas party. Before she had left that evening, wearing a pretty red dress and smelling of hairspray and perfume, she had asked him to think about what he would like Father Christmas to bring him. He didn't believe in Father Christmas anymore, and even if he had been real, he couldn't give Treasure the two things he wanted most in the world. Even God hadn't been able to deliver, and Treasure had been asking him for long enough. All he wanted was to rescue Star. And to be white.

10

Now

Billie sat in the trendy cocktail bar wearing half a glass of gunpowder pepper gin and artisan tonic water down the front of her favourite white shirt.

'Oh God! I'm so sorry!' One of her best friends, Julia, was trying to mop up the pool of expensive liquid on the table with a flimsy paper coaster, while the other, Annie, searched in her bag for some tissues, which she handed to Billie.

'That's the best part of twelve quid I'm drenched in,' Billie joked, dabbing herself with the tissues.

'I know. I know. I'm really sorry. It was just the shock. You could have broken it to us gently. I can't believe you haven't said anything before now.' Julia sipped what was left of the drink she had knocked over in surprise when Billie had shared her latest news with them.

'I was working out what to say. And anyway, I haven't known for that long myself.'

'Well, I'm going to buy myself another drink, and then you have to tell us *everything*!'

Julia headed for the bar.

'Are you okay?' Annie was rarely ruffled by anything. She was a lecturer at the university where Billie had worked. They had met in the refectory on Billie's first day and had been friends ever since.

'I think so. I mean, it was a hell of a shock at first, but now it just feels weird. I'm not sure what to do about it, or even if I should do anything. Sleeping dogs and all that . . .'

Annie fixed her with the steady gaze she used on her students when they tried to fob her off with some bullshit answer to one of her questions.

'What?' Billie shrugged, and busied herself with more shirt dabbing.

'I hope I haven't missed anything.' Julia arrived back with her drink and a cloth to wipe up the rest of the spillage. 'The barman was very sweet. He gave me another gin and tonic on the house.'

'Of course he did. But not because he's sweet – he's a good businessman. We're new customers and he wants to make sure we come back.' Annie was ever the pragmatist. Julia pulled a face. 'Well, I think it was very nice of him. Now, Billie. Start at the beginning – we need all the details.'

It didn't take Billie long to tell them everything she knew.

'Is that it? Don't you even know where you were found? What you were wearing? Was there a note left with you?' Julia was beginning to be genuinely upset on Billie's behalf.

'Yes, no, no and no. And it's fine, I'm fine, honestly Julia.'

Annie considered the facts carefully as she always did.

'Well, you probably think you are, but quite frankly it would be a bloody miracle if that were true. And anyway, you've already told me that it feels weird.'

'There, see! I knew I'd miss something.' Julia removed the pink grapefruit slice from her drink and took a swig. 'Weird in what way?'

'I feel like a question mark,' Billie replied. 'I only have Dad's letter, and I completely understand why they did what they did. I don't blame them in any way. But I don't know anything about where I came from. Who I came from.'

'Whom,' Annie teased her. 'If you're going to be melodramatic, at least be grammatically correct.'

Billie smiled, but the smile didn't reach her eyes.

'I do know that I was found at the seaside on the prom. But not exactly where. Nor by *whom*,' she added.

'Do you want to know?' Julia was swirling the ice cubes in her drink thoughtfully. 'It could be quite exciting. You might be the child of someone famous.'

'Or infamous,' countered devil's advocate Annie.

'Or just some poor, terrified teenager who got pregnant, panicked and disposed of the unwelcome result on the street wrapped in newspaper like the remains of a fish and chip supper.' Billie was beginning to realise exactly what a can of worms this whole thing might be. The possibilities were infinite and some of them inevitably quite unsavoury.

'You *could* have been wrapped in newspaper.' Julia's second gin and tonic was slipping down very easily, and her words escaped before she could properly censor them.

'Oh God – I'm sorry, Billie. I didn't mean that.'

Billie shook her head. 'Don't be sorry. Listen, I need to be able to talk about it to someone. I need to talk about it honestly. It's true – I could have been wrapped in newspaper. My birth mother could have been a slapper, a saint, or a member of The Nolan Sisters for all I know!'

'She couldn't have been one of The Nolan Sisters. They weren't formed until 1974.'

Billie laughed properly for the first time that evening. 'How on earth do you know that, Julia?'

'Pub quiz. Our team won the league last year, remember?'

Annie had no idea who The Nolan Sisters were. 'So, what about your name? Did you come with it, or was it your parents' choice? I mean, your adoptive parents.'

Billie winced. 'Let's not call them that. I know that it's technically correct, but to me they were – *are* – just Mum and Dad.'

Annie raised her hands in an apologetic gesture. 'Just trying to be clear about . . .' Her words trailed away.

This wasn't turning out to be the fun evening that Billie had hoped for, and she blamed herself for deflating the mood like Miss Havisham at a hen party.

'Ladies. I'm sorry. God – if any of us says that one more time tonight, I swear I'll tip every drink I can lay my hands on over them. Even at these prices! You don't have to be gentle with me, or polite, or sensitive. That makes me feel weirder than being adopted. Feel free to take the piss like you usually do. Just be normal.

I want to talk about it, because I don't know what to do, and I trust you guys to be honest with me. I don't need empathy, I just need your usual, and frankly often completely inappropriate, but much appreciated advice. Oh – and another one of these arty-farty gin and tonics.'

As she stood at the bar waiting for their drinks, she watched her friends conferring and wondered what they were saying, if they were talking about her. Bloody hell! Since when had she become so self-obsessed? Or was that just too much gin on an empty stomach? They were probably discussing the barman again – Julia eyeing him up and Annie putting him down. Once their drinks were served and Billie was seated back at the table, Annie returned to her earlier question.

'So, what about your name? Where did it come from?'

'Don't you mean, from whence or from whom?'

Annie grinned. 'Touché, smart arse. Now answer the bloody question.'

'I'm not sure. Of course, I always assumed that it was the name given to me by Mum and Dad. They had me christened Billie Marie – Marie after Dad's sister – but come to think of it, Billie seems an unlikely choice for them.'

'Maybe after Billie Whitelaw, the actress?' Annie offered.

Billie laughed. 'Definitely not. Mum couldn't stand her. Said she had cold eyes.'

'I know exactly what she meant.' Julia shuddered. 'She was so creepy as the nanny in *The Omen*. What about Billie Jo Spears – the country singer? Were your mum and dad fans?'

Billie recalled the records that had been the soundtrack to her childhood, but couldn't remember any Billie Jo Spears amongst them.

'I don't think so.'

'Well maybe that's the one thing your birth mother did give you.' It was Annie who voiced what they were all thinking. 'Maybe *she* gave you your name.'

Billie wondered if that changed anything.

'So, what do you guys think? Should I leave well alone, or try and find out who she was?'

Julia frowned her thinking frown. 'What about your birth father, or whatever you want to call him. Wouldn't you want to know who he was too?'

'Well, I suppose so. Although he might not even know I exist. The most likely explanation is that my mother was some young, unmarried girl who got pregnant and couldn't keep me. Maybe he knew and couldn't or wouldn't stand by her. Or maybe she never told him.'

'Maybe he was married,' Julia added helpfully.

'I think you should do whatever you think you need to.' Annie returned to the original question and answered it. 'If it were me, I'd want to know. But you have to be ready for the possibility of drawing a complete blank or finding out things that you'd rather not know.'

Billie had already made her decision. In fact, despite all the doubts she had been expressing, she had known from the moment she had read her dad's letter that she couldn't do nothing. She had to try and find out who she really was.

'And what do you think, Julia?'

Julia finished her drink and got up to buy another round.

'I think you should be very careful.'

11

Now

Billie recalled Julia's words as she reread the letter in front of her for the umpteenth time. The radio in her flat was tuned to Classic FM and the sweet strings and lilting melody of Czibulka's 'Love's Dream After the Ball' were completely at odds with her emotional turmoil. She had felt so much better after last night – finally sharing her news with her closest friends. Their company had made her feel normal again and dispelled the strange sense of displacement that had haunted her since she'd discovered her dubious pedigree. Had the letter arrived yesterday, its contents could have been debated too and Julia would, quite possibly, have spilled an entire round of drinks over her. This letter had also been forwarded by her dad's solicitor – he'd be charging her for postal service soon – with a covering note explaining that the sender had been an acquaintance of Billie's father for many years but had always communicated with him via the solicitor's office.

Who the hell was Imelda Burova?

She was, according to her letter, someone who had information to share that would be to Billie's advantage.

She suggested that they should meet in a café on the seafront at Brighton on Thursday of next week. God – it sounded like an episode of *Poirot*! And Imelda Burova was certainly a name worthy of an Agatha Christie character. It was a brief letter that concluded with the words . . .

Of course, if you would prefer not to pursue this matter then I understand completely. It is your choice and I shall abide by your decision whatever it may be. I shall wait for you at the café and hope that you are prepared to trust that I wish you no ill. In fact, I should very much like to meet you.
  Kindest regards,
  Imelda Burova

A quick Google search had confirmed Billie's knee-jerk suspicion that this woman was almost certainly a charlatan. Imelda Burova – aka Madame Burova – was a tarot reader, palmist and clairvoyant who had traded in Brighton for many years. Billie knew that Julia would tell her to keep well away. Annie would probably take it less seriously – *go, if you like, it might be quite interesting. But she's probably just touting for business.* And usually Billie would agree with Annie. But this woman – this Madame Burova – had exchanged correspondence with her dad for years and yet Billie knew nothing about her. She'd never heard her name mentioned once. Madame Burova had been her dad's very well-kept secret. But secret what? Lover? Friend? Relation? And why the silence? Why was she a secret?

Billie scoured the letter for further clues. The note-paper was thick, ivory in colour and obviously expensive. The writing was bordering on flamboyant and the sparse words appeared to have been carefully chosen. The envelope had a Brighton postmark and a first class stamp. Billie's parents had always been the bedrock of her world and she had never doubted their unconditional love. Now she had to face the fact that not only had they concealed her adoption, but there were other things about her dad she didn't know. A part of his life that he had kept from her, and possibly from her mum too. Madame Burova. Was keeping such a secret the same as lying, she wondered? Could trust be incremental or was it an absolute that, once licked by a flame of deceit, crumbled like paper into ashes? Billie folded the letter carefully and tucked it back inside its envelope. There were too many questions and not enough answers. It was time to go and have it out with the people who knew the truth. Billie stood up and fetched her coat.

The cemetery was a damp disarray of fallen leaves and bedraggled trees flailing in a cantankerous wind. Billie's mum and dad were buried together, and their grave was marked by a simple white marble headstone. Billie had stopped at a petrol station on the way and bought a bunch of carnations and chrysanthemums as a peace offering, or perhaps as a salve to soothe the guilt that was contaminating her for doubting her parents. But surely she had a right to? She flung the flowers down.

'I'm not sure you deserve these anyway!'

She wished that her parents' plot had been more conveniently situated – closer to a bench or even a tree stump that she could sit on. She squatted down, feeling her knees protest, and addressed the headstone.

'What the hell do you two think you're playing at? First the adoption – *my* adoption, and now this Madame What's-her-face! Did you know about her, Mum? Or was she just Dad's little secret?' She paused to allow the gravity of her words to sink in, and felt her thighs beginning to ache. She really must get to the gym more often. Or maybe she could try yoga? She stood up and thrust her hands into the pockets of her coat.

'Mum, I understand why you didn't want to tell me about being adopted, but it wouldn't have made any difference. You will always be my mum. And Dad, I understand why you thought I ought to know, and you were right. But what did you expect me to do about it? And I'm talking to both of you now.'

Billie heard a noise and turned to find an elderly couple shoving dead flowers into the unattractive wire bin, which was inconveniently situated close to her parents' plot.

'Don't mind us, luv,' the old chap called to Billie with a cheery wave. 'You carry on. Always best to get it off your chest.' Billie smiled, but waited until they had wandered off before continuing.

'Now I know this much, I need to find out the rest. Or at least try. I just want to know who I really am and where I came from and I hope that you're okay with that, but also kind of glad that you can't tell me if you're not, because I'm going to try anyway. And as for the mysterious Madame B, I've not made my mind up about her yet. But you haven't heard the last of this, Dad.'

She half expected a crow to fly down and land at her feet or poo on her head as a sign; an answer from beyond the grave. But no portent was forthcoming, avian or otherwise. Billie straightened the flowers. She wanted to tell her parents that she loved them before she left, because she did. But the words caught in her throat. The love was still there, but the trust, for the time being, was broken.

12

1973

Grisha licked the back of the young woman's hand as tears pooled in her eyes and spilled down her cheeks. She had come to Imelda with questions about her twin brother. The Fool, a Seven of Swords and The Magician inverted in the tarot spread told the sorry story of a foolish young man, enthralled and excited by the company of a brash and boastful Jack the Lad and his friends. Their drunken brawling and petty thieving had eventually landed them in trouble with the law, and the Judgement and Justice cards revealed that they had had their day in court and got exactly what they had deserved. Imelda handed the young woman, who was called Nina, a tissue.

'He's always been easily led. It was the same at school. He tagged along with the troublemakers trying to make himself look big, but he's not really a bad lad. He's just a bit soft in the head.'

'And this time it went too far?' Imelda could see from the cards that it had, but also from the tears and the hands twisting the tissue into shreds that Nina needed someone to talk to.

'He met this lad at work. Rooster, they call him, because he's always crowing. I never liked him. He was always egging my brother, Andy, on. *Have another drink – a proper one this time,* he'd say – *else we'll call you Namby-Pamby-Shandy-Andy.* Andy thought the sun shone out of his you-know-where. It was always Rooster this, and Rooster that. He brought him home once, and Dad warned Andy that he was trouble – told him to steer clear. But he took no notice – of course he didn't!'

Nina wiped her eyes angrily with what was left of the tissue and Grisha nudged her hand with his nose in sympathy.

'Andy started wearing new clothes that I knew he couldn't afford, and when I asked him where they came from, he would just wink and tap the side of his nose. Bloody idiot! Then one night in a pub, Rooster started mouthing off and baiting another group of lads and it ended in a punch-up. The police were called, and all the lads were arrested, including Andy in his flash new clobber. It turned out that the clothes had "fallen off the back of a lorry" being driven by one of Rooster's mates. The police knew they'd been stolen and so Andy, Rooster and all his stupid mates were charged with theft and fencing stolen goods.'

Nina looked up into Imelda's eyes, checking for disapproval, but found only sympathy.

'And Andy ended up in prison?'

Nina confirmed that he was serving a two-year sentence.

'But Mum and Dad won't visit him, and they won't let me either. They say he's brought shame on the family. But he's my brother. He's a complete bonehead, but he's still my twin. I can't just abandon him. He tries to act all cocky like Rooster, but underneath it all he's still a big kid.' Nina's eyes filled with tears again. 'He'll be so frightened,' she whispered.

'The cards say he's holding on, but he needs to feel loved. He needs something to hold on for. Can't you write to him?' Imelda handed her another tissue and Grisha rested his head in Nina's lap.

'I do. But Mum and Dad won't let me read his replies. They just burn them.'

Imelda gathered up her cards from the table and returned them to their velvet pouch. She could hear Shunty-Mae's voice warning her not to make the offer she was about to, but she did it anyway.

'Would you like to ask him to send his letters here, to me? I could keep them for you and you could collect whenever you're able to.'

The café was bustling, and the tables outside were full of customers basking in the burgeoning warmth of the late-spring sunshine. Imelda and Grisha had had a busy morning seeing clients and she was looking forward to a mug of strong tea and a slice of Madeira cake, while he was hoping for a bacon sandwich. Diamond was looking hot and flustered behind the counter, fanning herself with a tea towel, but she greeted them with a broad smile and took their order.

'Are you ready for the grand opening at Larkins then?' she asked as she sploshed tomato ketchup onto Grisha's bacon. 'That's all we hear about from our Jeanie these days.'

'Well, can you blame me?' Jeanie appeared at Imelda's side and began gently scratching Grisha behind his ears. 'It's the most exciting that ever happened in my life!'

The holiday park had been open to a steady trickle of guests for the past few weeks, but the holiday season proper began that weekend, along with a full programme of on-site entertainment. Imelda was to begin regular sessions on Saturday evenings, as well as a couple of afternoons a week.

'The mermaids' aquarium was installed yesterday, and I saw them practising. Their costumes are amazing! And Cillian is coming tomorrow to supervise the construction of the Wall of Death.'

Imelda felt the hairs on the back of her neck prickle at the mention of his name. She had tried not to think about him too much since the Christmas party at Larkins, but with little success. When she closed her eyes, his face appeared in the blackness like a magic-lantern slide, and his voice would whisper to her in the wilderness between sleep and waking. But with the prospect of his return in person, Imelda recalled the words of Jeanie's imperious friend and their barely veiled threat concerned her. Vivienne was little more than a spoilt brat and as a woman, Imelda was more than a match for her. But Vivienne's wealth gave her an arbitrary advantage, which, when coupled with her ruthless sense of entitlement, it would be foolish to ignore. And then there was the man himself. How could such a brief encounter have made such a lasting impression on her? He was trouble, she was sure of that, but her instinct and her cards told her that he was also a good man, and she trusted both. Which was just as well, because she couldn't deny that she was excited to see him again and she was damned if she was going to let Vivienne keep her away.

'Come along, Jeanie. Are you going to walk me back to prison? Miss Sharp will be whinging all afternoon if I'm late back for her intolerable shorthand class.'

Imelda hadn't noticed Vivienne seated at the table where she and Jeanie had been eating their lunch and now she had joined them at the counter to reclaim her friend. Vivienne peered over her designer sunglasses at Grisha and wrinkled her nose.

'Isn't it a little unhygienic to allow dogs into a café?'

Imelda refused to be provoked. She smiled at Vivienne and handed Grisha half a slice of his bacon sandwich. Vivienne took Jeanie's arm and swept out of the café without another word. Once Vivienne's back was turned, Diamond flapped her away with her tea towel.

'And bloody good riddance, Miss Knightsbridge Knickers!' She leaned over the counter and spoke to Grisha. 'I'd much rather have you in here than that snooty cow any day.'

'Now, now. That's no way to speak about a customer.' Jack turned from the frying pan where he was turning sausages and wagged his finger in warning at his wife. 'But in her case I'm prepared to make an exception.'

Diamond sighed. 'We had hoped that when Jeanie left the secretarial college to start at Larkins, she might lose touch with that wretched girl,' she told Imelda. 'But she's started meeting Jeanie here for lunch. Our Jeanie's a lovely girl and I can't help thinking that she's being used. I'm not sure why or how, but I've just got a bad feeling.'

'Well, so far "Miss Knightsbridge Knickers" has warned me to stay away from "her" man and insulted both me and my dog. I'm certainly not a fan.'

Jack shook his head in feigned disappointment. 'And there was me thinking she was single, and I might be able to woo her with my irresistible charm and Tom Jones impersonation.'

Diamond snorted. 'The only thing men could woo her with is their wallets.'

'I'm not so sure about that.' Imelda fed Grisha the last of his sandwich and wiped the tomato ketchup from her fingers with a paper napkin. 'I think the man she is claiming to be hers is none other than the Wall of Death rider himself, Mr Cillian Byrne.'

'But I thought she'd only met him once – with Jeanie – at the Larkins Christmas party.'

'Apparently, once was enough.'

The bell above the café door clanged and three young women wiggled in, chattering and giggling. They were all blonde hair, bosoms and broad smiles, with disarmingly similar features – like a Technicolor trio of Marilyn Monroes.

'You must be Jeanie's aunt,' said the first one to arrive at the counter, offering in greeting a beautifully manicured hand with iridescent turquoise polished nails. 'I'm Dolly, and this is Daisy, and Dixie. We're the mermaids from Larkins. Jeanie told us to come here for the best bacon sandwiches in town.'

Recalling his Diana Bass and The Sardines joke, Diamond shot a warning look at Jack before taking their orders. Imelda introduced herself to them and promised that she would try to see their act before she started work on Saturday evening.

'And we'll definitely be coming along to you for readings,' Dolly replied. 'If that's allowed, what with us being staff.'

'Only I decide who I do readings for, and you'd all be very welcome.'

'How are the rehearsals going, ladies?' Diamond asked, handing them their sandwiches. 'Jeanie was very impressed.'

'They'd be going a damn sight better if Mr Mount would leave us to it and keep his hands to himself.' This time it was Daisy who spoke, but her girlish voice was almost indistinguishable from Dolly's. 'He keeps claiming to see a loose sequin or pearl that's come adrift on our costumes, but really he's just trying to stroke our bums, or brush up against our boobs.'

'Well, that's not right, is it Jack? It's a bloody disgrace is what it is!' Diamond wondered if Ruby and Jeanie were getting the same treatment.

'Certainly not! If ever you ladies want me to come and sort him out for you, just say the word.'

Dolly smiled sweetly at him. 'That's very kind of you, and we'll certainly bear that in mind. But the problem is, we've only just started and it's a good job. It's guaranteed work for the whole season – maybe longer – and the money's not bad. We don't want to cause trouble and he *is* the manager. We're just hoping that the novelty wears off, or he finds someone else to lech over.'

Grisha had wandered over to Dixie who had yet to speak. She stroked his head gently and confessed in a completely unexpected and rather menacing contralto, 'If he touches me again, I'll grab his gooseberries and twist them 'til he shouts.'

13

1973

Grisha was in full flight along the pebbled beach – an elegant, blond-furred streak of ecstatic exuberance finally released from the confines of the dukkering booth. Imelda followed him at a more relaxed pace. It had been a busy day and she had been called upon to relate some difficult truths to several of her clients. Her cards were the story and she was teller. She never altered the plot to make it more pleasing or amended the characters to render them more appealing. But honesty and its aftermath were sometimes hard to bear, and what she did was who she was – a vocation from which there was no vacation. The warm, fresh air and sound of the waves foaming across the pebbles were both soothing and cleansing to her weary and cluttered mind. The gulls swooped overhead and fidgeted in feathered rows along the blue metal railings of the promenade above. In the distance, a figure stood on the shoreline – a lone sentinel staring out to sea. His stillness marked him out from the other people wandering along the beach. He seemed oblivious to everything and everyone except the infinite expanse of water and sky before him. As Grisha approached him, his pace slowed to a trot and he halted several yards away from the man and stood, statue-like, with his long nose in the air, sampling the breeze like a sommelier savouring a particularly fine Barolo. As if sensing the dog's presence, the man turned around and Imelda saw his face. Cillian Byrne.

For a split second she was tempted to turn and walk away, whistling Grisha to follow her. She wasn't ready to see him. Emotions that she had yet to fully understand, let alone command were still unfettered and too near the surface for her to be comfortable in his presence. He unsettled and excited her. He appealed to the wild side of her nature that, for the most part, she attempted to suppress for fear of where it might lead her. By Saturday, she would be fine. Prepared. Today was only Thursday. When he raised his hand in greeting it was too late to escape. But she was glad.

'You're late. What have you been up to?' Shunty-Mae narrowed her eyes and looked her daughter up and down as though searching for incriminating clues.

'Leave her alone, *lyubimaya*. She's a grown woman with a life that's her own. You were never like this with our boys.'

Alexei kissed his wife on the cheek and poured Imelda a glass of vodka from the open bottle on the table.

'And look what happened to them! Paul and Peter deserted us to live on the other side of the world and Mark married his driving instructor.'

'But Damian joined his father's business.'

'Yes! Because he's the only one with any sense.'

Shunty-Mae scowled at Grisha and took a swig from her own glass.

'Your father's been slaving away over a hot stove making dinner and you are so late that it's almost ruined.'

Alexei laughed out loud.

'Please don't fret on my behalf, my love. My stroganoff is a forgiving dish – more forgiving than you. It's quite happy simmering away.'

Imelda sat down and Grisha slumped at her feet, drooling slightly at the rich, tantalising smell that filled the kitchen.

'I went for a walk on the beach to clear my head. It's been a busy day with some tough readings. I had to tell some poor woman that her husband's probably cheating on her with her sister, and a man that his business will close before the year is out.'

Shunty-Mae raised her eyebrows. 'What business?'

'A pawn shop.'

'Serves him right!' said Shunty-Mae, banging her glass down on the table 'Making money out of other people's misery.'

Imelda sipped her vodka. 'For once I'm inclined to agree with you. He turned really nasty when I told him what I saw in the cards – said that they were lying and that I was talking rubbish. Grisha had to help me kick him out.'

Shunty-Mae topped up their glasses. 'Well, at least he's useful for something,' she muttered.

'He's brave and handsome, like me.' Alexei began laying plates and cutlery on the table before ladling the stroganoff into a large blue and white china tureen. A couple of spoonfuls also found their way into Grisha's bowl and he slunk out from underneath the table to where Alexei had surreptitiously placed it on the floor by the back door.

'I hope you got his money before he went,' said Shunty-Mae, helping herself to mashed potatoes.

Imelda shook her head.

'He insulted my cards. I didn't want his dirty money. Besides – I didn't get a chance to tell him, but I saw something much worse in store for him than unemployment.'

Shunty-Mae raised her glass. 'Well that's something worth drinking to.'

Once Alexei was seated, she said grace.

'Dear Lord, bless this food, our home, the vardo and all those we love. And may the pawnbroker get what's coming to him. Amen.'

There was a moment's silence while they all savoured the delights of Alexei's delicious food before Shunty-Mae remembered something.

'So, tell your mother – who were you walking with on the beach?'

Imelda sighed. She had thought they had left that topic of conversation safely behind them.

'Grisha, of course.'

Shunty-Mae put down her fork and looked directly into her daughter's eyes, which were the same astonishing colour as her own and inscrutable to all except the woman who had borne her. She reached across the table and placed her hand over Imelda's. 'Be careful,' she said.

14

1973

Treasure was white. Except for the tracks of his tears. He stood perfectly still on the edge of the school playing field dripping with paint and tears, an upturned bucket at his feet. He was ashamed of who he was. Not the colour of his skin, but that he wasn't brave enough to be proud of it. Proud like his dad with his stories of how he sailed to England from his home in Jamaica on a big ship called *Empire Windrush*. How they'd arrived at Tilbury Docks in the summer of 1948 and his dad and many others had had to stay in an old air-raid shelter until they could find somewhere to live. Treasure had heard the stories so many times that he knew every detail. His dad always spoke about it as though it had been a great adventure – sailing halfway across the world to start a new life in what he always called the 'mother country'. He never talked of being scared or being treated badly, only about how exciting it was. But Treasure had worked out that his dad had been only eighteen at the time – just seven years older than he was now. Treasure couldn't imagine going to London on his own, let alone another country. And how was he supposed to be proud of who he was when so many people seemed to hate him just for being himself?

'You need to come to the school as soon as you can, Mrs Campbell. The headmaster would like to have a word with you.'

'Is Treasure all right? Has something happened to my son?'

Ruby was breathless from rushing back to answer the phone – she had just left the house for work – and now her heart raced at the sound of the school secretary's anxious voice. The hesitation before the reply was almost imperceptible, but distinct and deafening to Ruby's ears.

'It's nothing to worry about. He's just had a bit of a mishap. I think it's best if Mr Scrait explains the details when you get here.' The line went dead. Ruby glanced at her watch. The timing couldn't have been worse. Tomorrow was the first day of the summer holiday season at Larkins and over two hundred guests were checking in to the park. There were a million things to do before then, and now Ruby was going to be several hours late for work and Marty would be furious. But Treasure was her son. He was more important than any job. She wondered if she should ring Randall, and get him to come with her, but decided against it. Fridays were always busy at the garage and if it was only a minor mishap, there was no point in dragging him away.

But when Ruby arrived at the school and saw her son at the end of the long corridor outside the headmaster's office, she wished that her husband was by her side. Barefoot and sitting on a chair that was protected by a sheet of newspaper, Treasure looked strangely disjointed and horribly desolate, like a discarded ventriloquist's dummy. He was completely covered in white paint. At the sound of her footsteps, he lowered his head a fraction. Ruby crouched down in front of him and gently lifted his chin with her hand. His blue eyes were framed by ghostly lashes clumped together with the chalky white paint. There were no tears now – in fact no discernible emotion at all. Treasure had switched off and shut down.

Miss Jenkins, the school secretary, ushered her into the headmaster's office where Ruby took a seat without waiting to be asked. Mr Scrait was studying some paperwork in front of him and took a moment before deigning to look up and acknowledge her presence.

'Mrs Campbell. Thank you for coming. I think you need to get *Treasure* home and into some clean clothes. He's had a bit of an accident – no real harm done – but I'm afraid he's going to need a new school uniform.'

Ruby flinched at the supercilious inflection of his voice as he spoke her son's name. How dare he.

'And I'm going to need an explanation of what precisely has happened to him.'

Mr Scrait sighed and spoke again with exaggerated patience.

'One of the teachers found him standing on the playing field next to an empty bucket. The paint is used by the groundsman to mark out the football pitch and it seems likely that your son tripped and fell, spilling the paint over himself.'

It was all Ruby could do to stop herself leaning over the desk and slapping Mr Scrait's smug and shiny face.

'Really? That seems *likely* to you, does it? It seems *likely* that Treasure tripped for no apparent reason and managed to roll himself around in spilt paint until he was covered from head to foot, and then he just stood there doing absolutely nothing about it until a teacher came and found him?'

'What is it, Mrs Campbell, that you're implying?' The headmaster's veneer of insincere civility was disintegrating in the face of such an unexpected challenge to his authority. 'Are you trying to suggest that someone else was involved?'

'I'm suggesting that your version of events is about as likely as Prince Charles announcing his engagement to Elsie Tanner! What does Treasure say?'

Mr Scrait smirked. 'Nothing.'

Ruby stood up. She'd had enough. 'You've not heard the last of this. My husband and I will be in touch.'

Mr Scrait didn't bother to rise from his chair.

'Ah yes, Mr Campbell. He's from Jamaica, I believe.' He returned to his paperwork, before adding as an afterthought, 'Of course, it's never easy for children like Treasure having parents from such *different* backgrounds.'

Ruby resisted the temptation to slam the door on her way out. Miss Jenkins was waiting with a carrier bag containing Treasure's ruined shoes.

'I'm so sorry. He's a lovely boy. So well behaved.' She turned to Treasure. 'I hope you're feeling better soon.' He gave no indication of having heard her attempt at kindness, but Ruby thanked her and then took Treasure's soiled hand in her own.

'Come on, son. Let's get you out of here.'

Randall sat at the kitchen table with his head in his hands. Eventually he looked up at Ruby and she was scared by what she saw. Her husband was usually a genial man. He rolled with the punches – took everything in his long and loping stride. But she knew that at his core burned a pride that was absolute. It had been hard won and sorely tested. The 'mother country' that had invited him, one of her sons, to make it his home in 1948 had denied and humiliated him more times than Ruby wanted to remember – far too many times for her to be able to forget. But Randall had refused to be broken by his country's betrayal. He had never allowed the demeaning treatment he had endured, nor the filthy words flung at him in ignorance and hate, to define or diminish him. He knew who he was. He was an honourable man, who worked hard and loved his family. He was proud of where he came from and the life that he had built. But this was different. This was his son.

'Someone is going to pay for this,' he growled.

Ruby placed her hand over his.

'We don't know what happened.'

Randall smashed his fist down onto the table and stood up, knocking his chair flying across the kitchen.

'We do know what happened! Of course we know! Some vermin racist kids at that school tipped paint on our son, and that bastard headmaster did nothing about it apart from telling you to get him a new school uniform!'

'But we can't prove anything. Treasure won't say what happened. He hasn't spoken a word since I went to pick him up.'

Randall went to the fridge and yanked out a can of beer.

'He will. Give him time. And when he does . . .'

Treasure was supposed to be in bed, but he was sitting at the top of the stairs listening to his parents talking, and there was one thing that he was certain of now. He was never going to tell.

15

1973

'Are they real mermaids?' A little girl sucking an ice lolly and clutching her dad's hand stood wide-eyed, staring into the aquarium where Dolly, Daisy and Dixie were performing an exquisitely choreographed underwater waltz. Their golden hair fanned out and trailed behind them like veils of silken seaweed and their pearlescent sequinned tails flicked and swished, sending bright bubbles bobbling to the surface like the contents of an uncorked champagne bottle.

'I shouldn't be surprised.' The man was as mesmerised as his daughter, although probably for slightly different reasons. The mermaids' costumes certainly accentuated their voluptuous figures. The little girl finished her lolly and handed the stick to her dad.

'Where did they get them from?'

The man pocketed the stick without taking his eyes from the aquarium. 'Somewhere exotic, I reckon. Probably Bournemouth.'

Imelda overheard their conversation in passing and smiled. The mermaids were proving to be very popular and had attracted quite a following. Larkins was teeming with holidaymakers and many of them were spending their first day exploring all the delights it had to offer. The Wall of Death was one of the highlights and the tiered seats of the auditorium were packed with an excited audience. Vivienne was, predictably, in the front row, but Imelda stayed at the back with Grisha by her side. Cillian was prowling the floor like a prize fighter waiting for the bell. He wore jeans and a T-shirt, but no helmet. His motorcycle stood ready – blood red with a chief in a feathered headdress painted on its tank. He scanned the audience once more and then signalled for the show to begin. The ferocious roar of the bike, the smoke, and the fumes of engine oil were a potent cocktail. In that moment, as man and bike began to climb the wall in ever-accelerating circles, Imelda understood why he did it. When she had been younger, her mother often took her to visit Romany cousins who kept horses. The children would gallop across the fields bareback and Imelda always insisted on riding a wild-eyed white stallion called Crazy Horse. Her mother had always protested but never actually stopped her. He was the fastest and least biddable mount and to experience the thrill of riding him meant embracing the danger that came with it. For Imelda it had always been, and still was, an irresistible combination. Fear and excitement were two sides of the same coin and a man like Cillian Byrne was willing to risk death to feel truly alive. He was riding around the top of the wall and then swooping down, almost to the floor and back up at a dizzying speed. Eventually he slowed and while the bike was still moving, he switched to riding side-saddle.

Accelerating once more, he climbed the wall and raised one arm in a triumphant salute. Imelda's heart was pounding and her ears ringing. She needed to be outside, but had to see Cillian safely dismounted first. As he relished the applause she slipped away and headed off to her booth to prepare for that evening's readings.

In the entertainment lounge, she was greeted enthusiastically by an older woman who was seated at the bar drinking a large gin. The woman looked vaguely familiar. She waved Imelda over to join her.

'Let me buy you a drink to celebrate our first day.' It was barely six o'clock, but the woman looked as though she'd already been celebrating for quite a while. Imelda was about to politely refuse her offer, but then thought better of it. She had plenty of time to get ready and the woman was only trying to be friendly.

'Thank you. That's very kind.'

The lounge was crowded but Imelda managed to find a free stool and as she squeezed in next to her new colleague, she recognised her as the extraordinary contortionist, Sara-Jade Virtue.

'Cheers!' Sara-Jade clinked glasses with her and swigged her gin. 'I know you from the posters. You're Madame Something-or-another – the fortune teller.'

The reception hall at Larkins was bedecked with brightly coloured posters advertising all the activities and acts that the guests could enjoy. Marty had insisted that the entertainment staff have their pictures taken for use in Larkins' publicity material. Cillian had been photographed astride his motorbike wearing a black leather jacket and a sultry scowl. Someone had already christened it with a lipstick kiss. Imelda had posed inside her booth, hands hovering over a crystal ball with Grisha beside her.

'Call me Imelda. And yes, I'm a palmist and clairvoyant, and I read tarot cards.'

'Do you do curses as well? There's a few people I'd pay good money to have cursed.'

'Anyone I know?' Imelda joked.

'Well, that Marty Mount for starters. He needs to learn to keep his hands to himself. And the bloke in my corner shop who smells of kippers. He's always scratching. I can't stand a man who's always scratching. I reckon he's got fleas.'

'When are you on this evening?' Imelda asked, wondering if the effects of the gin would have worn off by the time Sara-Jade shimmied out on stage.

'In about an hour. Should have time for a couple more of these before I have to go and get changed and warm up.'

Her answer caught Imelda off guard, and her consternation was momentarily evident before she managed to regain a more neutral expression. Sara-Jade laughed out loud.

'Don't worry, love, it lubricates my joints. I always have a few drinks before I do my act. I'm never that bendy when I'm stone cold sober.'

Imelda had been surprised when Ruby told the entertainment staff that they would be permitted to drink in the entertainment lounge along with the guests. It was, apparently, Marty's idea. He thought that the paying guests might welcome the opportunity to 'rub shoulders with a little bit of stardust'. Imelda finished her drink and wished Sara-Jade 'good luck' for tonight's performance.

'At least you didn't tell me to "break a leg". Most people think it's hilarious to say that to a contortionist. As if I haven't heard it a million times before. It makes me want to break their silly necks!' She winked at Imelda, who was pretty sure she was joking . . .

Inside her booth, Imelda laid a velvet cloth over the table and placed her crystal ball onto its golden stand. She removed three packs of tarot cards from their silk pouches and sat down to await her first client. Grisha circled the booth as though he were checking that everything was in order, and once he was satisfied, he settled at her feet. Her thoughts returned to Cillian Byrne. The evening she had found him staring out to sea, he had walked back with her along the beach. As they walked, a connection had arced between them. It crackled and flashed through the salty air. It couldn't be seen or heard – but it was palpable. Imelda was certain that they had both felt it. They had exchanged pleasantries, but mostly they had strolled in silence. And when they parted, Cillian had simply smiled at her and walked away.

A nervous cough came from the other side of the curtain draped across the doorway.

'Come in.'

Imelda's first client was a large woman with red hair and a very pink face. She had clearly been making the most of the glorious weather on the first day of her holiday without the protection of suntan lotion or a shady hat. She looked sticky and uncomfortable in her going-out dress, but perhaps she was simply nervous at the thought of having a reading. Imelda tried to make her feel more at ease. She invited her to sit down.

'How can I help you? Would you like me to read your palm, the crystal ball, or perhaps you would like to ask a question of the cards?'

The woman wriggled a little on her chair.

'Can I ask anything?'

Imelda smiled at her and nodded. 'Choose one pack from the cards on the table, and as you shuffle them, ask your question out loud.'

The woman pondered for what seemed like an age and Grisha sighed heavily, as though urging her to get on with it. At last, having made her choice, she shuffled the cards as expertly as any poker player.

'I want to know who keeps stealing my undies from the washing line.'

The Magician inverted, the Fool and the Ten of Cups revealed the knicker thief to be the woman's bumptious neighbour who had developed an obsessive crush on her. Imelda couldn't decide if the woman was flattered or furious, or maybe a little of each. After two and a half hours of readings, Imelda was exhausted and decided to call it a night. She packed up her things and woke Grisha, who was snoring gently on his blanket. She could hear Jeanie's voice coming from the entertainment lounge. She was belting out Shirley Bassey's 'Big Spender', and judging from the applause that followed, the crowd loved it. Imelda wished that she could avoid any more people tonight, but she had to walk through the bar to get out. The room was hot and noisy, and very crowded. Ruby was chatting dutifully to some of the guests, but she looked tired, almost haunted. Imelda made a mental note to seek her out and see if there was anything that she could do to help. But not tonight. She edged her way along the line of palm tree lamps, skirting the pink flamingos that Grisha sniffed with worrying interest. She urged him on, fearful that he might decide to relieve himself against one of their spindly legs. She saw Jeanie weaving through the crowd, receiving many well-deserved congratulations on her performance as she made her way to the bar followed by her accompanist, Charlie Martin. Waiting for them, dressed in a very tight, very short red dress was Vivienne. She was perched on a bar stool with a drink in one hand and a cigarette in the other, chatting to Sara-Jade, but her eyes kept darting across to a nearby table where three men were drinking beer and trading card tricks. One of them was a stranger to Imelda, perhaps a guest at the holiday park, but to his left sat Titus Marlow, the hypnotist, and the man dealing the cards was Cillian Byrne.

Imelda walked on through the noise and lights, eager to be outside beneath the unconfined canopy of a star-studded sky and feel the cool air on her face. But as she reached the door, she couldn't resist a brief backward glance. He was looking directly at her. He held her gaze for just a moment and then returned to his cards.

16

Now

'They'll start putting up the Christmas decorations any day now, I expect,' said Henry, stirring sugar into his flat white. Billie was on her way to Brighton but having made her customary visit to her talisman, Sir John Betjeman, she had stopped to have a coffee with Henry before catching her train. She pulled a face.

'It's too soon. It's only just November. It stops it being special when it drags on for too long. Christmas shouldn't start before the first of December.'

Henry laughed. 'Don't be such a grump! I love it. All the glitter and tinsel and twinkling fairy lights – it's magical. And in this life, we must take the magic where we can find it. Besides which, if they waited until December, by the time they'd finished it would be time to take it all down again!'

The air inside St Pancras was chilly and seated at his piano, Henry was cosy in a tweed woollen coat, mustard felt beret that matched his customary bow tie, and fingerless knitted gloves.

'So, my dear – are you all set to meet the mysterious Madame Burova?'

Billie had told Henry about the second letter she had received and today was the day of the rendezvous. She was nervous, excited and wishing that she'd worn more comfortable shoes. The metallic DMs had been an impulse buy, and although they looked great with her bowler hat and the rest of her carefully chosen outfit, the inside seams were rubbing, and she could feel a blister threatening. She sipped her cappuccino and emerged from her cup deliberately sporting a foam moustache. Henry smiled.

'Nice deflection, but tell me honestly, are you okay?'

Billie wiped her top lip with the back of her hand. 'Honestly? I've no idea. But I have to go. I need to find out what I can. If all else fails, I can always ask her to read my palm. Maybe I'll get some answers that way.'

Henry's expression was serious for once. 'Try not to judge her before you meet her, Billie. I knew her once briefly, a long time ago. She was a good woman.'

Billie was gobsmacked. 'You never said anything when I told you where I was going. What do you know about her?'

Henry shook his head. 'Very little. Of course, I know she has a booth in Brighton – it's on the prom. But I haven't seen her in person for many years. All I'm saying is don't think the worst. Wait and see what she has to say.'

Billie finished her coffee, kissed Henry on the cheek and left him playing 'That Old Black Magic'. She was sure he did it on purpose. Passing the flower stall on the way to her platform, she stopped and, on impulse, bought a posy of yellow roses and purple heather. As she reached the bottom of the stairs the Brighton train was just pulling in and she managed to find a window seat facing in the direction that the train would be travelling. Perhaps it was a good omen.

Madame Burova sat staring out of the window at the heaving waves of a sea buffeted by a bullying wind. She had been coming to the café for most of her life and she felt comfortable here, which is why she had chosen it as their meeting place. If the meeting took place at all. It was twenty minutes to two and she had asked Billie to join her at two o'clock, but she had no idea if she would turn up. On the table in front of her lay the brown envelopes and a tiny silver bracelet inscribed with the name 'Billie'. It had been over forty-five years since she had seen Billie – since she had cradled her in her arms. But she had never forgotten the unbearable softness of her baby skin and the brush of her downy hair against her lips as Madame Burova had kissed her head for the last time before handing her over to the strangers who would reinvent her life. Of course, she had the photographs that Billie's adoptive father had sent every year until Billie was eighteen and then the final picture of her in a graduation cap and gown. It had been very kind of him. He was under no obligation to honour her request, but the pictures had arrived, nonetheless. Madame Burova wondered if she would recognise the woman that Billie had become. If she came.

At twenty past two, Madame Burova stood up to put on her coat, but just as she was lifting it from the back of her chair, the bell above the door rang and a woman wearing a bowler hat and brandishing a bunch of flowers burst into the café. Her comic entrance was reminiscent of a scene from a Charlie Chaplin film. Madame Burova sat down. She really hoped this was Billie. The woman was obviously looking for someone. She surveyed the tables and then stood, uncertain, in the centre of the café, as though waiting for a sign. When none was forthcoming, she made her way to the counter and asked for a cup of tea and a slice of carrot cake. Having placed her order, she came straight over to Madame Burova's table.

'Are you Madame Burova?'

Madame Burova looked into her face, searching for some familiar feature. But she saw nothing that she recognised and was both disappointed and relieved.

'How did you guess?'

'You're the only person in here who looks like a Madame Burova.'

Madame Burova smiled. 'Please, have a seat.'

Billie sat down and shrugged off her coat. 'I'm sorry I'm late. I'm hopeless at directions. I went the wrong way down the seafront.'

'I was about to leave. I wasn't sure that you would come.'

'Neither was I. But in the end, I couldn't resist.'

Madame Burova admired her honesty. 'I don't blame you for being suspicious. I imagine it's been rather a lot for you to take in since your father died. But I'm truly glad you did. I'm afraid I have some more revelations for you.'

They lapsed into silence as Billie's tea and cake were served. Madame Burova had rehearsed this moment so many times in her head, but now that it had arrived, she hardly knew how to begin.

'How much do you know about what happened before you were adopted?'

Billie poked at her cake with a fork but appeared to have lost her appetite.

'Virtually nothing. I know I was abandoned – presumably by my birth mother – but I have no idea what her circumstances were. I don't know if she couldn't keep me or simply didn't want to.'

Madame Burova winced at the understandable hurt that whetted Billie's words. She wanted to provide some comfort, but she had to be cautious about how much she revealed.

'She left you here deliberately, on the promenade. She chose a place where she thought you'd be safe. A place where she knew someone would find you.'

'How do you know that? And how the hell do you know my dad?' There was no malice in her tone. A touch of anger perhaps, but mainly bewilderment.

Madame Burova sighed. She caught the eye of the waiter and ordered a pot of Earl Grey. It was going to be a long and tricky conversation.

'I'm sorry Billie, but please understand there's only so much that I can tell you. It's complicated and I want to help you, but in certain aspects my hands are tied. Let me start with what I hope will be some good news for you. Your mother has left you a generous trust fund, which is now yours to do with as you please. I have all the paperwork here.' Madame Burova pointed to a substantial six-figure sum on the bank statement she was holding, and then waited for the news to sink in.

Billie appeared to be considering what her reaction ought to be. She drummed her fingers along the brim of her hat, took it off, placed it on her lap and then put it back on.

'I suppose I ought to be pleased. No, I am pleased. Of course, I'm pleased. Who wouldn't be?'

Madame Burova sipped her tea and waited patiently for the 'but'.

'But it feels like a consolation prize. Or maybe even hush money. Is it because she feels guilty for dumping me or is she paying me off so that I don't look for her?'

'Perhaps this is all she *can* give you. Perhaps this is the only way that she is able to show you that she cares about you.'

'Is she still alive?'

'I have no reason to believe otherwise.'

'But you can't tell me who she is?'

Madame Burova shook her head.

Billie had discarded her bouquet on the table, and now she picked distractedly at the petals on one of the roses, lost in her own thoughts. There was a crackle on the café's sound system as the album that had been playing finished and the needle hiccupped on a speck of dust. The Tea Leaf was run by Jack and Diamond's granddaughter, Amber, and her partner, Kip. Since they had taken over, the whole place had been remodelled and was now a bastion of cool retro chic, and the only music played was either live or on vinyl. As the first track on the new album began to play, Billie's face was transformed by a sheepish smile.

'What a bloody idiot! Here I am being a complete

misery guts when you've just told me I'm rich! Well – certainly not poor. I had a wonderful childhood with parents who loved me, and maybe even my birth mother cared a bit. I suppose I really ought to give her the benefit of the doubt – for the time being at least. I apologise for being a complete misery guts.'

She handed the bouquet to Madame Burova with an extravagant flourish.

'A good friend of mine told me that this whole thing could turn out to be an exciting adventure. Maybe he was right. What have I got to lose?'

Madame Burova wasn't surprised that it was Charlie Chaplin's composition 'Smile' that appeared to have lifted Billie's mood. Certainly, it was a beautiful melody, but she had a feeling that it held special memories for Billie. And when she smiled, Billie's face became faintly familiar to Madame Burova. She felt a fleeting recognition, like fragments of a recurring dream. She examined the flowers. 'Heather for a gypsy – very appropriate.'

For a moment Billie's smile faltered. 'I didn't mean anything by it . . .'

'I'm teasing you! They're lovely. Thank you. Why did you bring me flowers?'

'I'm not sure. I didn't want to come empty-handed, but I was slightly worried that you'd be wearing a head-scarf and gold hoop earrings and demand that I cross your palm with silver before you told me anything. I certainly came prepared not to believe a single word you said.' Billie blushed as she realised how judgemental she sounded.

'But now you do?'

Billie grinned sheepishly. 'I'll let you know when I've been to the bank!'

Madame Burova nodded approvingly. 'Smart. Very smart.' She liked this woman, and she was hugely relieved. It hadn't been a given, and if she hadn't, it would have felt like a tragedy.

'I have some things to give you which may help you to understand a little more about where you came from.'

She pushed the small silver bracelet across the table towards Billie.

'It's yours. You were wearing it when you were left by your mother. It was too big for you then, and it must have slipped off. It wasn't found until after you'd gone away to start your new life. I've kept it all these years in the hope that one day I might be able to return it to you personally.'

Billie picked up the bracelet and inspected it closely.

'So she gave me my name? It was my birth mother who called me Billie?'

'It would seem so. I'm sorry to be vague, but I made a promise many years ago and I'm a woman of my word. I agreed that I would tell you as much as I am permitted, and that I would give you the money and what's in this envelope. But the most important part of my promise concerned the things that I can't reveal, however much I might want to. That's not to say that you couldn't find out in other ways, but that's up to you.'

'What's in the envelope?'

Madame Burova pulled out a photograph and placed it in front of Billie.

'Your father is one of the men in this picture.'

The photograph was a group shot of men and women standing on stage in the entertainment lounge of Larkins Holiday Park and the caption read 'Larkins Entertainment Staff 1973'. In the centre of the photograph, smiling directly at the camera, was Cillian Byrne.

17

Now

'Nice hat!' shrieked one of a gaggle of young women tottering along the promenade dressed in pink PVC mini-dresses, feather boas and flashing tiaras. The bride-to-be was easily identifiable by her silver sequinned L-plates and was grappling with a giant inflatable penis that was in danger of being wrenched from her grasp by a feral wind whipping in from the sea.

'They'll catch their deaths,' Billie lamented to Madame Burova. 'Not a coat or cardigan between them, and I'll bet their underwear barely covers the essentials. And now I sound exactly like my mother. Well – one of them.'

Madame Burova was taking Billie to see where she had been found. She had hoped against hope that Billie wouldn't ask, but of course she had, and Madame Burova couldn't reasonably refuse – particularly as it was just next door. It would soon be the shortest day of the year, and it was already almost dark. The coloured lights on the pier, the snatches of music and smell of doughnuts and hotdogs drifting through the air were beacons, calling her home to her booth. But the booth looked a little forlorn now, shut up, and in darkness – missing out on all the fun. She found it difficult to stay away. It was so tempting to open it up for just a couple of hours. To see just a handful of clients. But she was trying hard to make a life for herself away from work – the work that had become her whole life.

'It was here,' she said pointing to the doorway.

Billie seemed surprised. 'But it's so busy,' she said. The promenade was filling up with people going home from work, visitors arriving for long weekends, and hens and stags determined to drink their own bodyweight in alcohol to achieve the humungous hangovers that would be testament to the amazing time they had had.

'It was very early in the morning. There was hardly anyone about. Nobody saw anything.'

Billie tried the door to the booth. 'Can we go inside?'

'I don't have the key with me.' The key was always in Madame Burova's bag, but she couldn't face it today. 'But next time. When you come again, we'll go inside.'

Billie tipped her head to one side and once again, Madame Burova was reminded of Charlie Chaplin – or at least a female version of him. 'But how do you know there'll be a next time?'

'Because I'm a fortune teller. Remember?'

Billie laughed. She fished around in her handbag and retrieved her mobile.

'I suppose I'd better take a selfie in situ.'

'Would you like me to take it?'

Billie handed the phone to Madame Burova and posed in the doorway grinning broadly, with one hand on her hip and the other on the brim of her hat. After the photo shoot Billie asked if they could go for a drink somewhere.

'I've got a couple of hours before my train, and I'd like to ask you about the photograph if that's okay.'

Madame Burova led the way to The Lanes. As they climbed the steps from the promenade, they were greeted by a man who was carefully looping coloured elastic bands over the posts of the metal railings.

'Good afternoon, Madame Burova, Tarot Reader, Palmist and Clairvoyant. How are you?'

'Good afternoon, Clive. I'm well thank you. How are you?'

'Busy, always busy,' he said, pulling more elastic bands from his pocket. 'Who is your friend?'

'This is Billie.'

'Good afternoon, Billie In The Bowler Hat.'

Billie smiled and tipped her bowler politely.

'Be careful how you go, ladies. They're watching. They're always watching.'

'We will, Clive,' replied Madame Burova. 'Take care.'

He nodded seriously and then moved on to the next post.

Soon they were seated in the cosy bar of The Cricketers sipping glasses of red wine.

'Who's Clive? He seems quite a character.'

Madame Burova smiled. 'That's one way of putting it. Clive – or MI5 Clive as he's generally known – is an extremely intelligent if somewhat unusual gentleman who claims to be working undercover for MI5.'

'And is he?'

'It seems unlikely, but then, who knows?'

'What's with the elastic bands?'

'He's leaving coded messages for his contacts. He says it's safer than using more conventional methods of communication. Phones and computers can always be hacked but the language of elastic bands is virtually impenetrable.'

Billie retrieved from her bag the photograph that she had been given and laid it on the table. Madame Burova took a large swig of wine to steady herself for the questions that would now follow, but the first one was easy enough.

'What should I call you? Is your name really Madame Burova?'

'It's my professional name. But you can call me Imelda.'

'Imelda Burova?'

'Yes. My darling Papa was Russian.'

'And your mum?'

'Headscarf and hoop earrings Romany,' Imelda replied with a deadpan expression.

Billie smiled uncertainly, unable to tell whether Imelda was joking or not. She turned her attention to the photograph.

'Can you tell me which one is my father?'

'I can't. But only because I genuinely don't know.'

'Do you know anyone in this photo?'

Imelda stared at the smiling faces captured in a single moment of the year that had changed her life forever. She had looked at the photograph many times since it had been in her possession, and her eyes were always, inevitably drawn to Cillian. But now she looked at the others. Friends, colleagues and some merely acquaintances. It had been a long time ago, but she could still put names to some of the faces.

'I knew most of them back then. It was taken at Larkins Holiday Park, and I worked there for a while.'

Billie pointed to Cillian. 'Who's this? He looks like a matinee idol. I wouldn't complain if he turned out to be my dad.'

Imelda was grateful for the wine and took another sip.

'Cillian Byrne. He was a Wall of Death rider.'

'What was he like?'

'Handsome, charming, kind – and very popular. He drew people to him, like a log fire on a winter's day. But he had a dark side too. Danger excited him.' As she lifted her glass again, Imelda's hand shook just a little. 'He was a big hit with the ladies,' she added.

'I bet he was. What happened to him?'

'He died.'

18

Now

'He died! Oh God, Billie, that's awful!'

Thankfully, Julia just managed to return the forkful of spaghetti Bolognese to her bowl rather than drop it into her lap with shock at Billie's revelation. She and Annie and had joined Billie for dinner at her flat before she returned to Brighton, where she had been invited to spend a week with Imelda. Billie was sharing with them what she had managed to find out so far.

'Years ago, apparently. Just my luck.' Billie had shown them the photograph and repeated word for word what Imelda had told her.

'But you don't know for sure that he was your dad?' Annie picked up the photograph and studied it carefully, searching Cillian Byrne's features for any likeness to those of her friend. 'You don't look much like him.'

'Imelda said that she couldn't tell me who my birth father was, because she didn't know. But my mother gave her this to pass on to me, saying that he was in this photograph. Cillian Byrne is right in the middle. His face is the first one you see, and frankly, if I had to choose, I'd choose him. He's bloody gorgeous.'

Annie raised an eyebrow. 'That sounds a little weird, coming from his prospective daughter. And anyway, as I said, there's not much of a resemblance,' she teased with an arch smile. Billie pulled a face. 'Maybe I look more like my mother.'

'Did Madame Burova tell you who any of the others were?'

Julia had momentarily lost interest in her food and gestured for Annie to hand over the photograph.

'She said that she knew most of them when it was taken – she worked at Larkins for a while doing readings – but now she can only remember a few names. She wrote them on the back.'

Julia turned the picture over and read out loud:

'*Back row, third from left – Titus Marlow, hypnotist.* He looks a bit creepy. *Second row, far right – Sara-Jade Virtue, contortionist. Front row, far left – Marty Mount, General Manager.* He looks like a proper ladies' man. *Middle row, second from right – Jeanie Rogers, singer.* She looks so young.' The list continued, finishing with *Centre – Cillian Murphy, Wall of Death rider.*

'What makes you think that this Cillian was your father? Did Madame Burova drop any hints?'

'How could she drop any hints if she didn't know who the father was?' said Annie, refilling their wine glasses.

'She said she didn't *know,* but I got the impression that she had her suspicions. She also said that he was very charismatic and that the ladies loved him. Maybe that was a hint.'

'It sounds like she fancied him to me,' said Annie, helping herself to a slice of garlic bread. 'What did she tell you about how you were found?'

Billie had thought about little else since her trip to Brighton. She had gone over and over Imelda's words in her head, analysing them for any cryptic clues, but if there had been any, they remained as indecipherable to her as MI5 Clive's elastic bands.

'She told me that I was found in the doorway to her fortune teller booth on the promenade, and that it was very early in the morning and nobody saw anything.'

Julia had returned to her dinner and was twirling spaghetti around her fork. 'Who was it that found you?'

This was one of the things that had puzzled Billie and that she had fretted over like a kitten with a ball of wool ever since she had found out. Not the fact itself, but Imelda's obvious reluctance to divulge it.

'She did. Madame Burova – Imelda.'

'So why didn't she tell you that in her letter?'

'I don't know. I'm not sure she would have told me at all if I hadn't pressed her. It was only when I asked her how she knew my dad, my real dad – oh God, this is so complicated – Dad here, that she confessed.'

'But why wouldn't she want you to know?'

'Again, I have no idea. But she said that after she had called the authorities and they came to pick me up, she asked if someone could let her know what happened to me. She wanted to make sure that I was okay, and apparently when I was adopted, that message somehow got through to my dad and he wrote to her. She also made sure that they knew my name was Billie.'

Julia slammed her hands down onto the table, making the cutlery jump. 'I've got it!'

Annie rolled her eyes. 'Julia has a theory, God help us. Come on then, let's have it.'

'Madame Burova is your mother!'

The thought had crossed Billie's mind more than once, and even Annie didn't dismiss it out of hand.

'It's certainly a possibility,' she conceded. 'It would explain why she's been so cagey with the details, and why she was so concerned about your wellbeing. But is she wealthy enough to dish out so much money, and if she is your mother, why wouldn't she want you to know now?'

Julia was eager to back up her theory. 'Because she's ashamed of what she did and can't face the possibility that you might reject her. She's trying to make it up to you with the money because that's something practical that she can do right now to help you without revealing the truth. Maybe she's hoping that if you get to know her, and whatever her story was back then, the two of you can build a relationship.'

Annie shook her head. 'Julia! Where does all this come from? I swear to God you watch far too many docusoaps on TV.'

Julia rapped her over the knuckles with a breadstick.

'You've got to admit – it's possible.'

Annie shrugged her shoulders. She couldn't deny it was *possible*.

'Do you have a photo of Imelda? What does she look like?'

Billie shook her head. 'I don't have a photo, but for a woman in her seventies she looks extraordinary. Long, dark, wavy hair and sea-green eyes.'

She stood up to clear the plates. 'Imelda did say to

me that perhaps the money was the only way that my mother was able to show me that she cared.'

Julia grinned triumphantly. 'I knew it! Madame Burova is your mother. What's for pudding?'

As Billie served the tiramisu, something was clearly still troubling Annie.

'You do realise that if Imelda *is* your mother then she's either a liar or a bit of a hussy.'

Julia narrowed her eyes and waggled her dessert spoon laden with cream and sponge in Annie's direction. 'That's not a very nice way to talk about your friend's potential mother. You haven't even met the woman. If she finds out you've been bad-mouthing her, she'll probably put a curse on you!'

'And if you drop any of that tiramisu on my tablecloth, I'll put a curse on you!' warned Billie, laughing.

'I wasn't being unkind. I was simply assessing the facts objectively.' Drinking wine had the curious effect of making Annie more sober. 'I was merely making an extrapolation from the information that we have before us.'

'Come on then, Miss Marple. Elaborate on your extrapolation.' Alcohol just made Billie louder and more verbose.

'Well, *if* Madame Burova is your mother, then either she does know who the father is but won't tell you or doesn't know because she was sleeping with more than one man at the same time.'

Julia took a sharp intake of breath as she tried to conceal a splodge of dessert on the tablecloth by covering it with her napkin. 'Now you're accusing Madame Burova of having a threesome!'

'I didn't mean at exactly the same time, as you well know. And I saw that,' Annie replied, nodding towards Julia's napkin.

———————————

It was a little after 6.30 a.m. and Billie sat on the balcony of her flat cradling a mug of tea in her hands and waiting for the sun to rise. She had pulled on a winter coat over her pyjamas and wrapped a woolly scarf around her neck and over her head. It was freezing but she hoped that the crisp, sharp air would dispel the stupor brought on by last night's wine and her friends' interrogation. She had barely slept and had spent the night chasing thoughts of Imelda and Cillian Byrne around her head like a border collie attempting to herd a flock of errant sheep. The protectiveness she felt towards Imelda after their single encounter had taken her by surprise. She was sure that Imelda was not a liar or a hussy and had been uneasy when Annie had suggested it even jokingly, but she had neither the evidence nor experience to substantiate her faith in the woman's character. And she was equally certain that Imelda was hiding far more than she was revealing.

A watery light was just bleeding into the darkness on the horizon.

> *'Awake! for Morning in the bowl of night*
> *Has flung the stone that puts the stars to flight:*
> *And Lo! the Hunter of the East has caught*
> *The Sultan's turret in a noose of light.'*

There was no sultan's turret to be seen from Billie's balcony, but the majestic backlit silhouette of St

Cuthbert's church was almost as magical as the view described in Omar Khayyám's *Rubáiyát*, a poem Billie had loved since finding a battered copy in a second-hand bookshop when she was a student. In a neighbour's garden, a blackbird tested out a tentative warble, which was soon bolstered by other birdsong. A modest choir rather than a full dawn chorus, but nonetheless an avian overture to the new day. As the first sliver of sunlight surfaced above the horizon, Billie wondered if the whole truth about her own beginnings would ever be revealed.

19

1973

Imelda was surprised to see Ruby at her booth on the promenade, but welcomed her in and offered her a seat.

'I didn't want to see you at Larkins. You know how tongues wag. And I have to be so careful – Marty watches me like a hawk.'

Imelda took in Ruby's weary eyes and drawn features.

'Actually, I was going to ask you if there was anything I could do to help. Something seemed to be worrying you when I saw you on Saturday night.'

Ruby looked to be on the verge of tears.

'It's Treasure.'

Imelda picked up her favourite pack of tarot cards and handed it to Ruby.

'Give them a shuffle, and let's see what they have to say.'

The Moon, the Hermit, the Tower, Death and the Fives of every suit told of Treasure's troubles.

'He's stopped talking to you. He's not letting you in. Something bad happened, maybe at school, and now he's struggling with his emotions and afraid he's not good enough.'

Ruby nodded. 'Something did happen at school, but he won't tell us what. What can we do?'

'Ask the cards,' said Imelda, picking them up and handing them to Ruby to shuffle once more. Imelda placed the second spread on the table.

'Hang in there,' said Imelda, pointing to the Temperance card. 'Give him some time and space to sort himself out, but don't try to force him to talk to you. He's stronger than you think.'

Ruby pointed to the Death card that Imelda had turned over for a second time.

'Isn't that really bad?'

Imelda shook her head. 'It doesn't always mean death. It can mean a new beginning, a fresh start. Don't worry about Treasure. The cards say he's going to be just fine.'

A little of the tension seemed to have been smoothed away from Ruby's face. She checked her watch.

'Thank you so much, Imelda. I must get going. I'm due at work in a bit. How much do I owe you?'

'You can buy me a drink next time I'm at Larkins,' Imelda replied, gathering up the cards. 'It'll be a large one mind you!'

There was a loud 'tut' from behind the curtain at the back of the booth, but fortunately Ruby didn't notice it as she was being enthusiastically bid farewell by Grisha.

'Oh, and one more thing,' added Imelda. 'Don't be surprised if Treasure gets a dog from somewhere. They'll rescue each other.'

Once Ruby was gone, Shunty-Mae's head appeared from behind the curtain like a puppet in a Punch and Judy show.

'What have I told you about doing readings for free? That's not the way to do it! If you don't value your gift, then no one else will.'

Imelda pulled back the curtain so that her mother was fully revealed.

'And what have I told you about coming down here and poking your nose into my business. For heaven's sake, Mother! You're supposed to be retired. Haven't you got anything better to do? Can't you get a hobby, like making jam or playing bingo?'

Shunty-Mae waved her hand dismissively at her daughter. 'Your papa rules the kitchen. He won't let me so much as boil a potato.'

'That's because you can't even peel a potato, let alone cook one.' Shunty-Mae's culinary ineptitude had resulted in numerous blackened saucepans and several small fires before Alexei had declared himself sole chef for the safety of his family's home and digestive health.

'I have talents that he appreciates far more than root vegetable preparation.'

'What about bingo, then?'

'Gambling!' Shunty-Mae exclaimed in a melodramatic tone. 'The work of the devil. Besides, once the summer season is in full swing, you'll be grateful for some help.'

Imelda couldn't deny it. As soon as she was old enough, she had always worked with her mother in the booth for the summer season, and often one of her mother's sisters or cousins had helped too.

Shunty-Mae had tried in vain to teach her sons to read the cards, but they had neither the interest nor the aptitude.

'Well, it's not busy at the moment, so why don't you make yourself useful and take Grisha for a walk along the promenade?'

It was difficult to say who looked more horrified, Grisha or Shunty-Mae.

Imelda smiled and took hold of her mother's arm.

'As if I'd trust you with my precious hound!' she teased. 'Let's all go next door and get some lunch.'

On the beach, the pebbles were peppered with stripy deckchairs. Many were occupied by bodies recklessly exposing varying expanses of winter-wan skin to a brutal midday sun. The tide was on the turn, and where the waves frilled at the water's edge, children in swim-suits and sun hats splashed one another and squealed with delight. Sitting outside Jack and Diamond's café, a serious-looking young man was scanning the faces of passers-by and circling words and pictures in the news-paper that was spread out on the table in front of him. He had begun frequenting the seafront just a few months ago, and always appeared to be engaged in some significant but incomprehensible task. Imelda had been curious and had sensed in him a desire for human interaction that would be satisfied by passing pleasantries, but possibly perturbed by any obvious attempt at friendship. She had begun gently – a simple greeting – and it had been gratefully received and read-ily reciprocated. Grisha wandered over to him and pushed his head under his hand, demanding to be acknowledged.

'Good afternoon Grisha the Russian Dog Who Doesn't Have Fleas.' Imelda sometimes wished that Clive wasn't so literal. When she had first introduced Grisha to him, she had joked that he didn't have fleas despite being rescued from the streets. 'Good afternoon Madame Burova, Tarot Reader, Palmist and Clairvoyant. Who is your friend?'

'Good afternoon, Clive. This is my mother, Shunty-Mae.'

'Good afternoon, Mother Shunty-Mae.'

Shunty-Mae smiled in response and hurried inside the café.

'Jesus! He makes me sound like I've escaped from a nunnery!'

Imelda laughed. 'You – in a nunnery? You wouldn't need to escape. It'd be the nuns chucking you out!'

'Who's going in a nunnery?' Diamond was standing at the counter buttering slices of bread.

'No one. It was just something that Clive said to Mum on the way in.'

'Bless him. He's a strange lad, but a good customer and always very polite. Now what can I get you ladies?'

A young boy with light brown skin suddenly appeared from behind the counter. Seeing Grisha, his eyes widened, and the trace of a smile flitted across his face. He placed his hand gently on Grisha's neck and began to stroke him.

'This is my nephew, Treasure, Ruby's boy. He's helping me out during half term while his mum's at work. He loves dogs, don't you Treasure?'

The boy looked up at his aunt, to acknowledge that she'd spoken, but remained silent.

'He doesn't talk much,' Diamond explained, somewhat unnecessarily, to Imelda.

Shunty-Mae winked at Treasure. 'I expect he's the strong, silent type.'

After their lunch, Imelda left Shunty-Mae in the café playing rock-paper-scissors with Treasure, while she took Grisha for a walk. She had been tempted to ask Treasure to accompany them. Perhaps she might be able to persuade him to confide in her, particularly if she had the help of Grisha. His quiet, comforting presence often had the effect of relaxing her clients, particularly those who were nervous or distressed. He seemed to sense who would welcome the warm weight of his head on their lap or a furry paw to hold. Occasionally, he would get up as soon as a client walked into the booth and disappear behind the curtain. It was the awkward ones that he always left Imelda to deal with on her own.

Imelda stuck to the promenade. It was too hot for Grisha to race along the beach, and they would have had to weave their way through sunbathers and sandcastles. There was also the temptation of picnics and al fresco fish and chips that might prove too much for an ever-hungry borzoi. The promenade offered a patchwork of shade and snatches of sea breeze, but the heat was still intense, and a short stroll was enough to loosen Grisha's long limbs after a morning of lolling about, and Imelda led him, panting, back to the umbral calm of the booth. Leaning nonchalantly against the doorway, wearing a roguish smile and a well-worn white T-shirt that showed off his muscular arms, was Cillian Byrne. Grisha dragged Imelda towards him, his tail wagging furiously and his mouth open in a ridiculously goofy doggy grin. Imelda concealed her excitement a little more successfully than her hound. She smiled what she hoped was her mysterious yet seductive smile and trusted that Cillian would realise her pink cheeks were a consequence of exposure to the sun rather than to his considerable charm.

'Mr Byrne. What a pleasant surprise. Are you here for a reading?'

Cillian disentangled himself from Grisha and followed Imelda inside the booth.

'I'm not. I was just passing, and I thought I'd call in and see if I could take you for a drink or maybe an ice cream. I'm sure the big hairy fellow here would love one too.'

Imelda raised an eyebrow. 'I'm not sure that your girlfriend would approve. And besides, we've just had lunch, thank you.'

Cillian sat down and, despite the heat, Grisha snuggled up against his leg.

'I don't have a girlfriend.'

Imelda was delighted to hear it, but not entirely convinced.

'I'm quite sure that's not what Vivienne thinks.'

Cillian shook his head. 'She can think what she likes. Sure, we've had a few drinks and she hangs around at Larkins with Jeanie, but she's just a kid.' He looked up directly into Imelda's eyes. 'I prefer the company of a woman.'

'Well then, it's your lucky day. Because now you've got two of us!'

Shunty-Mae's timing was either auspicious, or more likely the result of eavesdropping at the door. She swept in a little over-dramatically and narrowly avoided tripping over Grisha, who had slid into a prone position with his limbs fully extended across the floor.

Cillian stood up, completely unfazed, and extended his hand.

'I'm delighted to meet you. You must be the original Madame Burova. It's clear to see where Imelda gets her good looks and *lively* spirit from.'

Shunty-Mae allowed him to shake her hand – but only briefly.

'It'll take a good deal more than flattery to impress me.'

Cillian grinned. 'I've no doubt of it. Perhaps you'd like to come and see my show sometime?'

'I most certainly would not! Why on earth would I want to see a suicidal madman hurling himself in circles around a wooden barrel on a motorbike?'

'Mother! I think the whole point of the Wall of Death is for the rider to try very hard not to kill himself. It requires a great deal of skill. And nerve.'

Imelda glared at Shunty-Mae. She was definitely going to have words with her about this later.

Shunty-Mae was unrepentant. 'Well now, are you here for a reading or are you just distracting my daughter from her work?'

'I was hoping to take Imelda and Grisha for some light refreshment, but I can see she's busy. I'm sure there'll be another time.'

'Are you afraid of what the cards might say?'

Cillian was not to be provoked. He smiled good-naturedly.

'I'm not afraid of much. It's just that I prefer to keep my future a surprise. It's more exciting that way, don't you think?' He glanced at Imelda and turned towards the door. 'I'll see myself out.' And then he was gone.

20

1973

The afternoon passed quickly, with a steady stream of readings. Nina called in to pick up a letter from her brother, and Imelda's final customer of the day was a smartly dressed man in his thirties who looked more like he was on his way to an appointment with his bank manager than someone wanting to have his palm read or ask questions of the tarot cards. Imelda invited him in. He sat down on the edge of the chair and adjusted his spectacles nervously.

'I've never done anything like this before,' he admitted.

Imelda smiled. 'Don't worry – I'll be gentle.'

He looked puzzled and realising that he didn't have much of a sense of humour, Imelda took a more businesslike approach.

'What can I help you with today?'

'I'm afraid I'm not really sure how all of this works,' he replied. He took off his spectacles and polished them with a pristine handkerchief before replacing them on a nose that was slightly too small for his face. He was called Neville – the kind of man that you could pass on the street every day without registering; his ordinariness

119

rendering him invisible. And yet here he was, doing something new and, for him, clearly quite daring. Imelda was curious to know what had driven him to such uncharacteristic measures.

'Do you have any specific questions you would like to ask, or would you just like a general reading?'

'I don't know how much I'm supposed to tell you. I'm looking for answers, but I'm not altogether sure I know what to ask you. What I mean is, I don't want to give away too much in the questions.'

Imelda heard an impatient sigh escape from Shunty-Mae behind the curtain. Neville looked startled.

'It's my dog.' It was the best Imelda could do, gesturing to where Grisha lay behind her. 'Perhaps we should start with a crystal ball reading?'

Imelda moved her cloudy crystal orb to the centre of the table and asked Neville to place his hands just above it. She allowed her eyes to drift just a little out of focus, looking through the ball rather than directly at it. Soon the pictures began to flash across its glassy depths like a slideshow of hazy film stills and Imelda flicked them on with her hand. There were several houses. All smart, semi-detached, red-bricked neatness with wooden-gated driveways and square lawn gardens edged by regulation borders. The epitome of comforting conformity, they were the residential equivalents of Neville. One house kept returning. It had a dark blue front door with a brass knocker in the shape of a dolphin, and a ceramic tile painted with a number nine fixed to the wall.

'Have you been house hunting, Neville?'

Poor Neville looked genuinely startled. 'How did you know?'

Imelda smiled but didn't look away from the ball. 'It's my job. There's one that keeps appearing. Are you thinking of buying a house with a blue front door? It has a dolphin door knocker and it's number nine somewhere.'

Neville shook his head in bewildered disbelief. 'We made an offer on it yesterday. Number nine Stoke Street. Miriam loves dolphins and she said the door knocker was a good omen. I don't believe in that kind of nonsense' – Imelda braced herself for a disapproving tut from behind the curtain and timed her cough perfectly to cover it – 'but it's a lovely house and very tidy inside and out. Do you think we'll get it?'

Imelda saw the house with packing boxes piled in the driveway, and then a key turning in the lock of the blue door before the images blurred and faded, and finally disappeared altogether.

'Yes, Neville. Your offer will be accepted.'

He looked pleased, but something was still troubling him. Imelda placed three packs of cards in front of him and asked him to choose. 'Shuffle the cards and ask your question out loud.'

'Will Miriam and I be happy together?'

Imelda dealt the cards onto the table. The King of Swords and the Queen of Cups lay crossed at the centre of the spread. The King was Neville with his dark hair and pale blue eyes.

'Does your Miriam have dark hair and brown eyes?'

Neville nodded. Miriam was the Queen.

The High Priestess, the Lovers, the Two of Swords and the Four of Cups followed.

'You will marry Miriam. Your marriage will last, and you will have a very happy home together. Yours is a true love.'

Neville looked relieved. 'We're getting married next month.'

Imelda was delighted to be able to give Neville the good news. But there was something else in the spread. The Hierophant, the Death card and the Three of Swords foretold the sacrifice that Neville was making for his bride-to-be. He assured Imelda that she was worth it.

––––––––––

At the end of the reading, Neville thanked Imelda profusely, paid and left. The rise and fall of Shunty-Mae's gentle snoring from behind the curtain was syncopated by Grisha's random groans and sighs in front of it. Imelda placed the two objects that Neville had given her inside the cubbyhole in the wall before slamming the picture that concealed it back in its place. She was still angry with her mother for the way she had behaved earlier and hadn't spoken to her since. The sudden noise had the desired effect and Shunty-Mae emerged, smoothing her hair away from her face as she stretched her long, elegant neck.

'I wasn't asleep. I was just resting my eyes.'

Imelda refused to look at her. 'It's a shame you weren't resting your tongue when Cillian Byrne was here earlier.'

Shunty-Mae stepped warily around Grisha and took her daughter's hand. Imelda's fingers stiffened and she tried to pull away, but Shunty-Mae held on tight.

'Let's walk,' she said. 'Lock up, and we'll go for a walk.'

The beach was quieter now. Above the pebbles, a heat haze still shimmered, but its ferocity had abated as the spent sun dipped lower in the cerulean sky. Shunty-Mae slipped off her sandals and headed towards the sea. Grisha raced ahead of her as soon as he was unleashed, plunging into the water – spinning and leaping in a joyful canine jitterbug.

Neither could Imelda resist the temptation to paddle. The cold, crimpling waves soothed her sweltering skin and the stones beneath massaged her tired feet.

'I know you're angry.' Shunty-Mae gazed out to sea, water lapping at the hem of her dress. She stood strong and straight, like a ship's figurehead, with the breeze tugging at her long dark hair. Imelda had never encountered a woman so beautiful, so powerful and so bewitching as her mother. Nor one so infuriating.

'Damn right I'm angry! Why do you have to interfere every time a man comes into my life?'

Shunty-Mae laughed. 'That last one was hardly a man. He was scared of his own shadow.'

Imelda's last boyfriend had been a talented art student who had broken into a cold sweat every time he had met her mother.

'Tom was just a bit shy, that's all. You made him uncomfortable with all your questions.'

'He was still a boy – even at twenty-two – and no match for you. But this one – this Cillian Byrne is different.'

Shunty-Mae turned and faced her daughter. 'I'm not going to stop you seeing him.'

'You can't!'

Shunty-Mae smiled but there was sadness in her eyes. 'I don't want to.'

'Then why did you talk to him like that?'

'Because I'm your mother. I look at you and it's like looking in a mirror.' Shunty-Mae scanned the horizon, as though the sky or sea might harbour the words she was scrabbling for.

'You believe that I'm invincible. Afraid of nothing. But I have one fear that taps me on my shoulder like a tight-fisted tallyman. The fear of seeing those I love get hurt. You are my only daughter, and I love you more than my own life. I want you to be happy. I want you to taste everything that life has to offer and to learn that salty tears and sour disappointments will only make joy sweeter.

Imelda was winded by her mother's ragged voice and raw emotions.

'But I still want to protect you, and if I do that, I'm clipping your wings. As your mother, my job is to see that you fly. But perhaps, one day, you will understand how hard it is.'

'I don't see what all this has to do with Cillian.'

Shunty-Mae kicked at the water in frustration, soaking her dress.

'Just remember, Imelda, I won't always be able to break your fall.'

21

1973

'Something's got to be done.' Sara-Jade was stone-cold sober for once, and unusually serious. Dolly, Daisy and Dixie nodded their blonde heads in agreement and there was a general murmuring of assent from the other women present. Sara-Jade and the mermaids had asked to meet Ruby in the café and had invited other female members of staff from Larkins to join them, including Imelda and Jeanie. When Ruby had asked why they couldn't talk at the holiday park, Sara-Jade had replied, rather ominously, that 'it wouldn't be safe'. Once they were all seated, and Diamond had served them tea and biscuits, Sara-Jade, who was clearly their elected shop steward, explained why they were there.

'Something's got to be done about Mucky Marty. We're all sick of his smutty mouth and wandering hands. It's not right that we should be expected to work under these conditions.'

Ruby wasn't surprised. She should have seen it coming. She spent most days dodging his unwelcome advances and flinching at his filthy comments. His behaviour around the guests was usually just the right side of appropriate, but with female members of staff it was open season. She felt her cheeks redden with shame at her own cowardice. She had known that this was happening and yet she had done nothing to stop it. Nothing to protect them. She hadn't even had the self-respect to call him out when he made her feel cheap with his constant pawing and pathetic innuendo. She began to wonder now if she deserved it, had even encouraged it, by not saying 'no' or 'stop'. She wished she had the guts to slap his face.

'If we complain to him,' began Dolly, 'his answer is always the same,' added Daisy.

'Remember who pays your wages,' they finished, in unison.

'I've a good mind to tell him where to stick his wages,' growled Dixie.

Diamond, who'd wandered over to eavesdrop on the pretext of bringing another plate of biscuits, was indignant on their behalf.

'I said it before. That man's a bloody disgrace! Do you want me to send Jack round to sort him out? I'm sure his offer still stands.'

Ruby shook her head. 'It's not that simple, Diamond. That's why I haven't mentioned it to Randall. His solution would be the same as Jack's and it wouldn't help. We stand to lose our jobs if we make a fuss and we all have bills to pay. Imelda, has he ever tried anything with you?'

'No. But he's terrified of dogs. He never comes near me.'

'Lucky you,' muttered Dixie, reaching under the table and scratching Grisha's ears.

'What about you, Jeanie?'

Jeanie blushed slightly. 'He's never touched me, but sometimes the way he looks at me makes me feel really uncomfortable.'

'And you're young enough to be his daughter – bloody pervert!' Diamond had been very close to her younger sister, Emerald, and was instinctively protective of her niece. 'You should report him, Ruby.'

'To whom? If we report him to the police, they'll just laugh at us. In fact, we'll probably get into trouble for wasting their time. He's not done anything illegal.'

'Yet,' growled Dixie.

'Well, what about his boss then? He must have a boss?' Dolly was on the verge of tears. She had felt his sweaty hands on her body and his hot breath on her neck more than most. Just the sight of him made her feel sick and the only time she felt safe at work was when she was in the water.

'Yes, Dolly, he does,' replied Ruby, gently, 'but I doubt very much that Mr Collins will be sympathetic. Marty is something of a golden boy in his eyes. Since Marty was appointed, guest numbers have doubled, and the books are looking extremely healthy for the first time in years.'

Sara-Jade banged the table in frustration, causing her teacup to shimmy in its saucer.

'So, what are you saying? That we do nothing? We keep our mouths shut and lie back and think of England like well-trained Victorian wives?'

'No, of course not. All I'm saying is that if we want to keep our jobs, we need to be careful.' Ruby despised herself for seeming so defeatist and reluctant to take any action, but on the face of it theirs was a simple but depressing choice between pride and pay packets. She had once seen a tiny blue butterfly with the tip of its wing caught in a spider's web. As it struggled frantically to free itself, the fragile blue membrane began to tear. But if it gave up the fight for freedom, it would certainly be prey for a passing bird. Damned either way.

Dixie broke a biscuit in half as viciously as if she were snapping Marty's neck.

'Well, if he touches me once more, that's it. He'll be singing soprano for the rest of his days by the time I've finished macerating his meat and two veg.'

Dolly's eye make-up was sliding down her face in a torrent of tears. 'You can't, Dixie. He'll sack us. And he's already told me that he won't give us references, and he'll bad-mouth us to every other fairground and holiday park owner in England.'

Mavis, an impassive woman whose moon face always bore the expression of a bewildered goldfish, was trying to follow the conversation whilst wolfing down as many biscuits as possible. She was employed at Larkins to clean the chalets and rarely saw Mr Mount. She had only come to the meeting in the hope of free refreshments.

'What's she going to do with his dinner?' she asked Jeanie, spraying crumbs from her thick lips. Diamond, who was still hovering, moved the plate of biscuits out of Mavis' reach before replying. 'Meat and veg isn't his dinner, you daft mare – it's his manhood. She said she's going to mince his cock and balls!'

Mavis digested this information with interest as she chewed a mouthful of Jammie Dodger. She was mildly affronted that Mr Mount had never so much as winked at her. Imelda passed Dolly a tissue. It looked as though Ruby might need one too at this rate. She had enough to cope with already, worrying about Treasure, and Imelda knew that Ruby had experienced Marty's lascivious management style first-hand. Her office had an adjoining door to his.

'Sara-Jade's right,' she said. 'We need to do something, and I have an idea.'

22

1973

The knobbly knees paraded round in a circle and then lined up for inspection like a row of misshapen potatoes. It was a gloriously sunny Saturday and Larkins was a frenzy of fun activities supervised by the entertainment staff. Sara-Jade was leading a keep fit session in the pool with the mermaids, Jeanie was helping with the children's races, Charlie was playing music for an outdoor tea dance, and Titus was calling bingo numbers with the grandiose gravity of an actor delivering a Shakespeare soliloquy. Cillian had been persuaded by Ruby to compere the Miss Larkins Lovelies contest, closely watched from the audience by Vivienne, who had denounced it as a 'cattle market for vacuous bimbos' but had decided to attend nonetheless.

Imelda was inside her booth with Grisha and Ruby, plotting.

'Is Marty in his office now?'

Ruby nodded. 'He pretends he's doing paperwork for half an hour or so around this time, but I'm pretty sure he takes a nap. Especially when he's had a couple of G and Ts with his lunch.'

'Perfect. Let's go!'

Outside Marty's door, Ruby hesitated before knocking. She was nervous. She hated being alone with him. Her face flushed and she felt a trickle of sweat run down the back of her neck between her shoulder blades as though fear was leaking from her pores. Imelda squeezed her arm.

'You can do this.'

Once Ruby was inside, Imelda waited until she heard them begin talking before knocking. Without waiting for a response, she barged straight in with Grisha by her side.

'Oh, I'm terribly sorry, Mr Mount. I didn't realise you were busy.'

Marty eyed Grisha warily. Imelda released his collar and Grisha advanced slowly, distracting Marty's attention just long enough for Imelda to do what she needed to do.

'Get that blasted dog out of here!'

Imelda smiled. 'Of course. I'll come back later.'

They left the office and hurried outside where bemused holidaymakers were beginning to be distracted by a conversation being broadcast on the public address system.

'I can't believe you're making such a fuss about nothing. I'm only being friendly. It's my nature. There's nothing wrong with that.'

'We've had enough, Marty. There's nothing friendly about the way you behave. It's disgusting. You're just a dirty old man!'

The knobbly knees were looking slightly discombobulated. Charlie had silenced the music and the tea dancers were suspended mid-waltz in one another's arms. Sara-Jade's water babies were treading water and the Larkins Lovelies were giggling nervously on the catwalk.

'The problem is that you ladies have no sense of humour. I suppose it's your hormones. Tell me, Ruby, have you got your monthly? Is that why you're being so oversensitive?' Marty's usual silky smarminess had slithered away, and his tone had taken on a nasty edge.

'We're not your personal harem. We're here to do our jobs. It's time you learned to keep your hands to yourself and treat your female staff with respect.'

Imelda detected a slight quaver in Ruby's voice, but otherwise she was doing splendidly.

'And I think it's time that you remembered your place. Your job is my assistant, and if you carry on like this you won't have that job for very much longer, and nor will any of the other troublemakers.'

'Are you threatening me?'

'I'm advising you that I'm not happy with your performance.'

The wife of one of the knobbly knees contestants nudged the woman standing next to her. 'I bet his performance is nothing to write home about.'

The outdoor activities had, by now, been freeze-framed by the developing hostilities being publicly broadcast. Most of the holidaymakers and staff were hanging on every word. Ruby was very popular with the guests and disapproving mutterings were growing in volume among the crowd. Inside, in the dining hall, the scrape of cutlery on plates had paused and chewing suspended. Chatter had ceased and slot machines stood silent in the bar of the entertainment lounge. Even in the chalets, radios had been switched off and children shushed.

'If you have any complaints about the way I carry out my duties, then I'll be happy to listen to them, but the last time I looked, my job description did not include having my bum or boobs groped by you.'

A man who had been waltzing with his wife at the tea dance laughed. 'Nothing wrong with a bit of slap and tickle. Just a bit of harmless fun.'

His wife backed away from him, took aim and landed a stinging slap across his cheek.

'Well, see how much fun you think that is!'

Imelda wondered if it was time for her to go and rescue Ruby, but then Marty began again.

'At the end of the day, Ruby Campbell, it's your word against mine. And the same goes for any of the other stupid bitches who want to make an issue out of nothing. I'm the boss and don't you forget it. I'll decide what your duties are and if I get any more trouble from you, I'll kick you out on your pretty little arse.'

At that moment in Marty's office there was the briefest buzz of feedback from the microphone. His eyes flicked across the room in panic and the glowing red light finally alerted him to the fact that his conversation with Ruby had not been private.

There was a brief pause before Ruby had the last word.

'I'm pretty sure you won't.'

23

Now

Billie sat staring at the sulking countryside through the porthole she had wiped in the condensation-misted window. Its wintry garb was a depressing palette of muddy browns and greys, occasionally relieved by a splatter of hawthorn berries or rosehips. It was too mild for a frost to camouflage the dreary trees and hedges with a dusting of sparkling white and stiffen the mushy furrows in the fields into crisp, earthen vertebrae. The train had been held at a red light just outside Hassocks for ten minutes. 'Hassocks' always sounded to Billie as though it should be in a limerick, but she could only ever think of 'cassocks' to rhyme with it. According to the driver, they should be on the way 'very soon'. His qualifying statement of 'So I'm told' didn't inspire optimism, but then there was a quiet judder and hiss and the train pulled slowly forward. A tangible if barely audible expression of relief rippled around the other passengers in the carriage. Billie checked her watch. She wondered if she should text Imelda and warn her that she was running a little late. Imelda was meeting her at the station and

Billie would be staying with her while she was in Brighton. Billie worried now if that was wise. After all, she had only met her once. But what if Imelda was her mother? Surely the closer Billie got to her, the more likely she was to find out. Surely if she spent enough time with her, she would just *know*. Some visceral mother–daughter connection would be revealed like a message in invisible ink when the notepaper it is written on is warmed beneath a light bulb or skimmed with a hot iron. She had debated with herself whether to ask Imelda outright, but had decided against it. To pose the question was tantamount to accusing Imelda of lying, or at least of deliberate deception, and Billie was reluctant to risk damaging their fledgling friendship for the sake of impatience.

As the train pulled into Brighton, passengers were reminded that this was their final destination and that they should take all their belongings with them. Billie thought that the rail company should find a way of rephrasing it. Final destination sounded so ominous, like the eponymous American horror film. She tipped her bowler slightly further back on her head so that she could see better what she was doing, retrieved her small suitcase from the luggage rack and joined the huddle of passengers waiting for the doors to open. Imelda was standing at the platform barrier elegantly swaddled in a long leopard-print coat. She was accompanied by a small, pigeon-grey Staffordshire bull terrier with a wrinkled frown and a slight underbite which made her look permanently grumpy. Her true disposition, however, was betrayed by a stumpy tail that whirled, rather than wagged, with frenetic enthusiasm.

'Meet Mabel,' Imelda introduced the little dog to Billie before giving her a brisk, welcoming hug. She led Billie to her car, which was parked just outside the station. Billie was delighted to discover that Imelda drove an ancient silver Jaguar. On the journey back to her house, Imelda explained that Mabel was her retirement present to herself.

'I had a dog years ago, a beautiful borzoi I rescued from the streets when he was a puppy. My heart was broken when he died, and I couldn't face having another.' She honked the horn furiously at an indolent young man wandering across the road while studying the screen of his mobile phone. 'But now, I have more time on my hands and I could do with a little company at home.'

Imelda had apparently visited the local animal shelter and asked to see the dog that had been there the longest. 'I'd made up my mind to take the one that no one else wanted, whatever size, breed or age.'

Billie clung to her seatbelt as Imelda swerved suddenly to overtake a Nissan Micra whose driver was dithering between two lanes.

'Mabel was always overlooked because of her original features, but I think they give her character.'

Mabel, who was safely harnessed on the back seat, barked approvingly at the mention of her name. They pulled into the driveway of a tall, semi-detached Victorian house and Billie unclenched her jaw, relieved to have survived the journey and Imelda's exhilarating driving. Inside, the house was exactly how Billie hoped it would be. A pair of enormous mirrors with ornate gilt frames faced one another on the richly coloured walls of the hallway. The polished wood floors were the colour of freshly shucked conkers and cut crystal chandelier lights hung from the ceiling. In the middle of the kitchen stood a large oak dining table surrounded by six chairs, and on an oak dresser sat a gleaming silver samovar.

'It was Papa's, and his mother's before that,' said Imelda, brushing it tenderly with her fingertips as she passed. 'Now, take off your coat and hang it in the hall. Would you like tea or vodka?'

After a mug of strong tea and a shot of icy vodka, Imelda showed Billie to her room at the top of the house.

'It used to be mine when my parents were still alive.'

The deep brass bed was topped with a velvet patchwork cover and strewn with silk-fringed cushions. A Persian rug was sumptuously snug underfoot, and glass candlesticks on the mantle over a cast-iron fireplace glinted in the soft pink light of the afternoon sun. The window looked out over the garden. And there under a canopy of skeletal winter trees, looking for all the world like an Arthur Rackham fairy-tale fantasy somehow conjured into reality, was a Romany gypsy caravan.

A couple of hours later, after Billie had had the chance to unpack and take a quick shower, the three of them were in a cab heading towards the seafront. They pulled up close to the steps that led down to The Tea Leaf. The café looked much busier now than it had been on the afternoon when Billie had first met Imelda. As Imelda paid the cab driver, Billie stood holding Mabel's lead, listening to the voice of Marvin Gaye coming from inside The Tea Leaf, and the swoosh of waves coming from the beach.

'Good evening, Billie In The Bowler Hat.'

Billie turned to see MI5 Clive removing elastic bands from the posts on the promenade. She was surprised that he remembered her. 'Good evening, Clive. How are you?'

He pushed the coloured bands into his pocket. 'I'm very much occupied with my work.'

Mabel barked, offended at being ignored. Clive bent down and patted her awkwardly on her fuzzy head. 'Good evening, Mabel Who Nobody Wanted.'

Imelda joined them. 'Good evening, Clive.'

'Good evening, Madame Burova, Tarot Reader, Palmist and Clairvoyant.' Clive scuttled away, seemingly unsettled by such excessive social interaction, and Imelda led Billie and Mabel into The Tea Leaf. She had reserved a table for them, and it was the only one free as they took their seats. Music nights at the café were very popular and Amber and Kip were busy serving drinks and taking food orders. In the corner of the room there were two 'old-school' record decks and piles of vinyl. The shadowy figure of a tall man was searching through the records, selecting a playlist. He raised his hand in greeting to Imelda and she waved back. Amber came over to take their order.

'Hi, Imelda. How's Mabel settling in?' Mabel was sitting on Imelda's lap looking very pleased with herself. 'Gran would love her.'

Imelda introduced Billie, and Amber went off to fetch their drinks.

'When I first began working in my booth here, this place was run by Jack and Diamond – Amber's grand-parents,' Imelda explained as she shrugged off her coat, trying not to dislodge Mabel in the process. 'Diamond's sister, Ruby, and their niece, Jeanie, both worked at Larkins. Ruby looked after the entertainment staff and Jeanie was a singer. She still is – sings at festivals all over the world now. Her two boys and her husband play in her band.'

Amber brought them a bottle of red wine and filled their glasses.

'Some of the entertainment staff used to hang around here in the café back then,' continued Imelda.

Billie's ears pricked up. 'Did Cillian Byrne come here?'

'Sometimes.' Imelda gazed into the depths of her wine glass, her eyes unfocused, as though she was look-ing into her crystal ball.

'Did Ruby and Jeanie know him?'

'Of course. They all worked together.'

Billie remembered the photograph. Of course they had. Stupid question. The fat, sassy opening notes of Stevie Wonder's 'Superstition' interrupted her train of thought for a moment. This track always made her want to dance.

'There'll be dancing later,' Imelda told her, as though she had read her thoughts. Or maybe she had just noticed that Billie was unable to keep her shoulders still. Their tapas supper was delicious, although Mabel was largely unimpressed and had only deigned to try a morsel of chorizo, which she had then pushed out of the side of her mouth with her tongue. The tables were cleared and moved out to the sides of the room to create a space for a rather intimate dance floor. The patrons of The Tea Leaf were, however, an uninhibited or perhaps slightly inebriated bunch, and the floor was quickly filled.

Billie's thoughts returned to their earlier conversation. She didn't want to push Imelda too hard on the first night, but the café had such a tangible connection to the past that she was trying to uncover, that she allowed herself a couple more questions.

'What happened to Ruby? Is she still around? Do you think she'd be willing to talk to me about Cillian and the others?'

Imelda cupped her ear to try and make out what Billie was saying above the music, which was louder now that the dancing had begun. She shook her head.

'Sadly, she died. Three years ago now. She had a stroke. Such a shame. She was a lovely woman.'

Billie sat watching the dancers who were lost in the music and one another's arms. It felt somehow voyeuristic to be merely a spectator instead of a participant. She wondered if there had ever been a jukebox in the café, and if the staff from Larkins had danced with each other here. If Cillian had danced here.

Eventually the music faded, and people began draining their glasses and gathering their things. As Billie stood up to retrieve her coat, it was whisked from the back of her chair and held aloft.

'Allow me.'

The DJ had emerged from the shadows and was standing behind her. He was a well-built man of mixed race, in his late fifties perhaps, with astonishing aquamarine eyes. Having helped Billie into her coat he turned to Imelda, threw his arms around her and hugged her tightly. Imelda pinched his cheeks affectionately.

'Billie – meet Treasure. Ruby's son.'

24

Now

Imelda lay in bed too exhausted to sleep. The tears in her eyes blurred the pristine sphere of a mother-of-pearl moon suspended in the black rectangle of sky revealed by the gap between the curtains. Mabel puffed and grunted contentedly as she snuggled in closer, tucking her head under Imelda's chin. Her paws twitched and her eyelids flickered; a dream her puppeteer.

Imelda was wondering whether inviting Billie to stay had been a mistake. She longed to get to know Billie better, but was afraid of the consequences. She had always known that there would be difficult questions. That no matter how little she chose to reveal, she would still be forced to resurrect memories that were deeply painful. She reached for the gold chain around her neck and stroked the tiny stars. She had expected to be asked about Cillian. But she hadn't anticipated that talking about him, even after all these years, would be like deliberately pressing down on a fresh bruise. Back then, she had recovered from the wounds. She was young and had found the courage and sheer bloody-mindedness to heal herself. But what about now? And what about the questions that *she* had chosen not to ask? Perhaps now the choice would no longer be hers, but Billie's, and there would be answers whether she wanted them or not.

Billie was pretending to read the novel that she had brought with her, but it was like pedalling a bicycle when the chain has come off. Her eyes passed over the printed words, but her brain was occupied elsewhere, examining the evening's events in search of clues about her birth. Ruby's death was a blow. She would almost certainly have been able to fill in some of the gaps. She had obviously known Cillian and might have remembered any girlfriends he had had. Perhaps her sister Diamond would be able to help. If she had run the café, she must have known some of the Larkins staff who were her customers, and maybe Ruby gossiped with her about the goings-on at the holiday park. Billie hoped so. She wanted to speak to Treasure too, although he would only have been a boy when Billie was born. Still, it was worth a shot. Maybe she could invite him out for a drink. She smiled to herself, imagining Julia's reaction to such a suggestion – raised eyebrows and a knowing smirk, followed by, 'You go, girl!' And then there was Jeanie. She would definitely need to speak to Jeanie. Billie abandoned her book and padded in bare feet over to the window. The naked trees and gypsy caravan were silvered by the light of an improbably large full moon, but the rest of the garden was a tangle of shifting shadows. Tomorrow, Billie would ask Imelda about the caravan. Perhaps she would allow her to see inside. Billie wondered if Imelda was still awake. She had been quiet in the cab on the way back and had gone straight to bed.

'Help yourself to anything you want – tea, coffee. Vodka,' she had told Imelda with a wink. But she had seemed depleted somehow. Not simply tired but almost melancholy, as though she were resigned to some painful yet inevitable disappointment. Billie resolved to be more careful tomorrow. However eager she was to find out as much as she could about how she came into this world, she was, for now, a guest in Imelda's home. Imelda had chosen to help her, and the last thing Billie wanted was for her to live to regret that choice.

25

Now

The Hermitage was a quaint, half-timbered bungalow at the bottom of a quiet cul-de-sac. When Henry had heard that Billie was going to be staying in Brighton, he had immediately invited her to visit him at home. She had only seen him very briefly at St Pancras since her first meeting with Imelda and he was as eager to catch up on her news as she was to share it with him. He had extended his invitation to Imelda, but Billie had been relieved when she had declined. Imelda had already admitted that Henry's name didn't sound familiar to her, and Billie wanted a chance to speak with him alone.

Henry opened the door almost as soon as she rang the bell. He was dressed more casually than usual, and minus his customary bow tie, in jeans, an open-necked white shirt and a charcoal grey soft woollen sweater with patches on the elbows. He kissed her on both cheeks and ushered her into a small hallway where he took her coat and hat.

'I'll put the kettle on and then I'll give you the grand tour.'

The sitting room was small and cosy with a log burner and a squishy sofa upon which was heaped a mismatched miscellany of cushions covered in richly patterned fabrics. The burgundy walls were hung with a seemingly random and wildly eclectic anthology of paintings. Portraits and landscapes jostled for attention with still lives, nudes and abstract works, many of their frames abutting one another so that little of the painted walls could be seen. In stark contrast the adjacent room, which was flooded with light that reflected off its bare, barely blue washed walls, contained only four objects. In the bay of the large window was a battered leather armchair. Centre stage stood a gleaming baby grand piano, accompanied by an Edwardian mahogany piano stool. On top of the piano was a single large photograph in a plain silver frame. It was taken on a beach somewhere sunny – the sea was almost turquoise and the sand white. In the foreground, a younger Henry, tanned, toned and bare-chested, stood smiling with his arm around an olive-skinned man, perhaps ten years his senior, who was wearing mirrored sunglasses and a short-sleeved pink flamingo print shirt. Henry picked up the photograph and handed it to Billie.

'Jocelyn.' A single word spoken with as much love and longing as an entire Elizabeth Barrett Browning sonnet.

'How long were you married?'

'Just three years. Jocelyn didn't want a civil partnership. He was holding out for a proper wedding and luckily, he lived long enough for us to have one. But we were together for much longer than that. I first met him when I was twenty-one. We used to joke that I was his toy boy and he was my sugar daddy. He bought me this piano for my fiftieth birthday. You wouldn't believe the palaver we had getting it through the front door.' Henry glanced towards the empty chair. 'He used to sit there and listen to me play,' he added, almost to himself.

The kitchen was a hotchpotch of painted pine cupboards. The floor was gently uneven as though at some point in the past a minor earth tremor had caused the quarry tiles to undulate, and as a result the small Formica-topped table was propped up under one leg with a slim volume entitled *Fish and Fowl Recipes for Thrifty Housewives* to keep it steady.

'Before I make the tea, you must come and see my girls.'

Henry led Billie through a glazed door at the back of the kitchen into the garden, which was an odd shape of more than four sides, the name of which Billie couldn't remember. Geometry had never been her forte. Positioned as it was at the bottom of the cul-de-sac, the bungalow's garden appeared to consist of the remnant of land that remained once the other gardens had been allocated. There was a small patio with a round table and two wrought-iron bistro chairs overlooking a rather ragged lawn and a couple of flowerbeds containing shrubs and rose bushes. Beyond that, attached to a brick-built shed, stood a large wood and wire fence enclosure. Inside, three plump chickens were contentedly preening, clucking and pecking at the wood chips scattered on the ground.

'Meet Minnie Caldwell, Hilda Ogden and Ena Sharples,' said Henry with obvious affection.

Billie smiled. 'I assume that you're a *Coronation Street* fan?'

'Not anymore. But as a kid, I was brought up on it!'

Billie squatted down to take a closer look. Minnie was the smallest of the three. She had blonde feathers speckled with white and retreated nervously as Billie leaned closer to the wire fencing. Hilda was a bright chestnut brown and, unable to contain her curiosity, she swaggered over to inspect their visitor. Ena was the size and shape of a small pumpkin and the colour of dark chocolate. She sat amongst the wood chippings watching Billie with unconcealed suspicion. Their names suited them very well.

'They're ex-battery hens. When I got them, they had hardly any feathers and Hilda had a horrible limp. That first winter, they all had to wear little woolly jumpers to keep them warm, even in their luxury cottage.' Henry gestured towards the shed. At that moment, the sound of a train passing somewhere very close startled Billie so much that she almost fell backwards from her squat onto the damp grass.

'The railway line runs right along the end of the garden. It was one of the reasons I fell in love with this place. I always wanted to be one of the Railway Children.'

Billie jumped up and went to look over the fence. She had to stand on tiptoe, but she could just about make out the train tracks.

'The music to that film has me in tears every time I hear it,' she confessed. 'Do you ever stand here and wave your hanky at the commuters?'

Henry winked at her. 'All the time!'

Back inside the kitchen, Henry made 'proper tea' as he called it, in a teapot. The teapot, milk jug, sugar bowl and cups and saucers were all beautiful shapes and patterns but none of them matched. Billie pointed to the book under the table leg.

'I hope you're not intending to cook your "girls".'

Henry raised his hands in horror. 'I never eat chicken!'

They returned to the sitting room and settled into the sofa.

'How are you getting on with Madame Burova?' Henry asked as he poured the tea.

Billie hesitated slightly before answering. 'Okay, I think.'

'You don't sound very certain.'

Billie shrugged. 'Imelda's been lovely. She took me to The Tea Leaf last night and introduced me to some people who might be able to help me.'

'So why do I feel there's a "but" coming?'

'Because I can't help feeling like a kid with a stick poking a wasps' nest.'

'You think you're going to end up getting stung?'

'Maybe. But that's not what's bothering me. If I get hurt, it's my own fault. I chose to start poking around. But what if other people get stung too?'

Henry stirred milk into his tea and took a sip.

'Well, why don't you start at the beginning and tell me what happened the first time you met Madame Burova.'

Billie told him everything, and when she had finished Henry sat in silence for a moment, considering her words before offering his advice.

'You have a right to know who you are, Billie. Besides, your birth mother started all this with her mysterious legacy of funds and a photograph. All you can do is tread carefully. More tea, vicar?'

Billie passed over her cup and Henry refilled it. 'That photograph,' he asked, 'did you bring it with you?'

'No. why?'

'I might have been able to recognise some of the faces, that's all. I worked at Larkins too for a while, but only very briefly. That's where I met Madame Burova a couple of times.'

Billie almost choked on her tea. 'That's ridiculous! What an incredible coincidence!'

Henry shook his head. 'Not at all. The holiday park was huge and catered for hundreds of guests. Back then, Larkins was one of the biggest employers in the area. They took on all sorts: chalet maids, cooks, waiters, bar staff and, of course, the entertainers. Everyone knew someone who worked there.

'What did you do?'

'Pretty much anything I was asked. I was young and needed the money, and you were expected to muck in with whatever needed doing. But all I really wanted to do was play the piano. I got to accompany some of the singers at Larkins, but it wasn't enough. That's why I left. I got a job at a club in London, and that's where I met Jocelyn.'

Billie's thoughts had returned to the photograph.

'Did you know Cillian Byrne?'

'Everyone knew Cillian Byrne! He was dashing, dangerous and devilishly handsome!' Henry teased. 'But do you really think he was your father?'

Billie shook her head in frustration. 'How do I know? It's just that he's right there, in the middle of the photo.

His face is the one you see first, and she, my mother, gave me the photo because my father was in it. But if he was my father, then there must be any number of women who could be my mother. According to Imelda, all the ladies loved him.'

'And so did some of the men,' Henry added. But not out loud.

Billie checked her watch. 'I must get going. I promised Imelda that I'd be back for lunch, and then she's going to show me inside her booth on the promenade.'

'Sounds wonderful!'

As Henry helped her into her coat, he asked Billie to remember him to Imelda, and suggest that the three of them meet for dinner before Billie returned home.

'For all his admirers and hangers-on,' Henry said, as he stood at the door to see Billie out, 'I always had the impression that there was only ever one woman that Cillian really cared for.'

'And who was she?' Billie asked as she pulled on her hat.

'Imelda Burova.'

26

Now

'What will happen to the booth now you've retired?' Billie asked. 'Will you sell it?'

Imelda hadn't yet decided what she was going to do with it, but she wasn't going to sell it.

'I'm not sure. I may lease it out if I can find someone suitable.'

Mabel was snuffling round at their feet, inspecting every corner of the booth. It was her first visit too and she was inveterately curious. Billie sat down at the gypsy table.

'Will you read my palm, or the cards, or see what the crystal ball has in store for me?'

Imelda took a seat opposite her and placed both palms flat on the table. She pushed them forwards over the velvet cover and pulled them back towards her, feeling the soft nap of the fabric change direction under her touch. It had been inevitable that Billie would ask.

'I'm sorry, but there's no point. I made a promise and I can't tell you some of the things I'm sure would be revealed.'

Imelda felt strange and unbearably sad being back in the booth. Billie had been very keen to come, and that was, of course, completely understandable. But Imelda still couldn't quite accept that she had retired, that she had given up the vocation that she loved. It had never been what she did – it had always been who she was. It was her identity and without it she was afraid she would become a nonentity, a hologram of herself with no substance or purpose. Perhaps retirement had been a fatal mistake.

'It's fine.' Billie reached across and placed her hand over Imelda's. 'I shouldn't have asked.'

They sat in silence for a moment and Imelda let her mind drift away like a balloon released from the grasp of a child. The secrets she had been trusted to keep, the confessions she had heard, the pasts she had revealed and the futures she had foretold returned, not so much as memories, but rather they seeped from the dark, draped walls of the booth and swirled around her and through her like ghosts. They were a part of her that she could never fully escape.

'Perhaps I could rent the booth from you.'

Billie's words startled Imelda back into presence with both their sound and content.

'What in heaven's name would you do with it?'

Billie grinned and shrugged her shoulders in a pantomime gesture that made Imelda smile. 'I'm not sure. But I love it. And it would be rather fitting, wouldn't it, considering it was where I was found?'

'But you'd have to move to Brighton if you were going to run it yourself.'

'Why not? I can afford to now, and I don't have any ties at home save for my friends. I'm sure they would be more than happy to visit me here.'

Billie appeared to be warming to her idea with every word she spoke.

'What do you think?' she asked.

Imelda had no idea. Did she really want this? Billie moving to Brighton? Billie in her booth? She could hear Shunty-Mae whispering in her ear, 'Be careful what you wish for . . .'

Mabel had found a cushion on the sofa at the back of the booth where Shunty-Mae used to snooze and began hurling it into the air and pouncing on it as it landed. Her antics were a welcome distraction. Imelda stood up.

'Well, it's certainly a possibility worth considering,' she conceded, hoping that she didn't sound as uncertain as she felt. 'Let's take Mabel for a stroll before she wrecks the place.'

Outside, the daylight was dwindling into dusk, and Kings Road was a steady stream of white and red head and taillights illuminating the snake of homebound traffic. As they made their way back to Imelda's house, she spotted a familiar figure in one of the glass and wrought-iron shelters that provided a sea view for those who preferred to eat their fish and chips in the fresh air. MI5 Clive was weaving a complex cat's cradle of coloured elastic across the metal fretwork on one of the benches.

'Good afternoon, Clive.'

He looked up, careful to keep his fingers still hooked through the intricate arrangement of elastic bands.

'Good afternoon, Madame Burova, Tarot Reader, Palmist and Clairvoyant, Billie In The Bowler Hat and Mabel Who Nobody Wanted.'

Mabel trotted over to greet him, but Imelda pulled her back, fearful that she might interfere with Clive's labours.

'I'm afraid I can't chat,' Clive said brusquely. 'The security of the nation's entire winter brassica crop is dependent on these messages being delivered in time.'

Imelda nodded. 'Of course, Clive. We completely understand.'

Later that evening, Imelda stood in her kitchen cooking dinner while Billie sat on the floor playing with Mabel, who was busily disembowelling a stuffed toy. Ever since Billie had arrived, Imelda had been studying her face, searching for a likeness to either one of her birth parents. Sometimes Imelda thought that the tilt of her lips when she smiled, the colour of her eyes or the way she wrinkled her nose when she was concentrating seemed familiar – reminiscent of someone else, but the recognition was always fleeting and Imelda wondered if it was little more than wishful thinking. Billie looked up from the floor and sniffed inquisitively. Imelda laughed.

'You look like Mabel when you do that.'

Billie scratched Mabel's chin. 'I'm flattered. She's such a gorgeous girl! And anyway, I can't help it. Whatever it is you're cooking smells delicious.'

Imelda poured them each a glass of vodka from the icy bottle that she had retrieved from the freezer.

'Stroganoff. It's Papa's special recipe.'

After they had eaten, Billie leaned back in her chair, sated, and Imelda poured more vodka. Mabel had snuggled down into her bed and was snoring contentedly. Imelda sensed that she and Billie were beginning to relax a little more in one another's company. The stiffness was softening like new shoes having been worn several times. Perhaps it was the vodka.

'If you can't read my cards, can you at least explain to me how they work?'

Imelda stood and went to the dresser. From one of the shelves she took a small velvet bag containing her oldest and favourite pack of tarot cards. She cleared a space on the table and spread the cards out in front of her.

'The cards must always be laid on cloth, not wood,' she said, as Billie picked up several of the major Arcana to inspect their exquisite illustrations. 'Each card has many different meanings depending on its context in relation to the question asked, and its position in the spread.'

Billie shook her head. 'It sounds very complicated.'

Imelda picked up the cards and shuffled them. It was a reflex, as natural to her as breathing. They slid through her fingers and reassembled themselves as a pack as easily as a waterfall cascading into a pool.

'You have to read the cards as a language,' she explained, 'and each spread tells a story.'

Billie sipped her vodka. 'And can anyone learn to read them?'

'Anyone can learn the meanings of each card, and the purpose and configuration of different spreads, but not everyone is able to interpret the stories that they tell. It's a gift that not everyone possesses, and it takes many years of practice and experience to perfect.'

'Did your mother teach you?'

'My mother and my grandmother. And my grandmother and her mother taught my mother. It's been passed on this way from generation to generation for many years.

'And who will you pass it on to?'

Imelda sighed. She had broken the chain. 'I tried to teach my niece – my eldest brother's only daughter – but she had no patience. No love for the language. But perhaps one day her daughter will want to learn.' Her great niece was her only hope.

'Did you never want children of your own?'

It was a loaded question and Imelda thought carefully before answering.

'This life – *my* life – has been wonderful. It's been full, rich and sometimes astonishing. I've had the privilege of helping so many people, but often what I do, and how much it takes from me, leaves little time or energy for anything else. I've had relationships, romances, flirtations, even grand passions. But I've never been able to commit to marriage, and perhaps that made me afraid of what sort of mother I might be.'

'Maybe you just never met the right man.'

Oh, I did, thought Imelda, but she kept it to herself.

'And what about you, Billie?'

'Ha! I tried marriage once. But in the end, I didn't like it much. Perhaps I chose the wrong husband. But kids? I've never felt strongly one way or the other. I've never heard that clock that everyone talks about ticking. So maybe motherhood wasn't meant for me.'

She stretched and yawned. 'I'm so sorry! I'm exhausted. It must be time for bed.'

Imelda got up from the table and the sound of her chair scraping across the floor woke Mabel, who stirred sleepily in her bed.

'Come on, young lady. Time for a final trot around the garden.'

Imelda and Billie stood just outside the back door watching Mabel search for a suitable spot to have a wee.

'Your caravan is so beautiful. Will you show me inside sometime before I go home?'

Imelda put her arm through Billie's. 'Of course. It's called a vardo. It was my mother's. She refused to let it go when she gave up her travelling life to marry Papa and insisted that it be kept in their garden. She used to sleep in it sometimes. And then one year she gave it to me as a birthday present.'

'It looks like something out of a fairy tale. Do you ever sleep in it?'

Imelda smiled. 'Sometimes. But not tonight.'

27

1973

Treasure sat on a bench at the edge of the playground scoring lines through a single sentence amongst the prolific graffiti that had been scratched onto the wooden slats by countless childish vandals. He knew most of it by heart because this is where he had spent every lunchtime since the white paint episode. He imagined the bench as his life raft in shark-infested waters. It wasn't much protection, but it was all he had, and today was the last day of term. He had managed to survive. The words he was trying to obliterate were a recent addition and revealed the light grain of the wood beneath the varnish.

'Treasure is a . . . The final word was now illegible on the bench but still rang in his ears.'

It was what they had called him on *that* day, and on every day since. Terry Arnold and his brother Brian fancied themselves as the Kray twins of Kingscroft Comprehensive. They had attracted a straggle of like-minded, bored and brutish teenage boys more interested in brawling and bullying than books to join them. They spent most days stalking vulnerable victims amongst their fellow pupils to rob of their sweets and pocket money or to frighten and humiliate for entertainment. On *that* day, they had found Treasure. But he had been a disappointment. He had ignored them, no matter how badly their taunts had hurt and bewildered him. Treasure hadn't flinched when they had mocked his mum and abused his dad. He had no idea what some of their words even meant. He only knew that they were being used as weapons, and that he was the enemy. Not because of anything that he had done, but because of who he was. His failure to respond to the boys' crass jibes frustrated them and violence was their only answer. Terry threw the first punch and once Treasure was safely on the ground, the others found the courage to spit and kick. Treasure didn't fight back. What was the point? He couldn't win. He was outnumbered and much smaller than any of them, and he couldn't make himself the one thing that might have saved him from their attention in the first place. White. But he wouldn't give them the satisfaction of seeing his tears or hearing him cry out. He simply lay there and waited until they had finished with him. A whistle from the playground signalled that the lunch break was over, and Terry and his companion thugs swaggered away in the direction of the school buildings without a backward glance. When he was sure that they had gone, Treasure stood up. As he wiped the blood and spit from his face, something on the edge of the football pitch caught his eye. He stumbled towards the pot of white paint that one of the groundsmen had left behind, forgotten, after marking out the lines. Treasure lifted the pot with both hands, raised it high and tipped its contents over his head. Now he was white.

Treasure continued scraping at the hateful words on the bench. Nearby, a group of girls had begun a skipping game, taking turns to jump in and out of the rotations of a rope held at either end by one of their classmates.

Never tell a secret, never tell a lie
If you break a promise you will surely die
Say your prayers at bedtime, God forgive your sin
Then when you get to heaven the angels let you in

Treasure had kept his promise that he would never tell his parents what had happened *that* day.

A shadow fell onto the bench next to him. He looked up into the smiling face of a girl he recognised as being in his year but not in his class. She had long brown plaits, hazel eyes and a small gap between her two front teeth. She sat down.

'I'm Janice.'

Treasure hadn't known her name. Most of the kids called her Flipper. Her arms finished where her elbows should have been, and her hands, misshapen and elongated, grew out of the stumps at odd angles, hence her cruelly depictive nickname. But neither the name nor the reason for it seemed to bother Janice. She pulled a packet out of her pocket and offered it to Treasure.

'Do you want a Spangle?'

They sat in silence for a moment sucking their sweets. Janice picked at the offending graffiti with her fingernail.

'You shouldn't take any notice of Terry and his stupid friends,' she said. 'They're tossers.'

28

1973

Jimmy Cox was weaving his way homewards along the pavement having closed the pawn shop early and spent the last couple of hours drinking in The Mother's Ruin. Business at the shop had been slow for the past few months and he blamed that bloody gypsy woman on the promenade, who had read his cards. She had told him that his judgement day was coming and that the shop would close for good, and he had told her where to shove her cards. But now, part of him wished he'd kept his mouth shut. He was beginning to think that she had cursed him. Bloody witch! He aimed a vicious kick at an empty beer can discarded on his driveway, missed and then steadied himself against the front door while he searched in his pocket for his keys.

Once inside, he went straight through to the kitchen, threw down the keys and reached for an open bottle of whiskey that stood on the table. He sloshed a generous measure into a dirty mug and took a gulp, swallowed and belched loudly. He couldn't decide whether he wanted a bacon butty or a fag. Or maybe both. But first he needed to take a piss. In the bathroom, he stared at his ravaged reflection in the mirror. The younger version of Jimmy Cox had been rakishly handsome with thick, dark hair and swarthy skin. Women had fallen readily for his good looks and smooth banter. But even his most ardent lady friends had dropped him once they'd got to know the brutal man behind the oleaginous smile and smarmy small talk. And now his grey hair was lank and greasy, and his skin pocked and purple veined. He zipped up his flies and returned to the kitchen where he retrieved a cigarette packet from his trouser pocket, flipped open the lid and cursed when he saw that there were only three left. He tipped one out, placed it between his lips and lit it from a gas ring on the filthy cooker. When his mother was alive, the kitchen had been kept spotless and she would have cooked whatever he wanted as soon as he got home. But it had been three years now since she'd died, and the house had descended inexorably into squalor. Jimmy Cox was an only child and he had been as much a bitter disappointment to his father as he had been treasured son to his mother. He had done everything to deserve his father's opinion and nothing to warrant his mother's. The pawnbroker's had been started by his parents when they married, and they had worked hard to make it profitable. Jimmy Cox had eventually inherited their business but never their work ethic nor their principles.

It was stifling indoors. He unbolted the back door and opened it. The garden was little more than a patch of scorched earth and weeds littered with rubbish. Jimmy Cox stepped outside and his foot slid on something slippery. He bent down to investigate but recoiled immediately.

'Fucking dog shit!' he roared. 'Where's that fucking dog?'

The dog had been a gift to his mother, the closest thing to a kindness that he had ever shown her. He had won the puppy in a card game at the pub when his mother was still struggling to come to terms with the death of her husband. Jimmy Cox thought it might cheer her up. Or at least stop her snivelling all the time. His mother had been thrilled and showered the little dog with all the love that she had previously wasted on her son. She had named the puppy Hope, which was to prove a cruel misnomer. Just three months later, Jimmy Cox's mother was diagnosed with terminal cancer. Her dying wish was that her son should look after Hope. She had made him promise.

The dog lay panting and trembling beside the broken remains of a cheap wardrobe that had been there so long that it was covered in bindweed. Left in the garden all day without any drinking water, she had sought refuge from the pitiless sun in the only patch of shade that she could find.

'Get here, you filthy bitch!'

She cowered, trying to make herself smaller. Trying to make herself disappear. She was so thin that her ribs poked through her matted fur. Jimmy Cox lunged towards her. He picked up a piece of brick and hurled it. It caught her on her hind leg and she yowled in pain. He looked around for another missile while the dog searched desperately for an escape route. Her eyes were wide and white-rimmed with fear. Jimmy Cox bent down to pick up a lump of rubble but instead clutched at his chest, wheezing. He tried to stand upright but with every attempt a violent fit of coughing caused him to buckle. Now it was his eyes that were wide with fear. He staggered back towards the kitchen. The dog lifted her head and watched him struggle. As he reached the door, she got up and followed at a safe distance, keeping low to the ground. She was still very wary, but her instinct told her that the balance of power between them had momentarily shifted.

Treasure ran upstairs and flung off his uniform. School was finished for the summer! He changed into a T-shirt and shorts. It was stifling indoors. He opened the window and saw Jimmy Cox in the garden next door. Saw what he did. Treasure raced downstairs fuelled by fury but without a plan. There was a passageway between the two houses that led to the gates into their back gardens. He jumped and managed to grab the top edge of Jimmy Cox's gate, which was always kept bolted. He hauled himself up until he was able to scrabble over the top and drop down into his neighbour's yard. A small window in the side wall of the house gave a view into the kitchen and Treasure peered cautiously through the grimy glass. Jimmy Cox was frantically searching for something in a drawer. He threw the contents onto the draining board with one hand, and with the other he clawed at his throat. He was sucking for air as greedily as a pup milking its mother's teat, and his lips were blue. He finally found what he was looking for, but as he grabbed it, it shot out of his grasp and pin-wheeled across the floor. Jimmy Cox collapsed onto his knees and then fell forwards, his arm outstretched in a vain attempt to retrieve what he had dropped. His fingers crept painfully over the linoleum like a sickly spider, but the object they were seeking was just out of reach.

29

1973

'I'd like to ask the cards which man I should choose.'

The woman sitting opposite Imelda was smartly dressed in expensive clothes and misted with Joy by Jean Patou. Her hair was salon-fresh and her make-up immaculate.

'Neither, I should think. They're usually more trouble than they're worth.'

Shunty-Mae emerged from behind the curtain at the back of the booth. 'I'm just off to the café for a bitter lemon. I shan't be long.'

It was high season and Imelda was so busy that she had finally been forced to accept Shunty-Mae's help. Imelda frowned disapprovingly at her retreating figure.

'Please excuse my mother. Now let's get started, shall we? Would you like to choose a pack of cards?'

The woman made her selection and then shuffled them as she asked her question again out loud. Imelda spread the cards on the table and then turned them over one by one. They dismissed a self-opinionated playboy with a country house as entirely unsatisfactory. The King of Swords, the Ten of Cups, the Five of

Wands and the Emperor described an old, overweight, demanding and taciturn businessman as being the better choice. Imelda couldn't quite see why until she turned over the Ten of Pentacles. He was also very rich.

'Are you considering a romantic relationship with either of these men?'

The woman looked aghast. 'God no! They're both married. It's more of a business relationship.'

That explained the Two of Wands on the table.

'Each one has asked me to be his mistress,' she continued, 'and I wanted to know who would provide the most favourable terms and conditions, so to speak.'

Imelda had to admire the woman's chutzpah, but she was glad that Shunty-Mae wasn't there to overhear their conversation. She was pretty sure that her mother would have some advice of her own to offer and it was unlikely to be as polite or professional as Imelda might wish.

'May I ask one more question?

'Of course.' Imelda gathered up the cards and handed them over to be shuffled once more.

'What will make him happy in the bedroom?'

'Are we talking soft furnishings or sex?'

The woman smiled for the first time. Imelda spread the cards and turned over the Devil, the High Priestess inverted and the Six of Wands.

'Tie him up and talk dirty to him,' she advised.

At the end of the reading the woman handed over her payment in crisp, clean notes.

'You know, you'd be surprised how little sex my job actually involves,' she confided, as she snapped shut her purse and returned it to her Hermès handbag.

'I minister to their egos far more than their erections. If they can get them.'

Imelda's next client was a very distressed elderly lady called Mildred, whose beloved cat had gone missing. Grisha sprang to attention like a jack-in-the-box at the mention of the 'c' word and was banished to the back room behind the curtain. Mildred's hands were shaking so badly that she could barely shuffle the cards.

'What's your cat's name, sweetheart?' Imelda asked gently.

'Corporal Jones. Jonesy for short. After that chap in *Dad's Army*. It's my favourite thing on the telly and Jonesy – my Jonesy – always sits on my lap and watches it with me.' She dabbed at her eyes with a tissue. 'Every week we have faggots for tea and then watch *Dad's Army*. But this week Jonesy didn't come home for tea or the telly and I'm worried sick.'

'Don't panic, Mr Mainwaring,' Imelda replied with a wink as she spread a Celtic Cross. 'Let's see if we can find out where he's got to.'

The cards suggested that Jonesy was stuck inside a wooden shed that stood under some trees.

'That'll be *my* garden shed!' Mildred sounded relieved but her tone soon changed. 'I'll bloody strangle that daft bugger of a son of mine,' she exploded.

Apparently, her daft bugger of a son, otherwise known as Malcolm, had been round at the weekend to cut his mother's lawn.

'I told him to check inside the shed before he shut the door, and he swore blind that he had. Jonesy likes to sneak in there whenever he gets the chance to look for mice. Well, I hope he's found some because the poor blighter's been in there for nearly two days now.'

Mildred couldn't wait to get home and left in a flurry of thanks to Imelda and threats of what she was going to do to the unfortunate Malcolm. Once she had gone, Grisha reappeared from behind the curtain and came and rested his head on Imelda's lap. They shared a moment's peace before Grisha twitched his ears and his elegant tail began to wag slowly like a ship's pennant fluttering in a sea breeze.

'Is it safe to come in?'

That familiar voice – *his* voice – was a startling but welcome intrusion into the shadowy cocoon of the booth. Without waiting for an answer, Cillian Byrne sauntered in.

'Are you alone?' he asked.

Imelda smiled and then cursed under her breath.

Shunty-Mae followed him in. 'Not anymore!' There was a brief silence before she continued. 'Imelda's just about to take a break, so perhaps you'd like to take her for that drink you promised her?'

They sat outside the café under the shade of one of the large umbrellas. Grisha leaned heavily against Cillian's leg, slobbering over the ice cream cone that Cillian was feeding him. Diamond brought them their drinks and winked theatrically at Imelda as she whisked away the empty tray.

'Well, this is very civil of you, Mr Byrne.' Imelda raised her glass towards him.

'It's my pleasure, Imelda. I'm delighted that your mother has allowed you to accompany me unchaperoned. Why don't you call me Cillian?'

Imelda met his gaze. 'I'm still deciding whether I want to be that familiar,' she teased. 'After all, I don't really know that much about you.'

Cillian leaned back in his chair. 'Ask away!'

'What makes you happy?'

'Life.'

'What makes you sad?'

'Life.'

Imelda shook her head. 'You don't give much away, do you?'

'But I'm an open book to you, Imelda. You can ask me anything.'

There was a clatter at the table next to them as man in small round sunglasses wearing a trench coat over his T-shirt and shorts knocked over a chair in his attempt to sit down. It was MI5 Clive.

'Good afternoon, Madame Burova, Tarot Reader, Palmist and Clairvoyant. Good afternoon, Grisha the Russian Dog Who Doesn't Have Fleas.' He paused for a moment and stared long and hard at Cillian before asking, 'Who is your gentleman friend?'

Cillian doffed an imaginary cap in greeting. 'Cillian Byrne. Wall of Death Rider.'

MI5 Clive nodded seriously to himself. 'Good afternoon, Cillian Byrne Wall of Death Rider.'

Pleasantries over, Clive turned away and took out his newspaper, a pen, a ball of string and a silver whistle. Imelda resumed her interrogation.

'Where are you from?'

'Baltimore. A little place near Roaringwater Bay in County Cork.'

'It sounds wonderful.'

'It is. Baltimore has a beautiful little harbour full of boats and there's a white beacon on the headland that we used to race to when we were kids and then we'd lie flat on the grass, puffing and panting, and stare up at the sky.'

'So why did you leave?'

'I wanted a bigger life. More excitement.'

'And danger.' It wasn't a question.

Cillian twisted the skull ring on his finger. 'It's how I am, Imelda.' For once he sounded serious, his tone a curious mixture of fatalism and defiance.

'So how did you end up riding the Wall of Death?'

Cillian's grin returned. 'I ran away and joined a fair. I know, I know! It's the worst cliché but it's true! An uncle of mine ran a Waltzer, and one year, when I was fifteen, his fair came to Cork. I hitched a ride up to see him and he offered me a job. When the fair left Cork, I went with it.'

As he told her how he had learned to ride and fix bikes at the fairground, every word he spoke was innervated by his passion for what had become not just his work, but his life. And Imelda understood, because it was the same for her. What she did and who she was were inseparable. She knew that the stink of exhaust fumes and the throb of an engine were as intoxicating and addictive for him as the silky chill of a crystal ball and the fall of cards like beating wings through her hands was for her.

She checked her watch. Reluctantly. 'I'd better get back. My mother can be trouble when left to her own devices for too long.'

Cillian stood up. 'Well at least that's something we have in common. But I haven't had a chance to ask you anything yet, and I was particularly keen to find out how you pulled off that stunt with the high and mighty Mr Mount.'

Imelda laughed. 'That can wait until next time.'

'So, there will be a next time? After all, I am now officially your *gentleman friend*.'

They were already back outside the booth.

'We'll see, Cillian.'

He placed his hands on her shoulders and looked directly into her eyes in a way that she found both exciting and disconcerting.

'Tell me, Imelda – honestly. Has he ever laid a finger on you?'

She shook her head. 'He wouldn't dare. He's a spineless little weasel. He only picks on women he has some hold over. He knows that Ruby and the others need their jobs. I have the booth, regardless of what I do at Larkins. And if he did try any funny business, I'd just follow my mother's advice.'

'Which is?'

Shunty-Mae's reply came loud and clear from inside the booth.

'Hit hard and aim low!'

30

1973

Treasure was positive that he had grown at least three inches taller in the past week. But perhaps it was because for the first time in his life he was standing proud with his shoulders back and his chin lifted. He was looking upwards to the rooftops and the sky, and forward to tomorrow and the future. It was a new and intoxicating feeling that took Treasure by surprise when he woke up each day. It was still early, but he couldn't wait to get up in the mornings now. And even if he should be tempted to lie in, a cold nose in his ear and a gentle paw on his chest would swiftly change his mind. His mother had given him a blanket for Star to sleep on, but he preferred to have her on his bed and she was happy to oblige. She trotted along beside him now, wearing a new collar and lead. She was nervous of almost everything: passing traffic, other pedestrians, even her own reflection in shop windows. But Treasure was determined to heal her broken spirit and teach her to trust. He had finally rescued her and now he was going to make her happy. Every time she wagged her tail, however slight or brief the movement, it was a tiny but significant victory for both of them.

Outside the corner shop, Mr Chowdhury was setting out trays of fruit.

'Good morning, good morning young man! You have a new friend, I see. You must introduce me.'

Treasure was a frequent customer, either shopping for his mum or spending his pocket money on comics or sweets.

'This is Star,' Treasure explained proudly.

'Well, it's a very lovely dog, but please don't let it urinate up my splendid Golden Delicious display.'

Treasure was affronted on Star's behalf. 'She's a girl! She doesn't cock her leg!'

Mr Chowdhury polished one of the apples on the front of his shirt before returning it to its tray.

'My apologies. But no squatting either. No puddles outside my shop.'

Treasure was about to walk on, but Mr Chowdhury asked him to wait before disappearing back inside the shop. He returned a moment later with a box of dog biscuits.

'To welcome your new and very fine friend, Star,' he said, handing the biscuits to Treasure. 'And to persuade her, perhaps, that if she does need to relieve her bladder, a most suitable place would be just outside the pawnbroker's.'

'Why?' Treasure didn't disagree but he was curious.

'Because that man, Mr Jimmy Cox, he's a bad egg. No, I should say even a rotten egg. He has no respect for his fellow shopkeepers.'

Jimmy Cox had frequently stubbed out his cigarettes on the pavement right outside Mr Chowdhury's establishment, but had never stepped inside to buy any, much to Mr Chowdhury's annoyance.

Treasure tucked the box under his arm and thanked Mr Chowdhury. 'You don't need to worry about Jimmy Cox anymore,' he added. 'He's dead.'

31

Now

'Za zdarovye!' Imelda raised her champagne saucer to the woman sitting opposite her at the kitchen table.

'Bottoms up!' Esther reciprocated. The two women had been friends since Imelda had walked into Esther's hairdressing and beauty salon thirty years previously, and they were spending New Year's Day together at Imelda's house as had become their custom since their respective parents and Esther's husband had died. The remains of a delicious fish pie were on the plates in front of them, and Mabel was sitting by the table sniffing the air expectantly with her retroussé nose. Esther offered her plate to Mabel and held it while Mabel literally polished off the pie with her pink tongue.

'You spoil her,' Imelda scolded. 'And they're my best plates!'

Esther laughed. 'I'm allowed to. I'm her favourite auntie!'

Over dinner Esther had been telling Imelda about her most difficult client on New Year's Eve who'd arrived half an hour late for her appointment and then demanded a full cut, colour and blow-dry despite the fact that she was only booked in for a dry trim and it was one of the busiest days of the year in the salon.

'What did you do?' Imelda asked.

'I did what she asked, of course,' replied Esther with a wicked grin. 'Although it may not have been the exact cut and colour she was expecting. I can't for the life of me think how burnished copper ended up being more like pillar-box red. And I did have to cut off slightly more than "just the ends" because her hair was in such bad condition.'

They had also been discussing Billie's visit and her offer to take over Imelda's booth.

'Darling, you don't have to do anything you don't want to,' Esther cautioned her. 'And you don't have to make a decision until you're completely ready.'

Imelda swigged her champagne and topped up their glasses.

'I've waited all these years to get to know her, worrying that she might want nothing to do with me, because after all why should she? And now she's here and she does. But sometimes I feel as though I just want to poke this particular genie back inside the bottle. And then I despise myself for being such a dithering old fool.'

Esther shook her head and laughed. 'Ha! Now you *are* being foolish. Firstly, you are the least dithery person I know. You decided to get a dog. The very next day you found Mabel. Secondly, you most certainly are not old. You're the same age as me and in your second prime, which is comparable to getting your second wind in the race of life – I just thought of that – it's rather good isn't it? You have hardly any wrinkles – just a few laughter lines – and not a single grey hair, although, admittedly that's down to me. Lastly, you are not being foolish. You're adjusting to a new and rather unusual set of circumstances. Fools rush in, my dear, but you are, quite rightly, taking time to consider your options. Have you thought about working at the booth part time? You could carry on doing readings for a couple of days a week – perhaps in the back room – and still lease it out. Look at me! I'm still working, and I wouldn't have it any other way. That salon is my world. Besides, if I wasn't there the bailiffs would be in and the sale boards up within weeks. My daughter-in-law might do a lovely set of gel nails and her Brazilians are very much in demand, but the staff run rings around her, and she has no idea when it comes to money, other than how to spend it.'

Imelda hoisted Mabel onto her lap and stroked her velveteen head. It was true that she hadn't realised quite how much she would miss her life on the promenade. The novelty of her retirement had quickly faded and the freedom it had brought felt empty and vaguely disappointing. The only good thing to come of it had been Mabel, and Imelda was sure that she would be happy enough to accompany her to the booth. To retire completely had been rash but was fortunately reversible. Esther was right, perhaps she *should* go back to work.

'Esther, you're a genius. Retirement is overrated.'

Esther smiled. 'Always glad to be of service. And maybe you could find yourself a new man now that you've got time on your hands?'

Imelda hiccupped with laughter as she tried to swallow her champagne. 'Oh, I think I'm done with all that!

I'm not sure that I could bear the trauma of a first date again or even be bothered, quite frankly. It's bad enough when you're young – exciting, yes, but awful as well. I remember the first boy I ever went out with. He was called Gareth Penny. My mother called him Spend-a-Penny because he spent so much time in the lavatory whenever he came to our house. Poor boy – I think she made him nervous.'

'Shunty-Mae would have made Her Majesty the Queen nervous!'

Imelda smiled, remembering how many of her early boyfriends Shunty-Mae had disliked or simply frightened away. But she had always been right. She had approved of Cillian.

Esther finished her champagne and stood up. 'Now darling, is it time for our annual cigarette?'

Outside, the garden air was thick with swirling mist and in the slate sky above them a crescent moon played hide and seek behind the drifting clouds. Imelda lit their Sobranie Black Russian cocktail cigarettes with a silver lighter. It was the ritual the friends enjoyed as much as the smoking itself, having both given up the habit years ago.

'Do you still think about him?' Esther asked and then blew a trio of perfect smoke rings into the mist.

'Cillian Byrne?'

Esther nudged her with her elbow. 'Yes, of course. Cillian Byrne.'

'More so now that Billie has turned up.'

'And are you okay with all this digging up of the past?'

Imelda sighed. 'She has the right to know, Esther.'

'Yes, but what about you? I'd hate to see you end up as collateral damage in this affair.'

She threw her arm around Imelda's shoulders. 'No pun intended,' she added and gave Imelda an affectionate squeeze.

'I'll be fine. It was all such a long time ago. And to be honest, I've never been sure if he was the love of my life or my biggest mistake.'

Esther took a final puff and then crushed out her cigarette underfoot.

'My Solomon was both. But I still miss him dreadfully. Every day.'

32

Now

'What's in here?'

Billie peered into a small cubbyhole in the wall that was revealed after she took down a framed print of an elegant woman walking a borzoi dog. Imelda emerged, closely followed by Mabel, from behind the half-drawn curtain that screened the back room.

'Secrets,' she replied.

It was late January and outside brutal waves battered the stony beach and gulls battled to pilot a course against the combatant gusts of a winter gale. Imelda had eventually decided to lease the front of the booth to Billie for a trial period of six months on the condition that she, Imelda, would continue dukkering in the back room and that Billie was able to come up with an appropriate business idea. Billie had proposed selling vintage seaside souvenirs, paraphernalia and ephemera and Imelda had approved.

'Secrets? What kind of secrets?'

Imelda sat down and once again the spectres of past clients returned to haunt her, as though they had been disturbed along with the dust that Billie continued to sweep from the shelves and brush from the curtains. Their voices whispered in Imelda's ears and their faces floated through her mind like images in her crystal ball. She had shared their hopes, their fears, their excitement and their despair, and vicarious though these feelings might have been for her, she had not always managed to protect herself from their onslaught. Her emotional armour had been dented, split and occasionally breached and she would always bear the scars. Billie's hand on her shoulder broke her reverie.

'It's okay. You don't have to tell me.'

Imelda placed her hand over Billie's and smiled.

'So long as you promise not to tell.'

'It's where I used to keep things for my clients – like a safety deposit box.'

'But why did they want to keep them here?'

Imelda raised her hands and gestured to the walls around her.

'This place is a confessional. People come to me for answers, for advice, for reassurance. But sometimes their questions are inextricably linked to confessions – an unavoidable quid pro quo – and they are prepared to trade their secrets for answers. For others, their secrets are too onerous to bear alone, but too dangerous or damaging for them to share with friends and family. Once people have learned to trust my cards and my crystal ball, they trust Madame Burova too. Here, alone with me inside the safety of these four walls, secrets roll off the tongue as easily as iced vodka slips down the throat. And they are sacrosanct. You were one of the secrets that I kept.'

'Did my mother visit you here?'

'I can't answer that, Billie, but I can tell you here is where I kept the things that she wanted you to have, the bank account details and the photograph.'

Imelda got up and began searching with one hand inside the hole in the wall. 'And there's something else.' She pulled out a bundle of photographs that were tied together with a piece of faded ribbon and handed them to Billie. Imelda watched as Billie leafed through the images of herself as a baby cuddling a teddy bear, a toddler taking her first steps, a schoolgirl in a pristine new uniform, and a proud graduate in a cap and gown.

'I don't understand.' Now it was Billie who looked as though she'd seen a ghost.

'Your father sent them to me. He was very kind; he didn't have to. But when I handed you over to the authorities, I wanted to know that you were safe and that you would be well cared for. I asked if someone could please let me know how you were getting on. I never really expected to hear anything, but somehow your father got the message. He wrote to me when he sent the first photograph to tell me that you were happy and settled, and very much loved.'

Billie handed Imelda the photograph of her as a baby.

'I still have that teddy bear.'

'And you still have all those happy memories of the wonderful man and woman who brought you up. They didn't need to be related to you to be the best parents you could have wished for. It takes more than blood to raise a child as well as they did.'

Billie resumed her sweeping. 'What were your parents like?'

'They were wonderful! Papa was an amazing cook and always full of stories about Russia and his family, and my mother was truly a force of nature. She was beautiful, strong and a little wild. And stubborn.'

'So, you take after her, then?'

Imelda laughed. 'It's true we sometimes clashed because we were too alike.'

'Over what?' Billie was curious about the young Imelda, not least because she would have been a contemporary of her birth mother.

'Well, she was against me working at Larkins.'

'Why?'

'She didn't think it was respectable. In fact, she likened it to Sodom and Gomorrah.'

'Blimey! Was it that bad?'

Imelda shook her head. 'But it was never dull. When people are on holiday, they like to let their hair down – especially when they've had a drink or two.'

'And the staff? Did they let their hair down too?'

'Well, I only really knew the entertainment staff. But yes, of course. They were a colourful bunch. There was a woman who could fold herself into a suitcase, Jeanie with her incredible voice, but I think the mermaids were my favourites.'

'Not the Wall of Death rider then?' Billie joked and then immediately wished she hadn't when she saw the smile fade from Imelda's face.

There was a sudden draught as the door opened and Treasure came in carrying a tray of drinks.

'I thought you ladies might be in need of some refreshment.'

'Earl Grey for you Imelda. Billie, I wasn't sure what you'd like. I guessed builder's tea with no sugar, but I brought some just in case.'

Billie tipped her bowler hat in gratitude. 'Spot on. And no, I don't take sugar, thank you.'

Mabel had sat down rather pointedly on Treasure's foot and was glaring up at him. When he failed to acknowledge her, she batted his shin with her paw and then grabbed the hem of his jeans and tugged it with her teeth.

'All right, all right! I surrender,' Treasure laughed. 'As if I'd dare to forget you, Mabel.'

He produced a brown paper bag from his jacket pocket containing two slices of best roast ham, which Mabel sniffed carefully, then wolfed down before burping loudly.

'Manners, Mabel!' Imelda admonished and Mabel whirled her tail, not in the least bit sorry.

Treasure surveyed the disorder inside the booth.

'So, what have you two been up to all afternoon?'

Billie brushed the dust from her clothes and picked up her tea.

'We're making room for my seaside stock.'

'Billie is going to be leasing the front of the booth to sell vintage seaside paraphernalia, and I shall continue with my readings in the back room as and when the fancy takes me,' Imelda explained.

Treasure placed his arm around Imelda's shoulders and gave her a hug. 'Sounds like a plan. I'm glad we're not going to be losing you from the prom completely.

And Billie, where will you be getting your stuff, sorry, stock from?'

Billie shrugged slowly. 'That's the part of the plan that I'm still planning. But I think maybe car boot sales, house clearances, auctions, that kind of thing. I'm not intending to open for business for a few weeks yet, so I've got some time.'

'Well let me know if you need any help, either with getting some stock together or sorting this place out. I'd be happy to lend a hand.'

Imelda smiled. She had been very fond of Treasure ever since he was a little boy, and now she hoped that he and Billie would be friends.

'And what about Mabel? What's she going to be doing?'

Imelda clicked her fingers and Mabel stood to attention and bared her teeth, her tail whirling furiously. 'I'm training her to be the bouncer.'

Treasure laughed. 'I'm not sure which end to believe, teeth or tail.'

'That's the beauty of it,' replied Imelda.

33

Now

Billie peered at a peculiar looking pufferfish in a glass-fronted case. It looked angry, as well it might be, with its corpse skewered by two metal pins and suspended above a wooden silhouette of blue-painted waves.

'Well, he's *unusual*, but I'm not sure many people would want him grimacing down at them from their mantelpiece.'

Brighton and Hove Auctions' saleroom was packed with a multifarious melange of antiques, collectables and miscellaneous *stuff* for their forthcoming general sale, and Billie had brought Henry along to help her search for possible stock items for the booth. She loved an auction house. They all had a similar smell – a combination of fried onions, musty furniture, damp carpets and stale cigarette smoke. She loved the thrill of sorting through shelves, boxes and tables rootling for hidden treasures that would make her heart beat just a little bit faster. When she was young, she had spent many happy Saturday mornings with her dad rummaging round junk shops and their local auction yard. His passion, ignited by his own father who had been a stationmaster, had been anything associated with steam trains: postcards, badges, lamps – even the crockery and cutlery that would have been used in the buffet carriages. There had been precious little money to spend on hobbies, and through necessity her dad had been an expert haggler and a disciplined bidder, never exceeding the limits he set himself. As she wandered up and down with Henry, noting the lot numbers of items of possible interest, Billie watched the dealers vying with one another in their habitual rituals that didn't appear to have changed much since the auctions of her childhood. Their superficial bonhomie as they prowled the saleroom floor camouflaged the cutthroat competitiveness that burned beneath. Some loudly denounced as worthless items that they would later bid for with ruthless determination.

'Look at that crack! If it's damaged, it's done for!'

'Nobody wants Whitefriars anymore!'

'Brown furniture! I wouldn't touch it with a bargepole!'

Others passed by items they were keen to purchase with barely a glance, feigning indifference so as not to draw attention to a potential gem. Another favourite trick was to hide promising-looking items included in a job lot behind or beneath the more commonplace, in the hope that they would go unnoticed by less canny customers.

'Ooh! Hello sailor!'

Henry clutched Billie's arm and pointed in the direction of a Pelham puppet dressed as a sailor, propped up against a hideous 1970s table lamp.

Billie inspected the toy carefully.

'He's still in his original box, and his condition's not bad considering his age. The strings are a bit of a muddle, but nothing that can't be fixed. What do you think?'

Henry smiled. 'I think his eyebrows are in a very strange position but other than that he's charming. If a little weird. And perfect for the booth, so long as he doesn't come with that appalling lamp.'

Amongst the bric-a-brac they managed to find a shoebox full of saucy seaside postcards, some W. H. Goss crested souvenir china and a child's push-along donkey on wheels that Billie couldn't bear to leave behind. When Henry questioned its seaside association credentials, Billie patted the donkey's head and defended her choice by declaring, 'Any seaside resort worth its salt has donkey rides!' They were about to sit down ready to bid when Billie spotted a framed photograph propped against a chair. The glass was filthy but a familiar name was just visible through the grime – Larkins Holiday Park. It was a picture of a little girl posing happily with three very glamorous young women dressed as mermaids. Billie noted down the lot number. She was determined to buy it whatever the cost – not for the booth, but for Imelda.

The rapping of the auctioneer's gavel on wood silenced the saleroom.

'Right then ladies and gentlemen, let's be having you!'

They stacked Billie's boxes of auction booty on the floor of Imelda's booth and Henry placed both hands on the small of his back and groaned. Billie had, on impulse, decided to bid on a collection of *Hornblower* books on account of their maritime connection, and their acquisition had made the boxes rather heavy. Billie took Henry's arm. 'Come on, I'll buy you a cup of tea and a slice of cake in The Tea Leaf as a reward for all your hard work. And then I've got something to show you.' The photographs that her dad had sent to Imelda were in her bag.

As they reached the café the door opened, and MI5 Clive greeted them.

'Good afternoon, Billie In The Bowler Hat.'

'Good afternoon, Clive. How are you?'

'Mustn't grumble. I have my work and a very nice piece of half-price smoked haddock for my supper,' Clive replied, holding his shopping bag aloft.

'This is Henry.' Billie pre-empted Clive's inevitable enquiry.

'Good afternoon, Henry I've Met You Before.'

Henry was clearly perplexed. 'Good afternoon, Clive. I'm terribly sorry but I'm afraid I don't remember.'

Clive stepped a little closer and lowered his voice. 'You said hello to me once, but we were never properly introduced. You used to come here when Jack and Diamond were in charge.'

Henry shook his head in amazement. 'I did, but only a couple of times. And that was years ago. How on earth did you remember me?'

Clive nodded proudly. 'I never forget a face.'

34

1973

It was early, a little after 6 a.m. Imelda could just hear the gentle tick of her alarm clock above the exuberant birdsong coming from the garden below. Already, bright sunshine sparkled on the open windowpane, and the cloudless blue sky beyond promised an idyllic summer day. But not for everyone. Imelda lay in bed and listened to the clock tick. It was the countdown to some destined but as-yet-unknown disaster. She closed her eyes and the darkness enveloped her. Not simply lack of sight, but a blackness that filled her, swallowed her up, crushed and choked her. She could smell sparking metal and coal dust. The clamour of her alarm going off rescued and returned her to the start of a bright, sunny day. Grisha stretched and yawned on the bed beside her, and then nuzzled her cheek. Imelda forced herself out of bed and went to the window. Outside, their tiny corner of the world looked picture-perfect. Nothing here was amiss. But somewhere there was always someone suffering.

By the time she had showered and dressed, Imelda felt better. She had all but shaken off the shadows. Downstairs, as usual, Alexei was cooking breakfast.

Shunty-Mae was dancing barefoot in the garden to a song that was playing on the radio she had left on the back doorstep. Alexei paused for a moment from frying blinis to gaze admiringly at his wife.

'She's still as beautiful as the day I met her.'

Imelda laughed and helped herself to one of the warm blinis. 'And just as awkward, no doubt.'

Alexei dropped another spoonful of batter into the pan. 'Certainly not. She's much worse now!'

Imelda sat down at the table and poured herself some tea while Grisha sat hopefully at Alexei's feet.

'Don't you feed that dog my breakfast!'

At the sound of Shunty-Mae's voice Grisha slunk under the table.

Shunty-Mae appeared flushed and slightly breathless in the doorway. She caught sight of her daughter and her expression became serious.

'What's the matter with you?'

'Nothing. Why?'

Shunty-Mae shook her finger at Imelda. 'I can see it in your face.'

Imelda shrugged. 'It's nothing, just one of those feelings. Whatever it is will happen anyway. There's nothing to be done.'

For once Shunty-Mae was silent, but she understood. The gift they shared could sometimes be a curse. Imelda finished her tea and stood up.

'Take some of these with you, Melda, if you're not going to eat a proper breakfast.'

Alexei began to spread soured cream on blinis. Grisha stirred reluctantly, ready to follow Imelda but disappointed that no one had thought to offer him a slice of the smoked salmon from the plate on the table. While Imelda was occupied wrapping her food parcel, a morsel of fish held tentatively between a thumb and forefinger miraculously appeared before Grisha's nose. He gently accepted the treat and then licked the fingers that had proffered it. Imelda kissed her father's cheek and then her mother's before striding down the hallway and stepping out into the glorious sunshine. Shunty-Mae stepped up to the kitchen sink and washed her hands.

The promenade was still quiet by the time Imelda arrived. Jack and Diamond were just setting up the tables and chairs outside the café.

'Morning, Imelda, luv. Looks like it's going to be a scorcher.' Jack greeted Imelda as he struggled to unfurl one of the sunshade umbrellas.

'Look out – here comes trouble.'

Imelda followed the direction of Diamond's gaze. A small boy was bounding towards them holding a collie on a lead. Treasure was followed at a more sedate pace by Ruby. Grisha sniffed at the collie, full of curiosity for this new canine, but she backed away nervously.

'Well, who is this beautiful young lady?' Imelda addressed her question to Treasure who was grinning proudly.

'She's mine. She's called Star and I rescued her.' He stoked her silky head and the dog looked up at him, momentarily reassured. Ruby checked her watch.

'I have to go,' she told Diamond. 'Now, Treasure, be a good boy and do as your auntie tells you.'

'And perhaps later you might like to go for a walk with me and Grisha,' Imelda added. 'He could show Star around and maybe they could be friends.'

Treasure nodded happily before Diamond whisked him inside for a chocolate milkshake. Ruby walked with Imelda towards the booth. Her face was pale and there were dark circles under her eyes. But Treasure seemed like a different boy. His transformation was astonishing and wonderful to witness. So, what could be troubling Ruby so badly now if it was not her usual concern for her son? Imelda didn't have to wait long to find out. When they reached the booth, Ruby asked if she could come in 'just for a moment'. Imelda unlocked the door and ushered Ruby inside.

'Can I talk to you about something in complete confidence? Something that must never be spoken about outside these four walls?'

'Of, course. Why don't you sit down?'

Ruby seemed exhausted. She perched on the edge of a chair and Imelda sat down opposite her.

'It's about Star. Well, Treasure and Star.'

Imelda waited in silence while Ruby marshalled her thoughts before arranging them into coherent sentences.

'Star belonged to our neighbour, Jimmy Cox, the pawnbroker,' Ruby began. 'He always was a poor excuse for a man and when his mum died, he got worse, coming home drunk and letting the house and garden go to rack and ruin. The dog was his mum's – God rest her soul – and once she was gone, he made Star's life a living hell. He left her outside in all weathers and rarely fed her. She's barely more than a bag of bones, and Treasure was forever feeding her scraps through a hole in the fence.'

Imelda instinctively dropped her hand to rub Grisha's furry head. She remembered well the cards that she had read for the pawnbroker but said nothing and waited for Ruby to continue.

'Treasure begged me to speak to Jimmy Cox about Star, and I tried over and again, but he wouldn't listen, just told me to mind my own business. Perhaps I should have tried harder. Or sent Randall round to see him.' Ruby was close to tears.

'What happened?' Imelda gently prompted her.

'Last week, Jimmy Cox was found dead on his kitchen floor. He'd had an asthma attack and the police said it looked as though he'd been searching for his inhaler when he collapsed.'

'Who found him?'

Ruby took a deep breath. 'Treasure. He came home from school and found Star wandering in the street. He checked Jimmy Cox's back gate and it was open, so he went into the garden and saw him lying on the floor through the kitchen window. He wasn't moving.'

'Did Treasure go inside the house?'

'No. He says he came straight back home to tell me, and then I phoned for an ambulance. The police were called because it was a sudden death, but they seemed quite happy that it was just an accident. Jimmy Cox had mislaid his inhaler. Probably dropped it on the way home from the pub, one of them suggested. It seems the local police knew him quite well and didn't have a very high opinion of him.'

'With good reason, I suspect,' Imelda added quietly. 'But Treasure seems fine. Children are often much more resilient than we give them credit for.' Imelda assumed that Ruby was worried about the shock her son may have suffered as a result of discovering a corpse.

Ruby shook her head slowly. 'But that's just the point. When he came home with Star that day and told me how he'd found Jimmy Cox he seemed almost pleased.'

Imelda could understand why he would have been. Jimmy Cox's treatment of Star had been brutal and as far as she was concerned, he deserved to be dead. But she could also see why Treasure's apparently blasé demeanour had made Ruby uncomfortable.

'He's just a boy,' she reasoned. 'All he could think about was Star. I'm sure he was just relieved that she was finally safe.'

'I hope so,' said Ruby, opening her handbag. 'Because I found this in the pocket of his shorts when I was sorting through the dirty laundry.' She handed Imelda an asthma inhaler.

Neville called in at the booth during his lunch break to pick up the things that he had left with Imelda for safekeeping. Despite the heat, he was dressed for work in his customary suit and tie, and a sheen of perspiration glistened on his red face. Imelda took down the picture and searched inside the cubbyhole behind it. The asthma inhaler had been added to its contents. Imelda had told Ruby to forget that she had ever seen it. When Ruby had gone, Imelda had consulted her cards and her conscience, and decided that silence would protect those who deserved protection. She handed Neville his rosary and prayer book and he slipped them into his pocket but he seemed reluctant to leave.

'Is there anything else I can do for you, Neville? Is Miriam well?'

He smiled at the mention of his wife's name, but the tension in his face betrayed his unease.

'Do you think I'm being disloyal to her, Madame Burova? Do you think I'm a bad husband?'

Imelda had grown quite fond of Neville, who visited her once a week without fail. He was a decent man in a difficult situation, and she was touched by his sensitivity.

'I have no right to judge you, Neville,' she replied.

'But I would value your opinion, Madame Burova.' Always so polite; so formal.

Imelda placed her hand reassuringly on his arm. 'I think you are simply trying to be both a good husband and a good son.'

'Yes, but do you think that what I'm doing is wrong? In the eyes of God? I made a commitment when I converted. Miriam's family would only allow her to marry within the Jewish faith and I love her very much. I try my best, but in my heart, I will always be a Catholic.'

Imelda shook her head. 'When we look up, wherever we are in the world, we see the same sky. We each may have a different vantage point, but we are all looking at the same sun, the same moon and stars. That's how it works with God, in my opinion. I'm sure he doesn't care how we worship or what we call him. Perhaps simply having faith in him and living by it is enough, and the trappings of religion are only fripperies. So, no, Neville, I don't think what you are doing is wrong.'

Neville smiled and this time it reached his eyes.

The afternoon was busy, with many clients seeking refuge from the blazing sun as much as an insight into their futures. At just gone four o'clock, Imelda decided that the next client would be her last for the day. A middle-aged woman marched purposefully into the booth brandishing her stout handbag as though it were a weapon. She sat down without waiting to be asked and thumped the bag down beside her. Grisha hauled himself to his feet and trotted off into the back room.

'Traitor!' whispered Imelda in the direction of his retreating tail.

'I beg your pardon?'

Imelda turned to face her client. 'Just clearing my throat. How can I help you?'

The woman folded her arms and jostled her bosoms. 'I hope you haven't got anything catching. I can't abide germs.'

Imelda now wished that she'd made her previous client her last. She gritted her teeth and took a deep breath. 'No, no. It's just the weather. It's very hot today and I've been doing a lot of talking. My throat's rather dry. Now, would you like a palm reading, the crystal ball or do you have some questions for my cards?'

Imelda noticed that the woman's hands had squarish palms and long, balanced fingers. Earth hands, perhaps indicative of her boorish bossiness. But the woman didn't want her palms read.

'What should I call you?' asked Imelda, half expecting her to reply 'Ma'am'.

'The name's Agatha Strop. Mrs Strop to you.'

How apt, thought Imelda. She handed Mrs Strop the

cards and told her to ask her question out loud as she shuffled them.

'I want to know where the painting is.'

'You may need to be a little more specific than that.'

The woman tutted. 'The awful painting of a woman fawning over her pathetic pooch – looks more like a fluffy rat with a bow in its fur if you ask me – that belongs to my skinflint father-in-law. We haven't seen it recently and it was promised to my husband once the old man drops off his perch.'

Imelda laid the cards and turned them over, revealing the Queen of Wands first.

'Do you or your father-in-law know a woman with light or possibly red hair and light eyes?'

Agatha Strop pursed her lips and narrowed her eyes. 'What's she got to do with it?'

'Is she close to your father-in-law?'

'She's his housekeeper and a harlot. A devious, scheming trollop.'

The cards begged to differ. According to them she was kind, conscientious and genuinely fond of her elderly employer. More so, it seemed, than his family was.

'She looks exactly like that floozy in the painting,' sneered Mrs Strop.

'Which is perhaps why your father-in-law has given it to her,' Imelda replied, trying to conceal her satisfaction at this turn of events. Mrs Strop was apoplectic, but Imelda was a little bemused.

'But you don't even like it. What on earth would you have done with it?'

'Sold it!' spat the Strop woman. 'It was an original Giovanni Boldini and worth a small fortune!'

Once she had paid, reluctantly (bad news costs the same as good, Imelda had told her), Imelda locked up and went with Grisha in search of Star and Treasure for their promised walk. At the café, Jack was listening to the radio and looking unusually subdued.

'Those poor buggers. And what about their families?' He shook his head in disbelief as the newsreader continued.

'It is believed that due to a faulty braking mechanism, the descending cage failed to slow down as it approached the bottom of the mine shaft at Markham Colliery, killing eighteen miners and seriously injuring eleven more . . .'

Sparking metal and coal dust.

35

1973

Jeanie sat on the bed and watched as Vivienne pouted at the mirror, painting her mouth scarlet with a new lipstick. The bed was strewn with clothes and more spilled from the wardrobe. Boxes of shoes teetered in precarious towers on the floor, and jewellery and make-up covered the shiny surface of the dressing table where Vivienne sat. The overall impression was that of the aftermath of a burglary in an upmarket boutique. Vivienne had invited Jeanie back to her rented flat after the two of them had been shopping. Jeanie had splashed out on a new top from Chelsea Girl while Vivienne had bought several outfits that now lay discarded on the floor still in their bags.

'Don't you ever put things away?' laughed Jeanie, thinking how sparse and plain her own bedroom looked in comparison. She didn't own enough clothes to make even a fraction of the mess that surrounded her here in Vivienne's boudoir.

'I don't have to. A woman comes to clean once a week and she does it.'

Jeanie shifted uncomfortably on the bed. She was still very much in awe of Vivienne and flattered that she had chosen her as a friend. She was witty, clever and unfailingly generous – forever treating Jeanie to lunch and buying her make-up whenever she bought any for herself. But there was a coolness to her when she dealt with other people as though she thought herself to be above them. It was an arrogance that made Jeanie uneasy.

'Does your dad pay for all this?' she asked, jumping off the bed and inspecting the contents of some of the shoeboxes.

'He pays for the flat and I have an allowance for everything else.'

Jeanie tried on a pair of silver platform shoes and wobbled across the room in them.

'When will you be going home?'

Vivienne's course had finished, and she was waiting for the results of her typing and shorthand exams.

'Why? Are you trying to get rid of me?'

'No, of course not!' replied Jeanie, holding a shocking pink mini-dress up against herself and inspecting her reflection in the mirror on the wardrobe door. 'I'll miss you when you go.'

Vivienne smiled. 'Well then, it's lucky for you that I'm not going anywhere just yet, and you can keep that dress if you like it. I never wear it anymore.'

Jeanie put the dress down. It was lovely but it wasn't really *her*. Besides, her dad would have a fit if he caught her wearing something that barely covered her knickers. In Vivienne's company she still felt very much like a girl. Although only a few years separated them in age, her friend appeared to have acquired all the attributes of womanhood, coupled with the knowledge of how to use them to her advantage.

'But I thought that your parents were coming home this summer?'

'They were, but now Daddy's planning to expand his company in California and so they're staying for a few more months, maybe even another year.'

'California!' Jeanie sighed. 'Don't you want to go too? I'd love to go to America.'

Vivienne lit a cigarette and threw the lighter onto the dressing table where it landed with a clatter, scattering the pots of make-up.

'Maybe for a visit. I went at Christmas. But certainly not for any longer. Over there they'd be watching my every move, but here I can do as I please.'

'And what *are* you going to do?'

Vivienne laughed. 'I've told them that I want to attend a finishing school for a couple of terms. Learn to arrange flowers, plan dinner parties and select appropriate outfits for Ascot, Henley and Glyndebourne. All vital skills for securing a suitable husband. Mummy was delighted.'

'And will you actually attend?'

'I've enrolled. But it hardly matters. I've already found the man I'm going to marry.'

Jeanie couldn't believe that Vivienne was even thinking about getting married. There was so much more that she wanted to do before she settled down, if she ever did. She wanted to travel, see the world – sing all over the world. She had so many plans and yet Vivienne, for all her money and sophistication, had so few dreams. She could only see as far as getting herself a husband, the very thing that she denounced her parents for. Jeanie almost felt sorry for her.

'Who's the lucky man, then?' she joked. She assumed it was a joke. 'Charlie? He adores you. Or maybe you've got the hots for Mr Mount. You've certainly got him wrapped around your little finger.'

'Don't be ridiculous. Charlie's just a boy. He's very sweet, but he's a boy. And as for Marty – he's useful. I like a man with power, but he's not exactly my type.'

'Well, come on then. Put me out of my misery. Who is it?'

'Cillian Byrne.'

Jeanie laughed. 'Cillian? He's a fairground attraction. Your parents would never let you marry him!'

'I thought you liked him.' Vivienne's voice was cold and quiet.

'I do. I think he's amazing. But I can't imagine him ever getting married. I don't think he's the type. But if he did, it would be to someone more like him. Someone like . . .' The words dried in Jeanie's throat as she caught sight of Vivienne's face, set rigid with anger and determination.

'Someone like Gypsy Burova?' she sneered. 'Trust me, that's never going to happen. Haven't you seen the way he looks at me?'

He looks at you the way most men do, Jeanie thought, but she remained silent, smarting at the insulting way that Vivienne spoke about Imelda.

'It's obvious that he likes me, and I fully intend to make him mine whatever it takes. I can't bear the thought of being married to some rich, boring City drip who wants a pretty, well-behaved wifey to dangle on his arm, decorate his dinner parties and defer to him in bed. I want excitement and freedom – and Cillian Byrne. And I'm going to have him.'

Jeanie was astonished at her friend's naivety, or maybe it was simply ego. Vivienne was so accustomed to having her own way that perhaps it never occurred to her that love wasn't something that could be acquired at will. Jeanie was also a little afraid of exactly how far Vivienne would go to get what she wanted.

36

1973

'Happy Birthday to you!'

Imelda and Grisha had arrived at Larkins for an afternoon of readings only to be waylaid in the entertainment lounge by their friends, who were surrounding a large cake and waving a birthday banner and balloons.

'From all of us!' Ruby handed her a card and a beautiful bouquet of cream and pink roses and freesias trailing streamers of coloured ribbons.

'How did you know?' Imelda was as pink as the roses with surprise and delight.

'I'm afraid Shunty-Mae spilled the beans to Diamond,' Ruby replied. They all sang 'Happy Birthday', led by Jeanie and accompanied on the piano by Charlie.

'Make a wish!' Sara-Jade held up the cake for Imelda to blow out the candles.

'Where's Marty?' joked Imelda as Ruby cut the cake.

'He's sulking in his office, I expect. He still hasn't forgiven us for his inadvertent broadcast. But at least his behaviour has improved.'

'About time too!' Dolly and Daisy spoke in unison as they helped themselves to tiny slivers of cake.

'Come on, ladies,' said Sara-Jade, spooning more cake onto their plates. 'You need to keep your strength up for all that swimming.'

'We also need to squeeze into those skin-tight costumes,' laughed Daisy, something that didn't appear to concern Dixie, who sat quietly devouring an enormous helping of the cream-laden confection while Grisha drooled at her feet. Ruby popped the cork of a bottle of Asti Spumante so that they could make a birthday toast, but Sara-Jade refused a glass when offered one, preferring to stick to her usual tipple.

'I have a theory that gin dissolves fat,' she proclaimed, 'which means that I can eat as much cake as I like,' and helped herself to another plateful. Titus, taciturn as ever, returned from the bar with a gin for Sara-Jade. It seemed that he had developed quite a soft spot for the woman in the suitcase.

Later, as Imelda settled herself in her booth, which was now heady with the scent of flowers, she opened the card that Ruby had given her. Everyone had signed it – even Marty. Even Cillian. She traced over his name and the single 'x' beside it with her fingertips. But he hadn't been at the party. He'd been tinkering with one of his bikes over at the Wall of Death. Imelda had seen him on her way in. And he hadn't been alone.

Imelda arrived home to the smell of something delicious cooking in the kitchen, and her mother wearing a beautiful violet silk dress, make-up and her best earrings. 'Hurry up!' she chided. 'Get changed and do something with your hair.'

'Why? What's the rush?' Imelda followed her through into the kitchen to find a vase for her flowers. She kissed Alexei on the cheek. 'Hi, Papa. Why is my mother acting like a crazy lady?'

Alexei smiled. 'Good evening, Melda. Your mother *is* a crazy lady. But she's right. Go and put on your finery.'

Imelda turned and registered that the table, set with their best linen, cut crystal glasses and silver cutlery, was laid for four people.

'We have a guest? On my birthday? Who?' This was a family occasion; her occasion. She wasn't sure if she was pleased or irritated. It would depend on the guest.

'You'll see,' Shunty-Mae replied. 'Now, upstairs! Get ready!'

The doorbell rang just as Imelda was on her way back downstairs, and on the doorstep stood Cillian Byrne.

'What in God's name are you doing here?'

He smiled. 'Well, that's a fine welcome, I must say. I'm sorry I missed your little party earlier, but there was something wrong with the bike and I had to get it fixed before this afternoon's show.'

Imelda raised a single eyebrow. 'And no doubt Vivienne was there just to pass you your tools?'

Shunty-Mae came up behind her daughter. 'Imelda! What are you doing keeping our guest standing outside? Come in, Mr Byrne. What will you have to drink?'

Cillian followed Shunty-Mae through to the kitchen leaving a speechless Imelda to close the door. By the time she joined them she'd found her tongue.

'*He's* our guest?' she asked, her voice slightly shrill with disbelief.

'You sound disappointed,' Cillian laughed, grappling with Grisha, whose ebullient greeting made up for his mistress's reserve.

'Sure, she's thrilled,' said Shunty-Mae, handing him a glass of vodka. 'She's just not very good with surprises. Meet my husband and Imelda's father, Alexei.'

Alexei had been watching their guest's entrance and reception with quiet amusement. He shook hands with Cillian, and looked him up and down, wondering if this handsome man was good enough for his only daughter. Shunty-Mae had told him that there was only one way to find out, and that was why she had invited him to dinner. The fact that Cillian had brought with him a bottle of champagne had certainly made a favourable first impression. Imelda, meanwhile, had poured herself a drink and was attempting to gather her wits together, but it was as fruitless a task as collecting fallen leaves in a frisky wind.

'I heard that you were already getting flowers, so I brought you this.'

Cillian handed Imelda a square box tied with a black velvet band. Inside was an antique gold chain upon which hung two tiny stars and a crescent moon.

'Here, let me.' Cillian took it from the box and fastened it around Imelda's neck. The brush of his fingers on her skin was exquisitely unsettling.

'I saw it in the pawnbroker's window a while back and immediately thought of you.'

'And why would the pawnbroker's shop remind you of me?' Imelda's voice was sharper than she had intended but Cillian didn't appear to notice.

'It didn't. I just thought that you deserved the moon and stars.'

Imelda threw a napkin at him but couldn't help feeling ridiculously pleased.

Once Alexei had filled their plates, Shunty-Mae got down to business. Her interrogation was barely disguised as conversation, but Cillian answered her questions about his family and childhood in Ireland with good-natured humour. He was, however, less forthcoming about his future. 'I'm happy enough doing what I'm doing for the time being,' was as much as he could offer. Alexei entertained with stories of his parents' early life in Russia and their escape to England. Her grandparents' history was as familiar to Imelda as her childhood teddy bear. She was proud of both her Russian and Romany ancestry and never grew tired of hearing about it, and she was pleased to see Cillian getting on so well with her father, but she was also still in shock that he was there at all – and at Shunty-Mae's invitation!

'What was Imelda like when she was a little girl?' Cillian asked Alexei.

'Much the same as she is now,' he replied. 'Bright, beautiful, stubborn and impossible! She takes after her mother.' He paused a moment for Shunty-Mae's reaction, but mellowed by Cillian's champagne, his wife allowed his gentle teasing to pass without comment.

'We once had to fetch her home from school for allegedly putting a curse on a fellow pupil. The wretched child finished up vomiting all over a needlework lesson.'

Cillian whistled through his teeth. 'Wow! That's impressive. Can a curse really do that?'

Imelda laughed. 'It wasn't so much the curse, although I was pretty pleased with it at the time, but more the fact that I also told her I'd put a maggot in her milk at break time, after she'd drunk it.'

'And what had she done to rile you so much?'

'She had it coming,' Shunty-Mae muttered.

'She called me a gyppo.'

Eventually, after dinner, cake and more vodka, the conversation began to drift into comfortable silences and long-held looks across the table between Imelda and Cillian. Imelda had been hoping to spend some time alone with him, but it was getting late and everyone except Shunty-Mae had work in the morning. With uncanny timing, Shunty-Mae announced, 'We have one more surprise for you, Imelda.' She and Alexei both got up and headed towards the back door.

'Keep her entertained for a moment, Cillian, and don't come outside until we call you.' Alexei closed the door behind him as he disappeared into the garden with Shunty-Mae. Cillian pushed back his chair and stood up slowly. He took Imelda's hand and pulled her to her feet. He paused for the briefest moment and looked straight into her eyes before pressing his lips onto hers, softly at first but then urgently, almost bruising. Imelda ran her hands down his hard-muscled back and returned his kiss, meeting his hunger with her own.

'Imelda?' Her father's voice called just before the door opened. If he saw them break apart from their embrace, he said nothing to betray it. Outside, a trail of tealights in jam jars led down the garden and all the way up the steps to the door of the vardo, which was wreathed in ivy, flowers and fairy lights.

'Happy Birthday, Imelda!' Her parents stood with their arms around one another, smiling. 'It's yours now.'

37

1973

The following morning Imelda woke up with a thick head and a skittish heart. She felt for the chain around her neck and as she caught the moon and stars in her fingers, she smiled. It had been an extraordinary birthday, and she permitted herself the luxury of a few moments' lie-in to rerun yesterday's events in her head. Her twin brothers, Paul and Peter, had remembered to send her a card from New York where together they ran an Irish bar. Her eldest brother, Mark, had bought her a lava lamp for her bedroom, and Damian, the only brother who had joined their father's business, had bought her perfume that smelled of old ladies, but was in a very pretty bottle. She had been touched and genuinely surprised by the kindness of her friends and colleagues at Larkins. The thought of Cillian on the doorstep bearing gifts and grinning with infuriating nonchalance made her stomach flip. And the fact that her mother had invited him was both astonishing and suspicious. She had questions to ask Shunty-Mae about that, but they would have to wait until this evening or else she would be late for work. She also had some questions for Cillian. She believed his story about having to fix the bike but what had Vivienne been doing there? She seemed to be intent on creating the impression that she and Cillian were a couple – something that Cillian had already denied. But if he genuinely wasn't interested in her, why did he tolerate her proprietorial attentions and her ridiculous femme fatale demeanour? Imelda had wanted to ask him last night, preferably before she had allowed him over the threshold, but Shunty-Mae had interrupted them.

And then there was the vardo. Imelda couldn't quite believe that it was actually hers. She knew how precious it was to Shunty-Mae; not simply as an object, but as a Romany reliquary for all the memories of her travelling life. It was a priceless gift.

Imelda had almost forgotten about the girl she had cursed at school until her father had brought it up last night. But once disturbed, the memories came flooding back, surprisingly sharp in detail. The curse itself hadn't been real – just some made-up gibberish garnished with the only swear words that her eight-year-old self knew, although Imelda had been pretty pleased with it at the time. But the hurt and anger that had triggered her reaction had been genuine enough. Once her class-mates had discovered Shunty-Mae's profession, the name-calling had become a popular pastime that had tailed her relentlessly in the playground. The chants of 'pikey' and 'gyppo' had become a daily occurrence, rarely challenged by any teacher and actively encour-aged by a small minority of ignorant parents. Imelda had never admitted the full extent of the bullying she had encountered. Even as a small child she had been confident but self-contained. The approval or even acceptance of her peers was something she had neither sought nor required. But she was fiercely protective of her parents, and the pain she felt on her mother's behalf had been fierce and raw. She knew that Shunty-Mae was different somehow, but in her eyes that made her special. Imelda hadn't revealed, then or since, that on the day of the curse and the maggot, her classmate had directed her insult not at Imelda but at Shunty-Mae, calling her a gyppo bitch. The following morning, her mother had taken her to school. Even now, Imelda couldn't really explain or understand exactly what had happened next. In the middle of the crowded playground, hand in hand with Imelda, Shunty-Mae had stopped. Her silence and stillness were unnerving and had gradually crept outwards like a freezing force field from her icy epicentre until everyone else was motionless and staring open-mouthed at them. Not one word was spoken, but back then Imelda had believed that her mother had truly cursed them as she stood strong and defiant, daring anyone to challenge or insult her. That night, her mother had given her a pack of tarot cards – her first – and began teaching her to read them. Imelda still had them, tattered and torn but treasured, nonetheless. She had taken them to school with her every day after that. They became her playmates and her protection.

Grisha rolled over onto his back and into the middle of the bed, his long front legs flopped over at the knees, and wriggled, almost nudging Imelda onto the floor. Of course, there was one more birthday memory that Imelda hadn't yet replayed. That kiss. But she wasn't going to think about that yet. She was going to keep it until later in the day for a treat, like saving the favourite chocolate in the box until last. She felt hot just thinking about thinking about it!

Imelda and Grisha spent the morning in the booth on the seafront. Holidaymakers basted in suntan oil roasted themselves in rows on the beach like sardines on a barbecue, or puffed and panted up and down the pier and promenade clutching dripping ice cream cones and punnets of vinegary chips. The queue outside the booth was rarely less than a dozen people and Imelda was delighted when Shunty-Mae turned up to lend a hand. She was also somewhat surprised to see the slightest flicker of Grisha's tail in greeting. Imelda was due at Larkins that afternoon, but by lunchtime the queue outside showed no sign of dwindling.

'We'll have to turn the rest away,' she told her mother, checking her watch. Shunty-Mae tutted disapprovingly. 'You can't do that. It's bad for business.'

'Well, I can't be in two places at once either!' Imelda was hot and tired and still a little hungover. She was also keen to get to Larkins and see Cillian, none of which she was prepared to admit to her mother.

'You go and I'll stay here.' Shunty-Mae was clearly enjoying herself. 'I'll close up as soon as things quieten down.'

Imelda gathered her things before her mother could change her mind, but Grisha, who was normally on his feet as soon as she moved, remained on his blanket. He opened his eyes a fraction and sighed heavily.

'Come on, lazybones!' Imelda chided him. 'We need to get going.' Grisha rolled onto his side and stretched, but still made no attempt to get up.

'Leave him with me. He'll be fine. It's too hot to go dragging him up to that holiday park.'

Imelda was speechless and not entirely convinced that she hadn't been mysteriously abducted and transported to a parallel universe. First her mother had invited Cillian to dinner and now she was volunteering to dogsit. Grisha looked perfectly happy with the arrangement.

'On your head be it!' Imelda warned him, kissing his long nose.

'You're welcome!' Shunty-Mae smiled wryly as her daughter rushed out of the door.

At Larkins, Ruby was in the entertainment lounge talking to the bar staff when Imelda arrived. She waved at Imelda and then came to find her once her meeting was over.

'How was the rest of your birthday?'

Imelda smiled. 'Lovely, thank you. Surprising and a little strange, but lovely.'

Ruby sat down. 'Well, now you're going to have to tell me everything!'

Imelda reprised the previous evening's events and showed Ruby her present from Cillian. 'I still can't believe my mother invited him.'

'But you like him, don't you?'

'Yes, but sometimes I don't know how to take him. I don't want to risk making it into something bigger than it is.'

'You don't want to get hurt? Don't you trust him?'

Imelda shrugged. 'My gut instinct tells me I should, but I still have doubts.'

'That's only natural. Especially if you *really* like him,' Ruby teased. 'Can't you ask your cards?'

Imelda shook her head. 'You shouldn't read for yourself or those really close to you. Your emotions get in the way and distort the interpretation. You can end up seeing what you want or what you fear instead of what's actually there.'

Ruby leaned forward to inspect the necklace that Imelda was wearing. 'It's beautiful – and it looks expensive. It's a serious gift. So, what has the man done to make you doubt him?'

'It's more what he hasn't done.'

Ruby raised her eyebrows in silent interrogation.

'Yesterday, just before my party, I saw him tinkering with one of his bikes. And guess who was playing with his spanners? He insists that it's just a one-sided infatuation, so why doesn't he tell her to get lost?'

'Perhaps it's not that easy.'

'It's two words.'

Ruby's face grew serious. 'Don't underestimate that girl, Imelda. She may be young and spoilt, but she's smart with it. She's cast her spell on Jeanie and has poor Charlie dancing attendance at the click of her fingers. She's not even a guest here, but Marty treats her like a VIP, sadly deluded that he stands even a cat in hell's chance of getting inside her Janet Reger knickers.'

Imelda had rarely heard Ruby speak about anyone other than Marty with such obvious dislike – and she hadn't finished yet.

'She's rich, and accustomed to all the privileges that Daddy's money can buy. She wants; she gets. And if anyone gets in the way, woe betide them.'

'So, are you saying that Cillian's right just to go along with her game?'

'No. I'm saying that maybe Cillian's playing poker. He can't change the cards she's dealt him, but he can play a clever hand. She's trouble, and I think he's trying to protect himself – and you.'

Imelda remembered her encounter with Vivienne at the talent contest and the vague disquiet she had felt looking into those cold, grey eyes for the first time.

'My mother did say she's got the devil in her.'

'I think she may well be right,' Ruby replied.

'Talk of the devil and he will appear!'

Cillian flung back the curtain and swaggered into the booth like a pantomime villain making his entrance. 'Now, who are you two ladies gossiping about?'

'Don't flatter yourself – it wasn't you!' Imelda couldn't help but smile.

'But you are just the man I wanted to see.' Ruby handed him a flyer from the folder she was holding.

'Now, that's supposed to be your line.' Cillian winked at Imelda. 'But Ruby, of course, I'm yours to command,' he added, scanning the piece of paper in his hand.

'That disco, next Saturday, can you be here?'

'Are you asking me on a date?'

Ruby shook her head. 'I wouldn't dare. The competition's far too stiff.' She shot a glance at Imelda, who glared back at her.

'So why am I going?'

'To be honest, I'm worried that Marty's bright idea to open up Larkins to young singles is a recipe for disaster. It's always been just families – nice and friendly – no trouble other than the occasional lost child and that granny who got tipsy on Campari and stood on a table in the entertainment lounge waving her roll-on girdle. These youngsters have a different idea of fun. They drink more than they can handle and that's when the problems start. We've already had a couple of dodgy incidents in the bar and the staff aren't happy. This weekend almost half the new guests are groups of singles. The disco will be their first chance to let their hair down, and I just want to make sure that there's no trouble.'

Cillian flexed his biceps. 'So, what? I'm to be the hired muscle?'

Ruby laughed, a little embarrassed. 'Well, yes, except you won't get paid any extra. I know it's cheeky to ask but I need some real men around to keep the boys and girls in order.'

'What about Marty? Will he be on security duty too?'

Ruby snorted. 'I said men, not mummy's boys! But if you see Titus before I do, would you ask him too?'

'It'll be my pleasure. But on one condition: that Imelda comes too. I'll ask her for the last dance. The guy who gets the last dance always gets to kiss the girl.'

'Again?' Ruby asked with a grin, as she got up and left them alone. As soon as Ruby had gone, and before Imelda had the chance to say anything at all, Cillian kissed her. Again.

38

Now

It was still dark, and Imelda lay cocooned in her duvet, listening to the huff and puff of Mabel's breathing and the tick of the clock on her bedside table. Outside, rain caught by the gusting wind splattered against the windowpane and the gnarled branches of ancient wisteria that clung to the side of the house tapped on the glass like arthritic fingers. Imelda felt for the chain around her neck and as she caught the moon and stars in her hand, her eyes filled with hot tears. The necklace had lain against her skin since the day that Cillian had fastened it there. She had never taken it off. For so long she had clung to the hope that the brief time they had shared together was as precious to them both as she believed it to have been. That the passing years had not hoodwinked her and burnished it to a brightness that it had never quite possessed. That he had looked forward to a future together with the same excitement as she had. Imelda hadn't wasted her life mourning what might have been, she had lived it to the full. But the absolute certainty that he had loved her as she loved him had always eluded her, and with it the sense of peace that knowing would have brought her.

The sound of footsteps on the landing woke Mabel and she lifted her head and rubbed her sleepy eyes with one paw. There was a tentative knock on the door.

'Are you awake? I'm making breakfast. Would you like some?'

Billie didn't come in and Imelda was glad. She brushed the spilt tears from her cheeks.

'Lovely. I'll be down in a minute.'

After breakfast Billie went straight to the booth. Imelda was going with Mabel to visit Esther at her salon for a morning of pampering and said that afterwards she would meet Billie in The Tea Leaf for lunch. The booth was filling up with stock and Billie wove her way through the cardboard boxes that were piled up on the floor.

She spent the next couple of hours sorting through the boxes and making an inventory of the stock that she had so far acquired. She had taken Treasure up on his offer of help and he was coming the following day to put up some extra shelving and help give the place a lick of paint. Imelda had moved her table and the other things that she would need into the back room and Billie had bought a beautiful heavy velvet curtain patterned with dark emerald leaves and blood red and purple roses to separate the two areas of the booth. She had decided to call her mini-shop Billie's Beside The Seaside and had ordered an A-board sign to stand at the door to the booth. Madame Burova's signage would, of course, remain.

Outside, the rain had finally stopped, and silver shafts of sunlight fell through breaches in the swollen storm clouds. Billie stretched and felt a painful but satisfying pop between her shoulder blades. She had been hunched over the boxes for too long. She shrugged on her coat, pushed her hat firmly down onto her head and set off for a brisk walk to clear the dust from her nostrils and loosen up her stiffened limbs. The promenade was quiet save for a few hardy runners, and dogs in designer coats looking considerably more cheerful than their wet and windswept walkers. Billie headed for the pier. The smell of warm doughnuts made her stomach grumble, but she resisted the rings of soft, sugar-coated dough. She would be meeting Imelda for lunch in less than an hour. The flags on the turrets that flanked the entrance to the pier were being whipped so viciously by the wind that their Union Jacks were barely visible; just blurred flashes of red, white and blue. Billie battled her way along the pier until she reached somewhere to sit and gaze at the sinuous, froth-crested waves. She found the sea's perpetual propulsion a soothing sight, and yet exhilarating to her other senses. The salt tang of it, the sting of it on her skin, the sound of water sloshing and crashing made her feel energised – her brio rebooted. Billie registered a figure in her peripheral vision and turned away from the sea to find MI5 Clive a little distance away stretching elastic bands across the fretwork of the metal railings. This time the design was simple: five green and two red bands positioned vertically, and eight blue running across them horizontally. Once the message was completed, Clive

straightened up and looked around, as though checking to see if anyone was watching him. Spying Billie,
he hesitated, seemingly unsure whether to acknowledge her or not. Billie waved. Clive appeared to gather
himself together, quite literally, by brushing down his
coat and shaking the bag in his hand, before approach-
ing her.

'Good afternoon, Billie In The Bowler Hat.'

'Good afternoon, Clive.' Billie wished that Imelda
had never told her about Clive's sobriquet. Each time
she encountered him she struggled to keep the MI5
prefix unspoken. Much to Billie's surprise, Clive sat
down next to her. She waited for him to say something,
but he was clearly more comfortable with the silence
than she was.

'I'm opening a little shop at the front of Madame
Burova's booth selling vintage seaside stuff.'

Clive didn't look at her. 'Why?'

For a moment Billie was thrown. There were so many
things that she could say about starting a fresh chapter
in her life; wanting a new challenge and the serendipity
of Imelda's semi-retirement. But if she were to strip
back her reply to match the candour of Clive's question
the answer was simple.

'Because my mother abandoned me in the doorway
of Madame Burova's booth when I was just a tiny
baby.'

'Why?'

Billie drummed her fingers along the brim of her hat
in a futile attempt to dissipate her discomfort.

'I've no idea,' she replied eventually. 'I don't even
know who she was.'

Clive bent down and adjusted one shoelace whose ends had become very slightly uneven in length. Once satisfied that perfect symmetry had been restored, he sat up straight, staring out to sea and placed his hands down carefully in his lap.

'I know,' he told Billie. 'I saw her do it.'

39

Now

They had settled on a shade of pale primrose. Once Treasure had finished constructing the new shelves, he and Billie began painting and Imelda and Mabel left them to it. The smell of paint made Mabel sneeze, and once she had approved of the redecorating plans, Imelda was keen to leave Treasure and Billie alone so that they could get to know one another better. She certainly wasn't matchmaking, she told herself. She was simply trying to help Billie make more friends in Brighton.

'And he didn't say anything else?'

Billie was discussing MI5 Clive's revelation with Treasure.

'He refused to say another word. Just got up, said goodbye and left.'

'What did Imelda say when you told her?'

'She seemed as shocked as I was. She said that if it was true, he hadn't said anything to anyone at the time.'

Treasure worked his paintbrush back and forth in even strokes, spreading sticky sunshine over the wall.

'He's a strange one, Clive. But I can't think of any reason why he would fabricate something like that. He's been hanging around the promenade for years, and I can certainly remember him being here when I was kid.'

Billie was trying to emulate Treasure's proficient painting skills, but she already had yellow splashes on her face and fingers. 'Do you remember the others too? The ones from Larkins who used to come to the café?'

'Vaguely.' Treasure frowned. 'Of course, Jeanie used to be there, but she's my cousin. She used to bring her snooty friend with her, the one from the secretarial place where she worked before she got a job as a singer. I didn't really pay that much attention to the others from Larkins. Once I got my dog, Star, I spent more time with Imelda and Grisha.'

Billie nodded. 'Imelda's first dog, the borzoi?' She'd seen photos at Imelda's house.

'That's right. Of course, I remember Cillian. As a Wall of Death rider, he automatically qualified as a small boy's hero. He was a genuinely nice bloke. Everyone seemed to like him, even Shunty-Mae, Imelda's mother, and she was a tough nut to crack. There was just something about him. Well, that's what I thought, but then I was only eleven. And I remember them talking about Marty, the manager, but I never met him. He had a real eye for the ladies, apparently.'

'What about the women? Do you remember any of them? The contortionist? Sara-Jade something? Or the mermaids? I found a photograph of them at the auction the other day, but I've given it to Imelda.'

Treasure smiled. 'Dolly, Daisy and the one with the very deep voice! What on earth was she called?' He thought for a moment. 'Dixie! Yes, I do remember them. They were so sexy that they scared me half to death.'

Billie climbed down from her stepladder and moved it along the wall. 'They all had such impossibly glamorous names. Even your mum and auntie.'

'Well, there's a story behind Mum's name. There was another sister too, Emerald, Jeanie's mum. She died before I was born. The three of them were named after the stones in my grandma's engagement ring. As for the Larkins lot, I suppose it was expected of the entertainment staff. Some of them were probably only stage names.'

Billie hadn't thought of that. 'What about Cillian? Do you suppose that was his real name?'

'It seems likely. It's a good traditional Irish name.'

They carried on painting in silence for a while, Billie wondering if perhaps her mother had been one of the mermaids. If so, Billie hadn't inherited any of her talent. The best she could manage was an inelegant and far-too-splashy front crawl. And now she thought about it, her arm ached, and she was desperate for a mug of tea.

'Time for a tea break, I reckon,' she told Treasure. 'My shout.' As she wiped her hands on an old towel, Treasure had just reached the cubbyhole in the wall.

'What's in here?'

'Secrets!' Billie whispered melodramatically, and then laughed. 'Imelda used to keep stuff in there for her clients. She said it was like a safety deposit box for secrets.'

'Anything exciting?'

'Hard to say. It's empty now. But Imelda kept the things from my mother in there for all those years, and a bundle of photos that my dad sent her.'

Treasure's hand was exploring the dark recess in the wall as Billie spoke. He touched cold metal. Not quite empty then.

'So, Imelda was in contact with your adoptive dad?' As he spoke, his fingers closed around the object he had found and then dropped it, startled by its familiar shape. Billie had turned away to fetch her coat.

'Yes,' she replied. 'It's a long story. Damn! Where on earth did I put my bag?'

While she searched, Treasure grabbed the object from the cubbyhole and shoved it deep into his pocket.

'Well, you can tell me all about it when I eventually get that tea you promised!'

40

Now

Over tea and carrot cake Billie explained to Treasure how Imelda had wanted to make sure that the baby she had found was well looked after. Her concerns had been assuaged and rewarded by regular updates and photographs.

'And then she ends up being the person who passes on the legacy left by the woman who gave birth to you?'

'Exactly! It's as though she's always been some sort of fairy godmother waiting in the wings.'

'And yet she never had any children of her own. I wonder why?'

'Ha!' Billie replied. 'You sound like a detective trying to solve a case.'

It was Treasure's turn to laugh. 'It's a fair cop! I spent thirty years on the force before I retired – the last fifteen in CID. Old habits die hard.'

'What on earth made you want to join the police? It can't have been easy, given your—'

'Colour?'

'I was going to say name, but okay, yes, your colour too.'

Treasure smiled. 'You're very—'

'Nosey?'

'I was going to say direct, but okay, yes, nosey. I joined because I needed to prove to myself that I could do anything. I had a tough time at school, and it took years for me to be proud of who I was. Back then, the police were desperate to recruit more black faces. Everything was "Equal Opportunities" and "welcoming ethnic minorities into the workplace". I didn't believe a word of it. My dad came over from Jamaica in 1948 and I know exactly what kind of welcome he had. But I figured if I got in and was the best that I could be, it would be the sweetest kind of "up yours" to all the racists and bigots willing me to fail.'

'And how did that work out for you?'

'Okay, I guess. I made DCI before I retired, but probably at the expense of two marriages and numerous relationships. The job always came first.'

'And now?'

'Now I get a decent pension and I get to play the music I love and make the people dance. It's not a bad life. What about you?'

'Gave up my job as a lecturer – history of art – a couple of years ago to care for my dad. Gave up my husband at the same time.' Billie sighed. 'It had got to the point where we were *really trying* to make our marriage work. But in the end, all that trying gets a little – well, trying. The sand was trickling through the hourglass and my life was about as exciting as boiling an egg.'

'And now?'

'Now it's much more fun. Slightly surreal with all this abandoned baby malarkey, but definitely much more fun.'

'Well, perhaps with my ex-detective skills, I might be able to help you find out a bit more about Larkins and the people in your photo. I may be retired, but I still have some tricks up my sleeve.' Treasure laughed – a deep, mellow laugh that reverberated in his chest.

Billie poured herself more tea. 'I tried good old Google, but I didn't get very far.'

Treasure went up to the counter and asked if he could borrow Kip's laptop. He brought it back to their table and started tapping away. After a couple of minutes, he turned the screen so that Billie could see it.

'Google's for amateurs,' he teased, 'but us professional sleuths have other options. This is a report in the local press from August 1973.'

The police were called to a disturbance at Larkins Holiday Park late on Saturday night and several arrests were made. There were some minor casualties and significant damage to property. The general manager, Mr Marty Mount, declined to comment.

Billie arrived back at Imelda's to find her clip-clopping energetically around the kitchen in a new pair of shiny black tap shoes. Mabel was watching from the safety of her bed, an expression of complete bewilderment rumpling her face.

'Oh, you're back. Good. I wanted to talk to you.' Imelda was a little out of breath from her exertions. She sat down. 'Aren't you going to ask about my tap shoes?'

Billie grinned. 'Imelda, why on earth are you wearing tap shoes?'

'Because Esther and I are joining a new tap dance class. There's only one problem, and that's what I was going to ask you about. The dance teacher needs a new pianist, and I was wondering if your friend Henry might oblige?'

41

1973

'I want to know if my friend Janet is trying to get off with the same bloke as me.'

Imelda smiled with forced patience. She had done at least a dozen similar readings already that afternoon. It was the Saturday of the disco and Larkins was teeming with rowdy, over-excited and evidently very libidinous young singletons. Imelda was beginning to understand why Ruby was so concerned. The new guests appeared to be interested only in getting drunk and getting laid. Gangs of youths doused in cheap aftershave and trippy on testosterone were peacocking around the holiday park taunting and teasing gaggles of brazen young women, slick with fruit-flavoured lip gloss and frosted eyeshadow, who sashayed past them in clouds of Charlie perfume. Imelda spread the cards on the table and turned them over.

'Does the boy in question have brown hair and brown eyes?' she asked, pointing to the Page of Cups. Debbie nodded. 'And Janet is fair with blue eyes?'

'Yes. But she's not a natural blonde,' Debbie added cattily.

Imelda sighed. The Page was followed by the Queen of Wands and the Two of Cups.

'I don't think he's the one for you,' she explained, trying to be tactful.

'Why not?' Debbie peered at the cards, narrowing her eyes. 'What do they say?'

Imelda was hot and tired, and her temples throbbed, threatening a headache.

'That Janet and this boy are together. If not already, then they soon will be.'

Debbie scowled. 'Bloody cow! She knows I like him. And I saw him first! Some bloody friend she is. She's ruined my holiday now. I might as well go home.' Tears glistened in her hazel eyes and threatened to spill through mascara-clumped lashes, running black rivulets through her mask of Maybelline foundation. Imelda wanted to shake her. Why did so many of these girls sell themselves short? They had barely discovered who they were as individuals when they became fixated on affixing themselves to someone else, as though they could only be whole as one half of a couple. When Imelda heard that Debbie was already writing off her holiday over a boy she'd only just met, the absurdity of it infuriated her.

'There's more to life than boys,' she heard herself saying, sounding scarily like her own mother. 'Don't you want to ask anything about you and your future?'

Debbie sniffed. 'What, you mean who I'll marry and how many kids we'll have?'

Imelda wondered why she was bothering, but having started she wasn't going to give up yet. 'No, Debbie. I mean about you! What do you want to make of your life? What would your dream job be, for example?'

Debbie looked as though she was sitting an exam in a subject that she hadn't studied as she frowned and inspected her pearly pink nails.

'I dunno. I work in a clothes shop. Well, it's a boutique really, that's what the boss calls it.'

'And do you like it?'

'It's all right. I get staff discount.'

'Wouldn't *you* like to be the manager one day?'

Judging by the expression of astonishment on her face, such an outlandish idea had clearly never occurred to Debbie before.

'I did once think about trying to get my own market stall.'

'Well, what's to stop you?'

Debbie shrugged. Imelda could have ended the reading right there. She was sorely tempted, but for some reason she couldn't let it go.

'Let's ask the cards if your market stall would be a success.'

As Imelda dealt the cards, she saw a flicker of curiosity animate Debbie's rather dull face, rousing her sluggish imagination like a dead car battery being jump-started. When Imelda turned over the Nines of both Wands and Pentacles, and the Chariot, she could barely believe her eyes. But once again her instinct had served her well and the tarot told her why. Debbie clearly had hidden depths, should she care to plumb them.

'Your market stall would be a great success,' she told Debbie. 'You'd earn a very comfortable living and, what's more, you'd love it!'

Debbie grinned. 'That's amazing! But now can you tell me when I'll get married?'

Once Debbie had gone, Imelda took Grisha outside for a walk. The air was sticky, and the park noisy and unbearably congested with bodies wandering this way and that, and once Grisha had found a convenient tree and relieved himself, Imelda was keen to return to the peace and quiet of the booth. They were waylaid in the entertainment lounge by Ruby, who was busy supervising preparations for the disco. All the chairs and tables were being moved to the sides of the room, and the DJ was setting up his equipment on the stage.

'You are coming tonight, aren't you?' Ruby asked her. 'I could do with some moral support as well as the hired muscle. These guests are going to be a proper handful. Besides, you wouldn't want to miss that last dance with Cillian,' she added with a wink.

Imelda still wasn't sure. Music and dancing were two of her favourite things, and crowds her least favourite. She found the cacophony of energies and emotions exhausting and disorientating. But what about Cillian? It was true that she hadn't specifically told him that she would be there, but then she hadn't said she wouldn't be. Her silence had implied acquiescence. And she really wanted to dance with him.

'Yes,' she told Ruby. 'I'll be there.'

Back in the booth, Imelda rested her head in her hands. Her headache was receding, and she began to think about what she might wear that evening and, rather annoyingly, about Debbie. Was she, Imelda, really so very different, mooning over Cillian? She allowed herself to think about what it might be like to be with him properly – coupled. And yes, she realised with relief, she was different. Nothing could ever induce her to give up dukkering for domesticity. Her mother never had. But then Shunty-Mae and Alexei had always remained undiluted individuals; united, but never shackled, by love.

Vivienne walked into the booth unannounced and sat down. Imelda hid her surprise admirably.

'Good afternoon, Vivienne. Are you here for a reading?'

'Hardly! I'm not so stupid as to be taken in by all your mumbo jumbo.' Vivienne flicked her talon-tipped fingers in a dismissive gesture towards the tarot cards on the table. Imelda gathered them up and returned them to the protection of their velvet bag, silently apologising to them for Vivienne's insults.

'Well, what do you want then?'

Grisha stirred and sat up, rigid by his mistress's side, sensing immediately the hostility in her tone. Vivienne smiled. It was merely a reconfiguration of her features rather than an expression of emotion. 'You're very fond of that dog, aren't you?'

An icy tingle trickled down Imelda's spine and goosebumps prickled the skin on her arms, but she said nothing.

'Well, I'd love to stay and chat, but I've got more interesting things to do. I just wanted to ask whether you're planning to go to the disco tonight?'

'And why would that be any of your business?'

Vivienne sighed. 'Because,' she explained with exaggerated patience, 'I'd hate to see you wasting your time and getting your hopes up about Cillian. It'll only end in tears. And I'm sure you wouldn't want to be a wallflower.' She leaned down and rummaged in the expensive handbag that was on the floor beside her, pulled out a compact and began powdering her nose. Imelda remained silent, denying Vivienne's opinions any credence or significance. What she really wanted to do was slap her. Very hard. But she remembered what Ruby had said and kept her poker face. Finally satisfied with her appearance, Vivienne snapped shut the compact, retuned it to her bag and stood up.

'Just a word of friendly advice before I go. Stay at home tonight.' As she reached the door, she turned and added, 'And take care of that dog.'

42

1973

Grisha stretched out his neck, lowered his head and began to retch and heave. His lean body shuddered with the effort and Imelda stroked him between his shoulder blades, trying to soothe him with softly spoken words of reassurance. She had caught him snuffling around under her table after Vivienne had left, and as soon as she realised what had happened, she rushed home with him. It was late afternoon and their local vet's practice was closed. The emergency vet was out on another call. Imelda had been distraught, but her mother knew exactly what to do. By the time they had managed to get Grisha to swallow enough salty water, both Shunty-Mae and Imelda were drenched, but now it was having the desired effect. As Grisha threw up in the flowerbed, Imelda wept with relief. The sticky brown substance was clearly identifiable as dark chocolate, and fortunately it hadn't been in his stomach long enough to have been digested. Grisha coughed and spat, and then wagged his tail weakly as he followed Imelda back inside. Shunty-Mae offered him some fresh water.

'Just a little,' she warned him. 'Drink too much too quickly and you'll be sick again. And if it's on my kitchen floor, there'll be trouble.'

Imelda sat down and Shunty-Mae poured her a glass of vodka. 'You're the colour of a shroud, girl! Get this down you. That great greedy dog will be fine. So long as he doesn't vomit in here,' she said, shooting Grisha, who had settled down on his blanket, a cautionary glare. Imelda lifted the glass to her lips. Her hands were shaking, but she couldn't say whether it was with fear for what might have happened, or anger about what already had. Shunty-Mae poured herself a drink and sat down at the table.

'Now, are you going to tell me what happened?'

As she knocked back the vodka in one gulp, the afternoon's events coalesced in Imelda's mind to form the explicit realisation that Grisha might have died. She stormed back outside into the garden and with her arms raised and her fists clenched she bellowed at the sky; an eruption of primal fury and frustration that continued until she could barely breathe. Alexei arrived home from work just in time to witness the spectacle. He kissed Shunty-Mae, poured himself a drink and waited for someone to tell him what the hell was happening.

Grisha was feeling much better now. And hungry. Imelda, Shunty-Mae and Alexei sat around the table eating fish and chips and discussing his attempted murder. Grisha rested his head on Alexei's knee – knowing that he was always a soft touch – and was rewarded with a small piece of battered cod. Shunty-Mae was holding forth, full of fire and brimstone.

'I told you that girl was trouble the first time I saw her. She drags it with her like a shadow wherever she goes. Men are taken in by her painted face and her fawning and flattery, but that one has no heart. She's an ice queen in her own cold world and everyone else is just one of her subjects to be commanded as she sees fit!'

'You don't like her, then?' Alexei joked as he stole a chip from his wife's plate.

'Like her? I'd like to push her under a bus!'

'Me too,' agreed Imelda, 'but as that's not really an option, what can I do? I can't prove she left the chocolate there. I didn't actually see her do it and Marty won't believe a word said against her anyway.'

'But no one else could have done it. Don't tell me that you're afraid to stand up to her too?'

'You know I'm not,' Imelda scoffed. 'But I'm beginning to be afraid of what she might be capable of.'

Ruby had been right – Vivienne was not to be under-estimated. She was clever, calculating and cold-blooded. Imelda could make sure that she never came near Grisha again, and she would happily take her chances if Vivienne tried anything with her. If fact, she would welcome it. But the thought of her hanging around Cillian – and especially his bikes – was now a cause for serious concern. Who knew how far she was prepared to go to get what she wanted and to punish those who tried to prevent her? Perhaps Cillian had been wise not to reject her outright.

'And what does Mr Cillian Byrne have to say about it?'

Imelda swore that her mother could read her mind sometimes. 'He says she's just a kid with a crush on him. That she'll get bored eventually.'

Alexei shrugged. 'He may well have more to say than that when he finds out that she deliberately tried to poison his girlfriend's dog.'

'Am I his girlfriend?' Imelda genuinely wasn't sure if either of them had consciously made that commitment yet. But she rather hoped they had.

'I saw you kissing in the kitchen. In my book, you're practically engaged.'

The taxi dropped Imelda at the gates of Larkins just before 11 p.m. She had spent most of the evening trying to decide whether to go to the disco or not. Shunty-Mae had been adamant that she should. 'Show that snooty gobshite that her threats are as feeble as a few snowflakes falling on a bonfire.' But Alexei had said that it must be his daughter's decision alone. Imelda had rehearsed every possible scenario in her head to see which one played out the most favourably. She couldn't tell Cillian about Grisha tonight. She didn't know how he would react, and she couldn't risk a confrontation of any sort. He was there to prevent trouble, not start it. And would Imelda be able to control her own rage face to face with Vivienne? She had told Ruby that she would be there to support her, and she had already let her down. In the end she decided that she would risk the eleventh hour only, like a contradictory Cinderella. Just in time to grant Cillian's wish.

She could hear the music, feel it pulsating in her chest, long before she reached the entertainment lounge. Outside, there were numerous couples grappling in ungainly embraces, whatever inhibitions they may have started the evening with now utterly absolved by alcohol. Imelda pushed through the doors into a maelstrom of flashing lights and deafening music. The disco floor was jammed with gyrating bodies; each one indistinguishable from another, merely a component part of a seemingly single writhing entity. As the music segued into Barry White's slow and sultry rendition of 'I'm Gonna Love You Just a Little More', the crowd reorganised into couples and the DJ declared this to be the last dance. Imelda felt someone tap on her shoulder. She turned to find Sara-Jade in a sequinned mini-dress, clinging tightly to Titus Marlow's arm. Sara-Jade leaned closer, a tad tipsily, in order to make herself heard.

'It looks like you missed your chance there,' she said, nodding towards the dance floor. Imelda shrugged, not understanding. Sara-Jade pointed, and as Imelda stared at the dancers one pair became painfully apparent. There, in the centre of the floor beneath the glitter ball, Vivienne was pressed closely against Cillian, her arms around his neck and her head resting on his shoulder. Imelda turned away and went home.

43

Now

'Shuffle step, shuffle step, shuffle step, shuffle ball change.' The tap dance teacher called out the choreography as she prowled the floor, checking her pupils' footwork. She was a striking woman in her mid-fifties called Gloria, with impressive curves and a swishy blonde ponytail, and her convivial enthusiasm was underpinned by a resolute professionalism. Her dancers might be 'mature' beginners, but she would make damn sure that they were the best 'mature' beginners in Brighton. She had already informed them that they would be expected to perform in an end-of-term show at a surprise venue. Henry was having a splendid time at the piano, reprising much of his St Pancras repertoire with Mabel sitting at his feet. Imelda and Esther were exhausted.

Gloria clapped her hands to signal the end of the class.

'Well done, ladies. And David. Same time next week please and practise every day in the meantime. Now, let's show our appreciation for Henry, our music man.'

Some of the ladies were clearly very appreciative and there was an enthusiastic round of applause before the class broke ranks and clattered off to change their shoes. Imelda and Esther emerged into the silvery winter sunshine with flushed cheeks and aching legs to find Henry and Mabel waiting for them.

'I wondered if you ladies might care to join me for some restorative refreshments at The Tea Leaf after all your efforts?'

'Sounds like just the job.' Esther took his arm and he offered the other to Imelda.

Revived by several cups of tea and slices of banana and walnut cake ('for energy', Amber had advised), Imelda and Henry began reminiscing about their time at Larkins.

'When Billie first mentioned you, I couldn't place you at all, but I do recognise your face,' Imelda told Henry. 'Did Billie show the photograph? Are you on it?'

Henry smiled. 'I am, but I was just a baby. I was eighteen and had never been kissed when I started at Larkins. By the time I left nine months later I was almost a man. It was certainly an education working and living there.'

'You lived there as well?' Esther had always been fascinated by Imelda's stories about the holiday park and was keen to hear more from Henry.

'Oh, yes. Staff who didn't live locally – and that applied to most of the entertainment staff – were offered accommodation with their jobs. Of course, our rooms were very basic, except for Marty's which was as good as any of the holiday chalets, but then we didn't spend much time in them. Mine was next door to your friend Cillian's,' he told Imelda.

Esther's face lit up. 'Ooh! Did you ever catch him sneaking Imelda in there?'

Imelda rapped her over the knuckles with a teaspoon and Henry laughed.

'There wasn't supposed to be any fraternising in the staff chalets, with guests or other members of staff.'

'But . . .' encouraged Esther.

'But rules are made to be broken,' Henry conceded. 'And, of course, they were.'

Imelda offered Mabel a small piece of cake. 'Did you know Cillian well?'

'Not really. We'd say hello in passing and I'd occa-sionally see him in the bar. The entertainment staff never had much free time. The Wall of Death shows were in the afternoon and early evening and I was generally working from noon to midnight. I used to play piano for Jeanie Rogers, the singer, most evenings.'

Imelda looked puzzled. 'But Jeanie's accompanist was a young man called Charlie Martin. He left to go and work in a club in London, and if I remember rightly, he got Jeanie a job there too eventually.'

'That's why you couldn't place me! I'm him. He's me. We're one and the same. Charlie Martin was my stage name. I hated Henry back then. It sounded like an old man. Charles was my middle name, so I became Charlie. Like Chaplin.'

'And the perfume,' offered Esther. 'I remember that so well. I used to drench myself with the stuff.'

'But you're Henry Hayward, now?' Imelda was deter-mined to get things straight.

'I took Jocelyn's name when we married. I liked the alliteration.'

Esther was keen to return to the more salacious gossip.

'So, did you ever sneak anyone back to your chalet?' she asked Henry.

'Now, that would be telling. I was quite the innocent back then, but I do remember that things got very rowdy once the management started allowing young single guests to stay. Saturday nights became like an everlasting happy hour in Sodom and Gomorrah.'

Imelda smiled, remembering her mother's words on her first visit to Larkins. Esther's eyes widened. 'Imelda! You never tell me the good stuff! What exciting lives you had.'

Henry shook his head. 'It wasn't much fun when you were trying to get a decent night's sleep. But it didn't last long. Head office had a change of heart and Larkins returned to a holiday haven for families.'

Esther looked disappointed, but Imelda, who remembered that time only too clearly, was keen to change the subject.

'Have you seen what Billie's done with the booth?' she asked Henry.

'Not yet. But I'll definitely be there for the grand opening.'

Mabel was beginning to fidget. It was time for her stroll. Esther excused herself to use the ladies before they left, and once they were alone, Imelda took the opportunity to ask Henry what he really thought about the photograph.

'Billie told me where it came from and that her mother said it was a photograph of her father, but that you couldn't say who he was.'

'That's right. Billie thinks it's Cillian. He's right there – centre stage – but who knows?'

Henry sighed. 'Unlike you, I don't know who Billie's mother is, and as I've already said, I didn't know Cillian well. But for what it's worth I always believed that it was only ever you that he really wanted.'

Imelda was grateful for his kind words, but it seemed now that she would never know the truth. 'Well, it was a long time ago. I'm not sure that it really matters anymore.'

Henry reached across the table and took her hand in his. 'Of course it does. Love always matters, no matter how fleeting, how messy, how painful. It always matters.'

When Esther returned, they gathered their things, wrapped woollen scarves around their necks and buttoned up coats against the seafront chill. At the door, they met Treasure. Imelda introduced him to Henry and Esther, and he lifted Mabel into his arms and kissed her head as she wriggled with delight.

'I was wondering if we could have a chat sometime?' he asked Imelda. She knew immediately that something was wrong.

'I'll be at the booth in the morning,' she said. 'Around ten-thirty?'

His tight parting hug did nothing to reassure her.

44

Now

Imelda turned the cards over and over in her hands. Their touch calmed and comforted her. Billie had taken Mabel for a walk along the prom and Imelda was waiting for Treasure. She had asked the cards what was on his mind, but they had, of course, simply confirmed what she already knew. She had checked the cubbyhole as soon as she got to the booth and the asthma inhaler was missing.

Treasure arrived at exactly ten-thirty and sat down without removing his coat or saying a single word. His face was drawn and there were grey bags under his eyes winged by deep lines as though what little sleep he might have managed had been with his eyes screwed tightly shut to keep the darkness out. Or in. He reached into his pocket, brought out the asthma inhaler and placed it on the gypsy table. His eyes were wary, like those of a wild animal, cornered.

'Where did you get it?' he asked. This was a secret that Imelda could no longer keep. She had been the one who had offered to take it off Ruby's hands, and in any case, Ruby was dead now.

'From your mother. She found it in the pocket of your shorts after Jimmy Cox died.'

'What did she tell you?'

'Not much more than that. She didn't know why you had it, but she was worried that it could get you into trouble.'

'Why didn't she ask me about it?'

Imelda hesitated, trying to find the right words. In truth, Ruby had been worried about what the truth might be. She had simply wanted to protect her little boy. But her silence implied that she had not been wholly sure of her son's innocence, and that might be hard for Treasure to hear. For Imelda, the truth was less problematic. Jimmy Cox had been an evil and malicious bastard who had got what he deserved. Whether it had been by the hand of God or Treasure made little difference.

'Ruby wasn't sure what to do for the best. You were so young, and she was worried about the effect the whole thing might have on you – seeing Jimmy Cox's body, and watching Star suffer until you could rescue her.'

'Did she think that I had anything to do with his death?' Treasure's voice cracked as he struggled to get the words out. How on earth could Imelda answer that? She couldn't possibly be sure what Ruby had thought.

'She knew that you would never lie to her. You told her what had happened, and she believed you. She didn't need to ask anything else.'

'So why did you end up with the inhaler?'

'I offered to take it to stop Ruby worrying about it. That's all.'

Imelda hoped that Treasure would be satisfied with her carefully edited explanation, but she could tell from the haunted expression on his face that there was more to come.

'I didn't tell her everything,' he said.

1973

*T*reasure ran upstairs and flung off his uniform. School was finished for the summer! He changed into a T-shirt and shorts. It was stifling indoors. He opened the window and saw Jimmy Cox in the garden next door. Saw what he did. Treasure raced downstairs fuelled by fury but without a plan. There was a passageway between the two houses that led to the gates into their back gardens. He jumped and managed to grab the top edge of Jimmy Cox's gate, which was always kept bolted. He hauled himself up until he was able to scrabble over the top and drop down into his neighbour's yard. A small window in the side wall of the house gave a view into the kitchen and Treasure peered cautiously through the grimy glass. Jimmy Cox was frantically searching for something in a drawer. He threw the contents onto the draining board with one hand, and with the other he clawed at his throat. He was sucking for air as greedily as a nursing pup milking its mother's teat, and his lips were blue. He finally found what he was looking for, but as he grabbed it, it shot out of his grasp and pin-wheeled across the floor. Jimmy Cox collapsed onto his knees and then fell forwards, his arm outstretched in a vain attempt to retrieve what he had dropped. His fingers crept painfully over the linoleum like a sickly spider, but the object they were seeking was just *out of reach. The dog was watching from the doorstep. As the asthma inhaler spun away from Jimmy Cox, she darted into the kitchen, snatched it between her teeth and ran out into the garden clutching her prize. All she knew was that for once she had a chance to deprive her cruel master of something he wanted and so she took it. Treasure watched in astonishment. For a moment he was frozen by fear and indecision. His trance was broken by the soft brush of fur against his leg. The dog was standing beside him, trembling, the inhaler still in her mouth. He reached down to stroke her head. She flinched but didn't move away. Treasure looked back through the window. Jimmy Cox was still lying on the floor motionless, but Treasure couldn't tell if he was breathing or not. He squatted down next to the dog and she crawled closer to him, pushing her head against his chest.*

'It's all right girl,' he whispered. 'You're safe now. I promise.' He wrapped his arms around her, cradling her gently until her shaking stopped and then he reached for the inhaler. 'Drop! Let me have it.' She released it into his hand. 'No one will ever know,' he told her as he shoved it into his pocket. 'Come on girl. We need to go.' He prayed that she would follow him. He unlocked the back gate as quietly as he could and when he checked, the dog was close behind him. Taking her by the collar, he let himself into his own back garden and walked into the house shouting, 'Mum! Mum! I think something's happened to Jimmy Cox!'

Imelda picked up the asthma inhaler and ran her finger over the faint indentations on its surface. She smiled. 'Teeth marks. I always wondered what they were.'

Treasure was looking at her expectantly, awaiting her verdict; absolution or reprobation. As a child, he had never given it a second thought. He had rescued Star and that was all that had mattered. He had worried briefly when he realised that the inhaler had gone missing but assumed that he had dropped it or lost it somewhere. As an adult, however – and a police officer – his conscience had developed, and with sophistication came censure. On the rare occasion that thoughts of Jimmy Cox had surfaced in his mind, he had managed, with a little effort, to bury them again. But since he had seen the inhaler in Imelda's booth, his sleep had been broken by nightmares relentlessly replaying the day that Jimmy Cox had died. Murder, manslaughter or misadventure? Had he acted sooner might a man's life have been saved? No matter how wicked the man and how worthless his life, Treasure had had no right to play God. And was there any chance that Star had known what she was doing? She had probably seen Jimmy Cox use the inhaler before, sensed that it helped him in some way. She was a collie after all.

'Let it go.' The verdict was in and Imelda was resolute. 'He was an alcoholic, chain-smoking asthmatic, who died of all of the above. He was also a complete and utter shit. A post-mortem was deemed unnecessary, but then I'm sure you know that. You will have checked.'

'But . . .'

'No buts. The inhaler was virtually empty, and it would have made no difference if the ambulance had arrived a few minutes earlier. Let it go.' Imelda had no idea how full the inhaler had been, but she knew that neither a small boy nor a terrified dog were to blame.

Treasure sighed. 'It breaks my heart to think that Mum might have doubted me.'

'She didn't. Not for one moment. She knew that you had told the truth.'

'But not the whole truth.'

'It makes no material difference. You were protecting Star, and God knows she deserved it. Ruby would have been proud of you.'

'I still miss her, you know.'

'Of course you do. She was your mother.'

Treasure smiled. 'Well, yes, I miss Mum too. But I meant Star.'

Imelda shuffled her cards.

'Then maybe it's time you rescued another dog. Let's ask, shall we?'

45

Now

Mabel was chasing a large white feather across the pebbles on the beach. The wind teased her, dropping it tantalisingly close and then whisking it up into the air again. Imelda had asked Billie to give her some time to speak to Treasure in private. Billie was curious to know what it was they needed to discuss, but she hadn't asked. Imelda had been right when she had described the booth as a confessional. It seemed that it was still keeping secrets safe inside its freshly painted walls.

Billie was quite glad to have a reason to wander down the prom. She was trying to bump into MI5 Clive. She hadn't seen him since he'd told her that he had witnessed her abandonment. She was hoping to persuade him to tell her more about it. Billie had reluctantly relinquished the idea that Imelda was her birth mother. For that to be true, Clive would have to be lying, and she couldn't think of any good reason why he would. And what justification could Imelda possibly have for not telling her? It was a shame though. Billie would have liked it to be Imelda. Mabel arrived back at her feet, panting but with the feather clamped firmly between her teeth. Her tail was spinning with proud excitement.

'Well done!' Billie praised her. 'You're a champion feather fetcher.'

Billie checked her watch. They had been wandering for just over half an hour. She wasn't sure how long would be long enough. The wind was skimming ribbons of grey cloud across a sullen sky and Billie's hands and feet were getting cold.

'Come on, Mabel. Let's go and get a cappuccino.'

The Tea Leaf was quiet, with few customers, but there in a corner, poring over an old telephone directory, was MI5 Clive. Billie hesitated, wondering how to play it. Asking to join him seemed too forward, so she chose the neighbouring table, pretending not to notice him until she had sat down. Once the customary protracted greetings had been exchanged, Clive resumed his scrutiny of the telephone directory and Amber came over to take Billie's order.

'No Imelda today?' she asked.

'She's seeing someone in the booth at the moment.'

Amber went off to make her coffee and Billie wondered if she had said the right thing. 'Seeing someone' sounded a bit odd, but then she didn't want to say it was Treasure in case their meeting itself was a secret.

'Did you want something?' Clive had no such qualms about careful wording.

'I'm sorry?'

'There are lots of empty tables, but you sat right next to me, which probably means that you wish to talk to me.'

Billie held up her hands. 'Guilty as charged.'

259

'That's a sort of joke, isn't it?' Clive replied without smiling.

Billie tried again. 'Yes, and yes. Please. I would like to talk to you if that's okay. Can I get you another cup of tea?'

Clive thought about it. 'Yes, and yes.' He paused for a moment. 'That's called speech mirroring,' he added. 'I did it to make you feel more comfortable. You seem nervous.'

Billie ordered his tea. She admired Clive's directness. Perhaps, she thought, she should mirror his approach. 'I wanted to ask you about the woman who left me outside Imelda's booth.'

'The woman who is your mother?'

'Yes.'

'Why?'

'Because I'd like to find out who she is. She left some things with Imelda – things that she wanted me to have – but she made Imelda promise not to reveal her identity.'

Clive considered the facts. 'Your mother doesn't want you to know who she is. She left you outside Madame Burova's booth because she didn't want to keep you. So why do you want to find her?'

It was a good question. 'Perhaps she couldn't keep me.'

'But even if that were true, she still doesn't want to be found by you, because she told Madame Burova to keep her a secret.'

Entirely uncluttered or complicated by emotions, Clive's logic was faultless. Why did she want to know? What good would it do? But still, she had to ask.

'Please, Clive. It's important to me, even if I can't really explain why.'

Clive frowned. 'Four,' he replied. 'Four is a safe number. You may ask four questions.'

'Do you know her name?'

'One. No.'

'Had you seen her before?'

'Two. Yes.'

'Where?'

'Three. Twice here, and three times on the promenade.'

'Did she work at Larkins?'

'Four. I don't know.'

Amber brought their drinks and Clive returned to his telephone directory and Billie cursed herself for not considering her questions more carefully. She should have asked what the woman looked like. She sipped her cappuccino and wondered if it would be safe now to return to the booth.

'I like your hat. Very much.' Clive had decided to engage her in a brief conversation as a 'thank you' for his tea. 'Charlie Chaplin had one just like it.'

Billie smiled and Clive stared intently at her face. The smile was just for him, a rare gift in his largely solitary life, and he wanted to remember and treasure it. Billie finished her coffee, fastened Mabel's lead and got up to leave. Clive wanted to give her something in return.

'She saw me watching her, your mother. And when she saw me, she did this.' He raised his forefinger to his lips. 'She wanted me to keep her a secret too.'

46

1973

The entertainment lounge was a disaster zone. Five palm tree lamps had been felled and several pink flamingos beheaded. One of the stage curtains had been ripped down and numerous chairs had been reduced to heaps of red and gold firewood. The shelves behind the bar had, under last night's bombardment, splintered into mirrored shards forming a maniacal mosaic of reflections echoing the chaos in the room. The floor was tacky with spilt drinks and broken glass crunched underfoot as Imelda walked in and surveyed the damage. Thank goodness she had left Grisha at home. She wasn't supposed to be at Larkins today, but she had gone to her booth on the promenade needing to work; needing to occupy her mind after the previous night. Diamond told her what had happened, and Imelda had come straight away to see what she could do to help. Ruby was organising the troops who were armed with brooms, mops and buckets. Dolly, Daisy and Dixie looked like ridiculously glamorous charladies with matching overalls and their blonde curls tucked under turban-tied headscarves. Determined to lift everyone's spirits, they were singing as they swept the floor side by side, occasionally throwing in a cancan step for good measure. Jeanie was helping to salvage whatever possible from the carnage behind the bar, hindered by Charlie who was nursing a horrible hangover, and Sara-Jade was sweeping the stage. Ruby's face lit up at the sight of Imelda.

'What can I do to help?'

'Imelda! You can come with me to the canteen and get a trolley of tea and sandwiches for this lot. They've already been hard at it for hours. We're trying to get it in a fit state to reopen tonight, but we might well need a miracle.'

The two of them set off in search of refreshments. 'What on earth happened? Diamond said that there'd been some trouble, but the place looks like a bombsite!'

Ruby pushed back her hair from her face. She looked exhausted.

'It started out as an argument at the bar. A couple of lads got lairy after a few too many lagers. A bit of pushing and shoving led to punches being thrown and then it all kicked off. Cillian and Titus did their best to contain it, but they were hopelessly outnumbered. Most of them didn't have a clue what they were fighting about, but after a skinful and a shot of adrenalin they didn't care. It was a teenage Armageddon. We had no choice but to call the police.'

In the canteen kitchen, Ruby commandeered a trolley and they began to load it with cups and saucers.

'Are you okay?' Imelda asked. 'Was anyone hurt?'

'Mostly walking wounded, thank God. I'm fine – just tired. I've hardly had any sleep.'

Neither had Imelda.

'Titus has a black eye coming and Sara-Jade lost a front tooth,' Ruby continued.

'Sara-Jade?'

'Yes, indeed. She broke a chair over the head of a lad that punched Titus and managed to whack herself in the mouth with one of the legs.'

Imelda piled sandwiches onto plates. 'And Cillian?' She didn't look at Ruby.

Ruby smiled. 'I wondered when you'd ask. He's got a few cuts and bruises and a fat lip, but don't worry, he'll live.'

Imelda winced at the thought of his injuries but said nothing. Ruby checked the trolley.

'Right, have we got everything?' They set off back towards the wrecked entertainment lounge, cups and saucers chinking merrily as the heavy trolley bumped along.

'What happened to you last night?' Ruby finally remembered to ask.

By the time Imelda had finished telling her about Grisha they were surrounded by hungry helpers eager for tea and sandwiches. Ruby started filling cups. 'I warned you about her. The awful thing is that we can't prove she did it. So, is that why you didn't come to the disco? Because of Grisha?'

Before Imelda had a chance to answer, Sara-Jade interrupted with a more pressing question.

'Where's Marty? Why isn't he helping?'

Ruby passed her a cup of tea. 'He's helping the police with their enquiries along with Titus and Cillian. They were told to call in at the station this morning and confirm their statements.'

Sara-Jade helped herself to a sandwich and bit into it gingerly. 'Well, Marty won't have much to say, will he? Where on earth was he hiding while all hell was breaking loose? He's about as much use as a fart in a bucket.' Imelda nearly choked on her tea.

After several more hours of work, some semblance of order had been restored. The stage was clear, and the curtain had been rehung. The palm tree lamps had been re-erected and the decapitated flamingos disposed of. The floor was glass-free, and if not gleaming, at least passably clean, and the surviving chairs had been set out in neat rows facing the stage for that night's show 'that must go on!' Ruby had declared.

'You should go home and get some rest for a couple of hours,' Imelda told her.

'Yes,' agreed Sara-Jade. 'You look knackered.'

Ruby shrugged off their concerns. 'There's no time. Besides, if I go home, I doubt that Randall will let me come back. But I might take a nap in one of the staff chalets in a bit.'

'Like that snooty friend of Jeanie's did last night.' Sara-Jade winked conspiratorially. 'I caught her coming out this morning.'

'She's not supposed to be in staff quarters.' Ruby's voice was suddenly stern, and she glanced at Imelda anxiously. 'Whose chalet was she in?'

Sara-Jade shrugged. 'Not sure. But it was definitely one of the men's.'

At that moment, Cillian and Titus walked in. Sara-Jade dashed over to Titus and, standing on tiptoe, planted a gentle kiss on his bruised cheek. Imelda wasn't sure whether she wanted to kiss Cillian or slap him. On his left cheek, a purple bruise was blooming, and his lip was split and swollen. He met her gaze with a weary smile and she felt herself weaken for just a moment. But then the memory of Vivienne's arms around his neck and her face nestled into his chest hardened her heart once more. Without a word, she handed him a cup of tea.

'You stood me up last night,' he said sadly. 'I was hoping we could have the last dance.'

'Me too,' Imelda replied. 'And I *was* here. But you already had a partner.'

47

1973

Imelda sat outside with Grisha on the steps of the vardo, waiting for Cillian. It was a perfect summer evening. The garden was bathed in mellow light and a warm breeze carried the scent of jasmine from constellations of tiny star-shaped flowers that cascaded over the pergola at the back of the house. Imelda felt sick; a muddle of shifting emotions, each taking turns to rise and fall in both intensity and significance, manifest in a single physical symptom. She felt excited at the prospect of seeing him, angry with him, guilty for doubting him, stupid for trusting him, frightened of losing him, frightened for wanting him. So badly. She felt as though she was falling but had no idea where she might land. Only Cillian had the answer. She had refused to talk to him about Vivienne at Larkins. It was now a crime scene to her in more ways than one. She hoped that here, on home ground, she might feel calmer, more in control. The vardo had always been a sanctuary – first for her mother, and now for her. The rich colours and fabrics of its interior glowed under the flickering illumination of a dozen or so tealights. Music played from an old radio, and a bottle of wine was chilling in an ice bucket. Whether one or two glasses would be called for remained to be seen.

'Listen first, think next and speak last,' her father had counselled her.

'Give him hell!' Shunty-Mae had demanded. But she had tempered her words with a smile. Grisha sat up and cocked his head to one side, listening. His tail twitched. Cillian appeared at the back door of the house and hesitated for a moment before walking towards them. His swagger hadn't entirely deserted him, but his certainty had. He looked relieved to see Grisha who charged to meet him, almost bowling him over before jumping up to greet him, paws on his shoulders, face to face.

'Steady on, big fella. I'm thrilled to see you too!'

Imelda didn't get up. She waited for Cillian to come to her.

'God, Imelda, I'm so sorry.' He reached for her hand, but she pulled it away.

'Sorry for what?'

'For everything.'

'You'll have to be more specific than that,' she replied coolly, but her heart was thumping.

'For Grisha. Ruby told me what happened. Is he okay?' He sat down on the steps but kept a respectful distance.

'He's fine. You can see that for yourself.'

Cillian sighed. 'Talk to me, Imelda.'

'I was there. I saw you.'

'It was just a dance, Imelda.'

'It was the last dance. Did you kiss her?'

He shook his head. 'How can you ask that? Do you really think so little of me?'

'What was I supposed to think?'

'I waited for you all night. Always one eye on the door hoping to see your face.'

'But you didn't wait quite long enough did you? Didn't see me when I *did* come through the door?' Her eyes prickled with threatened tears at the memory, but she blinked them away.

'I thought you weren't coming. That bitch' – he spat the word out like a fly – 'grabbed me for a dance and I didn't want to make a scene. If I'd known what she'd done . . .' He shook his head in disgust. Imelda was desperate to believe him, but she had to be sure.

'Look at me!'

He turned to face her. When Imelda read cards, she always trusted her instincts. Now she tried to read Cillian's face. She reached out and touched the bruise on his cheek, traced a line with her finger down to his split and swollen lip. He flinched.

'Don't ever lie to me,' she whispered.

He took her hand and kissed her palm with exquisite tenderness.

'Imelda, as soon as I met you, I was a dead man walking. I love you. Please tell me that you believe me.'

Imelda smiled. 'Let's just say I'm prepared to give you the benefit of the doubt. For the moment.'

Inside the vardo, she poured wine into both glasses and they drank. Imelda could feel the heat inside her flickering like the flames of the tealights. The anticipation of his touch, his kiss, was almost unbearable. A song began to play on the radio and Cillian put down his glass and turned up the volume. Al Martino was imploring a woman with Spanish eyes to wait for him.

'Dance with me.'

'Is this the last dance?' Imelda asked teasingly.

He took her into his arms and pressed their bodies together with fierce longing before releasing her just enough to look into her eyes.

'I'm hoping it will be the first of many. But I still get the kiss.'

As their lips touched Imelda tasted blood, but any pain that either of them felt was forgotten.

They sat naked outside on the steps of the vardo, wrapped in a blanket and blissfully exhausted. The night was balmy and still, and Grisha lay a few feet in front of them cooling his belly on the grass.

'Imelda.' Cillian trailed his finger lazily along the gold chain that he had hung around her neck and then let his hand slip lower, caressing her soft, warm flesh. 'Your name suits you.'

'And why is that?'

'Because you've a rare talent for melding.'

Imelda laughed and pinched his thigh. 'Is that what you call it?'

'I'd say you and I were pretty well melded now, wouldn't you?'

She kissed him in reply and then apologised as he winced.

'We'll have to stop kissing if your lip's ever going to heal.'

'Never!' he replied, kissing her back, but very gently. 'Let's go inside. I need to lie down. I was battered and bruised enough from last night, but now you've finished me off completely. Not that I'm complaining,' he added with a slow smile.

As they lay staring at the painted patterns on the ceiling of the vardo, thoughts of the world outside their enchanted cocoon began to trespass.

'What are you going to do about Vivienne?' Imelda finally asked.

Cillian rolled over to face her and tucked a strand of hair behind her ear.

'I have to go away.'

Imelda frowned. 'Isn't that a bit drastic?'

'No, I mean I have to go away for a few days. When I get back, I'll speak to her.'

'Where are you going?' Imelda didn't want him to leave her for a few hours, let alone a few days.

'I've a funeral to go to back home. I got a telegram yesterday.'

'On top of everything else! I'm sorry. Was it someone close?'

Cillian laughed. 'No need to be sorry. It was my great-granny Fionnuala who popped her clogs. She was ninety-seven years young, drank poitín from her own still, smoked a pipe and lived off black pudding and colcannon. She'd a grand life and died, happy as Larry, playing poker with a couple of her gentleman friends.'

'When are you going?'

Cillian checked his watch. It was past midnight. 'Tomorrow. Marty wasn't happy but he could hardly say no to a funeral. I'll be back Friday at the latest. You could come with me – meet the family!'

Imelda was tempted. Fionnuala's funeral sounded like it might be fun if it were any reflection of the woman herself. 'Maybe not this time. But one day – definitely. I'd love to see Roaringwater Bay and that white beacon of yours.'

'We'll go to Baltimore for our honeymoon then!'

'You haven't even asked me to marry you yet,' Imelda joked.

'I don't reckon I'll have much choice if your dad finds me in here!'

'It's not Papa you should worry about, it's my mother. She'll be chasing you off the premises with a sword-stick! But seeing as you're here, stay for today. And tonight, if you don't have to leave until Tuesday.'

'I'll need to pick up some stuff from Larkins, but I'm not working today, so I'll come back and stay on one condition.'

'Which is?'

'That you hide Shunty-Mae's swordstick!'

They dozed for a while, contentedly entwined, but Imelda was unable to banish thoughts of Vivienne. She couldn't help but feel that she was still somehow a threat to their happiness. That she had one final and ultimately damning card up her sleeve that she had yet to play.

'You will be careful how you deal with Vivienne?'

Cillian squeezed her hand. 'Not anymore. I'm done pussyfooting around with her, and if she runs to Marty, then let her. He's got more than enough on his plate at the moment trying to explain to the big bosses what happened at the disco and where the money's going to come from to pay for the damage. Now, go to sleep before the birds wake us up again.'

Several hours later, it was a knock at the vardo door that woke them. Outside on the steps Imelda found a tray set with breakfast for two.

'Thank you, Papa,' she called. He raised his hand and waved as he walked back to the house without turning around. But Imelda knew that he would be smiling.

48

1973

The skull ring was heavy and slightly loose on her middle finger as Imelda handed the cards to her client. Cillian had insisted that she wear it until he got back from Ireland. 'Then you'll remember me every time you look at it,' he said, as he had kissed her good-bye. She was hardly likely to forget him, but she was glad to have it; something that was so recognisably his. Something that signified their togetherness while they were apart. The woman sitting across from Imelda was in her late seventies perhaps, with enviable bone struc-ture and pure white hair swept into an immaculate French pleat. She had, no doubt, once been a great beauty, and would still be attractive were it not for the rigid expression on her face that had been calcified by bitterness and regret. The emotions around this woman were so strong that they were palpable. Imelda felt her chill, her resolute despair.

The woman shuffled the cards. 'I want to know about my granddaughter.'

Imelda lay a Celtic Cross. The Page of Wands, Death, the Ten of Cups and the Five of Swords told Imelda that a little girl with blonde hair had drowned, but that she was now safe and happy with the Emperor, her granddad. The woman nodded.

'It was over fifteen years ago now. She drowned in a pond. She was only four. Are you quite sure that she's happy?'

'Absolutely. She's with her granddad, and she loved him very much, didn't she?'

The woman bit her lip. 'May I ask you another question?'

'Of course.' Imelda gathered up the cards and passed them over.

'Has my husband forgiven me?'

The cards described a solid marriage inexorably eroded by internal anger. Furious words were followed by fewer and fewer conversations until meaningful communication between husband and wife was all but lost. The love had always remained, but sadly unspoken.

'Did you blame your husband for your granddaughter's death?'

The woman shifted uncomfortably in her seat. 'He was supposed to be watching her. They were in our garden and he was pruning the rose bushes. But he was supposed to be watching her too. I did blame him. Never in so many words, but he knew that I believed it was his fault. He was so angry with himself – and eventually with me too. Millie was gone; there was nothing we could do about that. But we should have been there for each other instead of allowing it to drive us apart. I just want him to know that I'm sorry.'

'Why now?' Imelda was curious. 'Why now, after so long?'

'Today would have been our golden wedding anniversary.'

After the woman had gone, Imelda sat turning the ring on her finger. She wondered why it was that so often people left important things unsaid until it was too late. She wished now that she had told Cillian she loved him before he left. He had rung her a couple of times from a payphone in the local pub, but their brief conversations had been overheard and punctuated by beeps signalling that the money was running out. Imelda consoled herself with the knowledge that he would be back in Brighton tomorrow. She would tell him then.

She was surprised to see Ruby in the café at lunchtime chatting excitedly to Jack and Diamond. As soon as Imelda pushed open the door, Ruby waved her over to join them.

'You'll never guess what's happened.'

'I'm sure I shan't. But something to cheer me up would be nice after my last client.'

Diamond was unable to contain herself. 'Well this is guaranteed to put a smile on your face. That bloody pervert at Larkins has got the sack!'

'And about time too!' added Jack, slapping the counter in satisfaction with the flat of his hand.

'Marty? When?' Imelda needed details. Grisha groaned softly. He needed a sausage roll.

'Mr Collins from head office arrived this morning. He wanted a full report about Saturday's shenanigans – spoke to most of the staff and the police too, by all accounts. Marty had tried to keep it quiet but apparently "a concerned member of staff" tipped off head office. It seems that they weren't consulted about Marty's idea to allow young, single guests, and they're certainly not too happy about it now. But there were other concerns about Marty's performance too, and the disco was the final straw.'

'Do we know who the "concerned member of staff" was?'

Ruby laughed. 'Not for sure, but my money's on Sara-Jade.'

'So, who's going to replace Marty?'

'Ruby!' Diamond announced proudly, before her sister had the chance to share the news herself.

'It's only temporary, until they appoint a permanent replacement,' Ruby added.

Imelda was delighted for her friend. 'Congratulations! And there's no reason why you shouldn't be the permanent replacement. You've practically been doing the job for the last few months anyway.'

'We'll see,' said Ruby modestly. 'How's Grisha?'

'In desperate need of a sausage roll, I expect, but otherwise unscathed.'

'Well, I'm very pleased to hear it.' Diamond rubbed his head affectionately before feeding him the largest sausage roll she could find.

'And what about you and Cillian?' Ruby asked pointedly, having spotted his ring on Imelda's finger.

Before Imelda could say anything, the bell above the door tinkled and Jeanie walked in followed by Vivienne. Hackles rose, and not just Grisha's. Imelda was the first to speak.

'Vivienne, I want to speak to you outside. Now.'

A mocking smile played across Vivienne's perfectly painted lips.

'I'm not particularly interested in what you want.'

'Well, you'll be off outside anyway.' Diamond came out from behind the counter and stood in front of Vivienne, blocking her way. 'You're barred from this café. We don't serve dog poisoners in here.'

Vivienne was completely unperturbed. 'I'm surprised you haven't poisoned anyone yourself with the disgusting muck you serve in here,' she sneered.

Jeanie looked completely bewildered.

'Don't worry, Jeanie. I only come in here because of you. I'm sure we can find somewhere better than this dump.' Vivienne turned and sauntered towards the door, followed by Imelda, while Jeanie stayed behind to remonstrate with her aunt. Outside the café, Vivienne lit a cigarette.

'How can I help you?' Sarcasm dripped from her voice like acid rain.

Imelda spoke quietly but with irrefutable menace.

'Never go near my dog again.'

Vivienne inhaled deeply and blew out a thin stream of smoke through pursed lips.

'Or what? You'll curse me?'

Imelda smiled. 'You're already cursed by your own nature. I'm not threatening you – I'm telling you. Stay away from my dog.'

Vivienne made a determined effort to look bored until she spotted the skull ring. Her composure was momentarily shaken but she quickly recovered her mask of indifference. And her voice.

'By the way, Cillian's all yours now. I had my fun, and so did he. The disco was quite a night, wasn't it?' She stubbed out her cigarette and began to walk away, but then decided to twist the knife. 'He was good. But I've had better.'

49

Now

The collie had a black patch over one eye. The rest of his head was white save for his ears. One was black and stood up, and the other was white with black spots and lay flat. His eyes were the colour of honey and sparkled with mischief. For Treasure, it had been love at first sight when he found him at the rescue centre. Mabel clearly felt the same way. Having just been introduced, she was licking his face industriously.

'Honestly Mabel, you could play a little harder to get!' her mistress admonished her. Mabel rolled over onto her back submissively and made cow eyes at the collie.

'He's certainly a handsome chap. How did he end up in a rescue centre?' Billie asked. Her shop opened tomorrow, and she was at the booth with Imelda and Treasure making final preparations.

'The sadly familiar tale of a family buying a cute, fluffy puppy with no thought of what would be required when said puppy grew up to be a whirling dervish needing training and exercise. He was a toy they grew bored of.'

Imelda stroked the young dog's ears. 'Well, thank goodness he's ended up with you. I seem to remember that you have quite a way with collies. What are you going to call him?'

'Well, he looks like a pirate with his eye patch, so I thought I'd call him Sparrow after Captain Jack.'

Imelda nodded approvingly. 'Good choice. I love those films! How old is Sparrow?'

'Almost twelve months. He's going to need a lot of exercise, but at least he'll keep me fit,' laughed Treasure, patting his own slightly rounded tummy. As if to illustrate the point, Sparrow began to chase Mabel around the booth barking excitedly and knocking over everything in his path. Treasure managed to corral him into a corner and clip on his lead.

'It looks like you need to learn some manners, young man. Maybe I should take you for a run on the beach to wear down your batteries a bit before you wreck the joint. Would you like to join us, Mabel?' Mabel was already by the door.

'You go too, Billie. Get some fresh air. I'll sort this out.' Imelda began picking up the things that Sparrow had upset.

The booth looked lovely with all its seaside artefacts now artfully displayed. Treasure had persuaded Billie to make room for several boxes of classic vintage vinyl, a somewhat random addition to the stock and not exactly 'on theme' but Imelda was glad. It made good business sense. Treasure knew his stuff when it came to music and there was always a market for these records. They might help to bolster the takings and attract a few regular customers. Imelda straightened one of the boxes that Sparrow had sent flying and began flicking through the singles it contained. There were some from the 80s, but most were earlier. Barry White, T. Rex, Donna Summer, Wizzard – this music was a fast track that took Imelda straight back to her time at Larkins. Discos in the entertainment lounge, palm trees and pink flamingos. The glitter ball and one particular night that she had fought so hard, but failed, to forget. Imelda continued to browse through the records and there, right at the back in its original paper sleeve, was a musical memory so precious that Imelda hardly dare pick it up in case her imagination had somehow conjured it. 'Spanish Eyes' by Al Martino.

Julia's Columbus 1493 was a miniature work of art served in a copper pineapple glass. She and Annie had come to Brighton for the opening of the shop and were now drinking cocktails with their friend, the proprietor, in the Victoria Bar at The Grand where the three of them were staying overnight.

'Cheers!' Annie raised her more conventional glass. 'May Billie's Beside the Seaside be a roaring success!'

Julia set down her pineapple and took out her phone to photograph it.

'God help us!' Billie exclaimed. 'Don't tell me that you've become one of those people who post everything they eat and drink on Instagram!' She knew that it was now a way of life for some people, but to her it seemed to be a way *instead* of life. No matter that your soufflé was sagging by the time you actually ate it, so long as its erstwhile perfection was photographically flaunted for the benefit of your followers.

Julia's phone flashed and she returned it to her handbag. 'Of course not. But it's so beautiful I want to remember it, and if I have too many cocktails, I'll be lucky if I remember my own name!'

'Well, just try not to spill it like last time,' Annie warned with a wry smile.

'If Billie's got any more shocking revelations, I'll sit on my hands,' Julia promised. 'Have you?' she asked Billie hopefully. Billie stirred her drink with a glass cocktail stick.

'Well . . .'

'I knew it!' Julia tucked her hands under her thighs. 'Come on, spill the beans!'

'I've found someone who says he saw my birth mother leave me in the doorway at Imelda's booth.'

'And you believe him?' Annie asked with her customary cool while Julia nearly knocked over the table in excitement.

'Why shouldn't she? Why would he make something like that up? Who is he?'

Billie smiled. How could she explain Clive?

'He's a chap called Clive who's been hanging around the promenade for years. He's a little eccentric, but I've no reason to suspect he's lying. I think maybe he has Asperger's or something similar. Imelda and Treasure have both vouched for him, and as Julia says, why would he make it up?'

'For attention? Maybe he's lonely and wants to feel part of something; wants to feel important?'

Billie considered Annie's words for a moment. Clive might be lonely, and it was strange that he hadn't said anything about it for all these years until Billie shared with him that she was the baby abandoned. But equally Clive wasn't a man who courted attention; if anything, he did his best to avoid it.

'That doesn't sound like Clive. He's a bit of a loner, and I get the impression that he likes it that way.'

'What do you mean by "hanging around the promenade"? Is he a vagrant?'

'Annie!' Julia had almost finished her cocktail and was beginning to relax. 'Don't be such a snob! Even if he is a homeless person it doesn't mean he's not honest!'

'I'm well aware of that. I'm just trying to build a proper picture of the man before I can decide whether or not he's a credible witness.'

Julia hooted with laughter. 'Who do you think you are? MI5?'

Annie shook her head. 'I'd rather be Vera. Only with a much better wardrobe, obviously.'

Billie had missed her friends' good-natured banter, but she felt uncomfortable hearing them discuss Clive like this. Of course she wanted to believe him, but it was more than that. Clive was the proverbial book so often judged by a shabby cover with a superficial synopsis. She couldn't help but feel that the man himself was a great deal more than that.

'He's not homeless. And I'm sure he's telling the truth,' she said quietly.

'Now, did he tell you what she looked like, pet?' Julia's approximation of TV detective Vera's Geordie accent was as wide of the mark geographically as Merthyr Tydfil.

Billie laughed. 'No. But he'd seen her a couple of times before in the café and on the prom. Unfortunately, he didn't know her name or whether she worked at Larkins.'

Annie got up to order another round of drinks. 'Well, it's all very interesting, but it doesn't really help much, does it?'

'I wanted it to be Madame Burova,' Julia added with a sigh.

'To be honest, so did I. But it's looking extremely unlikely now,' Billie conceded.

'Right! Does everyone want the same again, or shall we try something different?' Annie waved the cocktail list in front of them.

'Another copper pineapple for me please, and then when you get back Billie can tell us all about her Treasure!'

Imelda was sleeping in the vardo tonight. She had lit the small stove and Mabel was toasting herself on a rug in front of it. Tealights glowed softly in jewel-hued glass jars and cast dancing shadows on the walls and ceiling. The only sounds to break the silence were the crackle of burning logs and a fox barking in a nearby garden. Imelda took a sip from a glass of vodka and turned the skull ring on her middle finger. It was still loose. The silver glinted in the firelight. Imelda had retrieved it from her jewellery box having finally decided to wear it again as Cillian had asked her to. The record sat in its sleeve on her lap. She had nothing to play it on, but she could hear every note in her head and feel the rhythm in her body, nonetheless.

She closed her eyes and allowed the memories to engulf her until the past she was seeking was more real than the present she was escaping. She was with Cillian once again.

50

Now

Imelda, Mabel, Esther and Henry were on a grand day out to St Pancras. It was a Thursday and Henry was going to play the piano and then they were going for lunch in The Betjeman. Mabel, who was wearing a pink sequinned bandana around her neck for the occasion, was mesmerised by the views flitting past the window as she sat on Imelda's lap. The train pulled into Blackfriars and as they passed through glinting glass and over the Thames, its choppy waters flashing in the sunlight, Imelda felt a frisson of excitement. It had been a long time since she'd visited London, and it was a treat to be here with both her oldest and newest friends.

St Pancras was bustling with people travelling here, there and everywhere for Easter. Couples off on the Eurostar for romantic mini-breaks, students heading home from uni with bags of books and dirty laundry, families beginning holidays or crossing the country to visit far-flung relatives, and tourists and day-trip-pers here for the sights and shopping. Commuters and workers threaded their way through the pleasure-seekers and holidaymakers, marching through the meanderers, purposeful and brisk. This ever-changing peoplescape passing through the station was Henry's audience, if any of them could be tempted to stop and listen. Henry sat down at the piano with Mabel by his side. Mabel wasn't very keen on shopping and had made it quite clear that she would prefer to remain with Henry rather than risk being trodden on amongst the crowds. Imelda and Esther stood by the piano waiting for Henry to start.

'Don't you ever get nervous?' whispered Esther. Henry answered with a rousing arpeggio that ran the length of the piano. 'Never!'

A small group had already gathered, though whether that was in anticipation of Henry's piano-playing or Mabel's shameless playing to the crowd it was hard to tell. Henry began with 'Bring Me Sunshine', followed by 'Raindrops Keep Fallin' on My Head' and by the time he had completed his meteorological medley with 'Stormy Weather', Imelda and Esther were being jostled by a large crowd, many of whom were recording Henry and Mabel on their mobiles. Henry's accompaniment at their tap dance class and her vague memories of him at Larkins hadn't prepared Imelda for his showmanship. He was clearly a born performer and Imelda couldn't help but feel quite proud to call him her friend. Imelda and Esther eventually extracted themselves from Henry's fan club and went for a wander around the shops. They marvelled at the Easter display in Hamleys' window, spritzed themselves with perfume in Jo Malone, bought loose leaf tea and Florentines in Fortnum & Mason and at one o'clock they reconvened with Henry and Mabel in the bar of The Betjeman.

'You were wonderful!' Esther congratulated Henry. 'We could hear the applause all over the station!'

'Thank you. That's very kind. But there was someone else playing the other piano. Some of the applause was probably for them.'

Esther shook her head. 'I doubt it. They were playing Rachmaninov. Nobody wants Rachmaninov at Easter. It's far too miserable.'

'Well, never mind Rachmaninov. I'm delighted that you ladies came to hear me play and I'm going to buy us a bottle of prosecco to celebrate,' Henry declared.

As he stood waiting to be served, Esther appraised his trim figure and stylish outfit from behind. 'Has he always been gay, do you think?' she asked Imelda. 'It's such a pity. He'd just do for you – or me. Or maybe both,' she added, winking at Imelda.

'Don't listen, Mabel!' Imelda covered the dog's ears. 'Auntie Esther's being inappropriate again.'

Esther laughed. 'Don't be such a prude! All I'm saying is he's quite a catch.'

Henry returned with a bottle of prosecco in an ice bucket and three glasses.

'So, what have I missed?'

'Esther was asking me whether you've always been gay. Be careful, Henry. I think she may have designs on you.'

Henry laughed as he poured their drinks. 'I'm flattered! As for your question, Esther, I'm not really sure what to tell you. I happened to fall in love with a man, and he was the love of my life. But it's always been the person rather than their gender that's been important to me. I fancied boys and girls when I was young, but as corny as it sounds, Jocelyn was my soulmate.'

'So, there's still hope for me yet?' Esther joked.

Henry smiled. 'What about your Solomon? Was he your soulmate?'

Esther sipped her prosecco. 'I met my Solomon when I was seventeen. I thought he was a god and I worshipped him. We married when I was nineteen and I learned that he was just a man. A man who never ironed a shirt in his life, left the toilet seat up and grew hair out of his nose. Maybe I should have tried out a few more prospective husbands before I skipped down the aisle. Who knows? But Solomon was a good man who worked hard and loved his family. It wasn't all hearts and flowers but what relationship is? We survived forty-seven years as husband and wife without killing each other, and if I could have him back for a single day I would.' Esther drained her glass. 'But just the one day, mind.'

Henry refreshed their drinks. 'And what about you, Imelda? Did you ever think about marriage or having kids?'

'I thought you might have married that boat salesman,' Esther volunteered. 'The one with the deep voice and the Aston Martin.'

Imelda shook her head. 'God no! He was a pleasant enough companion for a while, but he ironed his socks. And his underpants!'

'What about that coroner chap? He was nice. You went out with him for quite a while. Edward, wasn't it?'

'Edmund. Yes, he was a fascinating man, but not very *physical*.'

'Or Laurence the firefighter. He looked very *physical* to me,' Esther teased.

'Well, it certainly sounds as though you've had possibilities,' Henry offered tactfully. 'I think we need another bottle before we delve any further.' He soon returned to the table with more prosecco.

'I'm not sure if I ever really wanted to get married,' Imelda began. 'My parents' relationship was extraordinary. They were very different people and sometimes I think they found being together really tough. They loved each other until they died, but more than that they remained *in love*. Their passion never faded into comfortable companionship. If I had ever contemplated marriage, theirs would have been my blueprint. And I'm not sure any man could have lived up to such high expectations.'

Esther was three glasses of prosecco down by now and asked a question that she had always wanted to but had never found the chutzpah to until now.

'Not even with Cillian?'

'You don't have to answer that,' Henry added quickly. Protectively.

'No, of course not,' Esther agreed. 'But I was just wondering . . .' Imelda had told her about Cillian years ago, but Esther always had the impression that Imelda had omitted some crucial detail.

'It's fine, it's fine.' Imelda took a deep swallow of her drink. 'With Cillian? Who can say? We were only together for a very short time. I thought we were in love. I know I was. I've never felt that way about anyone, before or since. But if he is Billie's father, then he lied to me. He betrayed me.'

'Do you think he is?' Esther was serious now.

'I don't know what I think. I can only tell you that back then, I would have trusted him with my life.'

291

'And now?'

Imelda's hesitation was infinitesimal. 'The same.'

Henry topped up their glasses. 'It must be hard for you having Billie around,' he said.

'Billie is a mixed blessing,' Imelda replied. 'If she is Cillian's daughter, then she has brought a little of him back to me, and whatever the circumstances, I'll treasure that. But if she isn't, it means that what I had with Cillian might just have been as perfect as I'd always believed it to be. Until Billie's mother sullied it with doubt. But either way, we'll probably never know.'

Esther frowned. 'But you know who her mother is. Can't you make her tell you?'

'Billie's mother is a clever woman. She knew full well that I would never break a confidence shared while I was reading her cards. She knew that I would always honour the rules of my profession. I can't use what she told me to find out more than she's willing to share.'

Esther sighed. 'You're a good woman, Imelda. My clients are always telling me their secrets in the salon. But it's a bit like those people who pick their noses while driving thinking that no one will notice because they're in a car. A secret shared in the salon might just as well be broadcast on local radio.'

Imelda laughed. 'That's hardly your fault. You only promise coiffures, not confidentiality.'

Henry poured the last of the prosecco into their glasses. 'It must have been heartbreaking for Billie's mother. I can't imagine how it would feel to leave your child in a doorway and walk away.'

'That's because you *have* a heart,' Esther retorted. 'Not everyone does. Did you ever want children, Henry?'

'I never really thought about it. When Jocelyn and I got together things were different. Adoption would have been our only option and we weren't considered to be "suitable parents".'

Imelda realised with relief that she had dodged answering the same question. Henry checked his watch.

'Come along ladies, drink up. We don't want to miss our train!'

51

1973

The bride looked every inch a princess in her fairy-tale dress as she glided down the aisle on the arm of her proud and distinguished father. Imelda stared blankly at the television screen, registering only moving images rather than the wedding of the Queen's only daughter to Captain Mark Phillips. There would be no wedding for Imelda now. No dress, no flowers, no fairy tale. No groom. On the day that Cillian should have returned, Imelda wore her dread, heavy and cold, like wet clothing. She didn't go to the booth or Larkins, but instead waited with Grisha in the vardo for the sky to fall. Her fingers pitter-pattered against the moon and stars on the chain around her neck – a fretful, capricious rhythm like the beat of a failing heart – marking time until the moment that she knew what she *knew*. Until the premonition was petrified into irrefutable truth by indisputable facts. Her mother brought her food that she didn't eat, and tea, which she drank. With vodka. But Shunty-Mae made no attempt to reassure or console her. She knew better than to raise false hopes. Only Alexei tried to make believe that all might still be well.

'He's been held up, that's all. He'll be back soon enough and then you can scold him to your heart's content.' But then Alexei didn't possess the gift that could sometimes be an affliction. The weekend passed with no word. Alexei suggested that they try to call the pub from where Cillian had phoned. Imelda ignored him, Shunty-Mae shushed him but Alexei tried anyway. The phone was out of order.

Ruby came in person on Monday morning, her face disfigured by news of the disaster that she was obliged to deliver. The details were almost irrelevant at that point. The single, solid, catastrophic fact that Cillian was dead filled Imelda's world, leaving no space for anything else, whilst simultaneously reducing it to a cavernous void. But later she had contemplated Ruby's every word with forensic obsession. She had tried to picture the events frame by agonising frame. The facts were that Cillian had been at his great-granny Fionnuala's wake, having the time of his life, when he had dropped down dead. They had been his mother's exact words when she had spoken to Ruby. Dropped. Down. Dead. Imelda had an indelible picture for each word. Cillian's heart had failed – not to love, but to live. The faulty mechanism of its warm flesh and blood explained by a cold, scientific epithet. Imelda had stayed in the vardo with Grisha, seeking comfort in the last place that they had been together. She had tried to invoke him: the touch of his skin on hers, his breath on her neck, his voice, his laugh, his smile. These were all just memories now, which slipped in and out of focus, impossible to capture and command. But the two things that she was able to recall with painfully constant clarity were that he had invited her to go with him and she had declined, and that she had never told him that she loved him. Now, she could only hope that somehow, he knew.

As the bride and groom on the television screen made their vows to one another, silent tears spilled down Imelda's cheeks and her hands fell to smooth her dress over her gently rounded stomach. Imelda thought that grief had scoured her hollow. But she had been wrong.

52

1973

'Well, I quite like the tiara, but the dress is horribly dull. And what on earth is that bridesmaid wearing?'

Vivienne and Jeanie were watching the royal wedding at Vivienne's flat. Since the incident with Madame Burova's dog, their relationship had faltered a little. Vivienne had vehemently denied any wrongdoing and Jeanie wanted to believe her, but the shadow of doubt remained. The news about Cillian had rippled through Larkins like wind through a field of whispering barley. He had been popular with staff and guests alike, a larger-than-life character whose youth and exuberance made his death all the more improbable and painful to accept. Most had been deeply shocked and saddened, but Vivienne's reaction had been strangely offhand.

'It's a shame,' she had acknowledged to Jeanie, 'and awful for his family. But I was already over him in *that* way. I can see now that it was just a crush,' she had added, dismissing him as easily as a once-favourite pair of shoes that was no longer a la mode. Jeanie didn't believe her. Vivienne had delivered the lines smoothly enough. But her nonchalance was too practised, too perfect to be credible. And something between the two of them had shifted. It seemed now as though Vivienne was more vulnerable, that she needed their friendship more than Jeanie did. These days they usually met at the flat. Vivienne had almost stopped going to her finishing school altogether and was less keen to go shopping or out to lunch.

'What are your thoughts on the captain then?' she asked Jeanie.

Jeanie wrinkled her nose. 'He's all right, I suppose. But I prefer David Cassidy.'

Vivienne got up to fetch her cigarettes from the dressing table. She offered the packet to Jeanie who, as always, refused.

'You're such a goody-goody,' Vivienne teased. Jeanie laughed. 'I'm just protecting my instrument,' she replied loftily, patting her throat. Vivienne lit one for herself and inhaled tentatively. After only a couple of puffs, she stubbed it out. Jeanie studied her friend.

'Are you okay?'

'Yes. Why wouldn't I be?' Vivienne replied tetchily.

Jeanie decided not to push it, but she was worried about her. Vivienne, who was so often and easily scornful of other less than immaculate women now seemed less than concerned about her own appearance. And then there was that smell. What was that smell like sour milk that had greeted Jeanie when she had arrived at the flat that day?

'Will your parents be home for Christmas?' Jeanie asked instead.

Vivienne shook her head. 'They've invited me to join them in California for "the holidays" as they now insist on calling it, but I'd rather make the most of my last few months of freedom.'

'So, they're coming home for good?'

'In May. And they'll want me back straight away so that Mummy can begin parading me around like a prize heifer in search of a worthy and, of course, wealthy bull.'

There was a resignation in Vivienne's tone that surprised and saddened Jeanie.

'You don't have to go back home, surely? Couldn't you get a job and keep your flat here? After all, you are a qualified secretary thanks to Miss Sharp.'

'What? And end up like her, a pathetic, wizened old maid who smells of lavender and cat wee?'

Jeanie flinched at the unnecessary cruelty of Vivienne's words. She hadn't liked Miss Sharp that much either, but the woman didn't deserve such vitriol.

'I don't think there's much danger of you ending up a spinster.'

Vivienne sighed impatiently. 'This flat costs a fortune. Without Daddy's allowance I'd barely be able to afford some squalid bedsit. And besides, we made a deal. I could have a couple of years' freedom in Brighton so long as I went home afterwards and made a "suitable marriage".'

'But you don't have to! They can't make you.' Jeanie was at a loss to understand Vivienne's uncustomary compliance.

'Oh Jeanie. You're such an innocent. Has it never occurred to you that I might *want* to go home? Perhaps

I *want* a nice, comfortable life, with a big mansion, cocktail parties, country house weekends and holidays in Scotland and the south of France.'

'And you'd be willing to settle for a bull for a husband to get it?'

'Plenty of women do.'

'What about love? You told me that you loved Cillian.'

Vivienne went to light another cigarette, but then thought better of it. Instead she pointed at the television screen. 'Do you think those two are in love?'

'Well, they seem happy enough.'

Vivienne shook her head. 'It's not a fairy tale. It's real life. He will have been thoroughly vetted and given the Queen's stamp of approval, and Princess Anne will have decided that he will do well enough as a husband. It's not about love – it's about lineage.'

'What happened to your escape plan? The one you told me about when I first met you?'

'Perhaps I realised that I didn't need one. Perhaps I grew up.'

Jeanie studied her friend's face – make-up free with dark circles daubed beneath her grey eyes – and she saw barely more than a girl. A girl she pitied.

'You could come to us for Christmas, if you like?'

Vivienne smiled wryly. 'That's very kind, but I can't imagine I'd be very welcome.'

'Well, I'll come over on Christmas Eve if I'm not working.'

Jeanie only wished that there was more that she could do.

53

Now

Clive sat in his dentist's waiting room staring at the glossy magazine that lay open in his lap. He studied the woman in the picture, matching hers with a face that he had seen many years before. His comparison was methodical and meticulous, checking features that remained largely unaltered by increasing age. Her high forehead, sharp cheekbones, strong jawline and pale, wide-set eyes all matched the picture that had been automatically filed in his memory so long ago. Clive had a facility for faces. His brain had an extraordinary capacity to process a composite of their visual characteristics and store it until it became necessary or desirable to recall it. This rare talent had been an invaluable asset in his undercover work and might now enable him to help Billie In The Bowler Hat. He couldn't say exactly what it was that made him want to please her. Perhaps it was because she was a friend of Madame Burova's, a woman who had always treated him with kindness and respect. Not everyone did. Or perhaps it was simply because of her smile.

Clive's reverie was interrupted by the receptionist calling his name. Once his teeth had been thoroughly inspected and cleaned, and he had swilled with red mouthwash that tasted of aniseed and dabbed his lips with a small, square tissue, he returned to the waiting room to pay. He had intended to retrieve the magazine and ask if he might be allowed to take it. It was an old edition that would no longer be available to buy, and he would have been happy to replace it with a new one. Unfortunately for Clive the magazine was in the hands of a young woman who was flicking through its pages and chewing gum with exaggerated belligerence. Clive hesitated, uncertain how best to proceed. Normally, he would have simply walked away, unwilling to engage in any social interaction with a stranger that wasn't strictly necessary. But on this occasion, it was different. He needed to do this. For Billie In The Bowler Hat.

'Excuse me,' he ventured.

The young woman looked up at him and twiddled her nose ring. 'Yeah?'

'Could I please have that magazine? I need it for a friend.'

The young woman raised her eyebrows. 'I'm reading it.'

'Yes, I know. I'm sorry. But could you perhaps read one of the others?' Clive gestured to several piles of various publications neatly stacked on the table in front of her.

'Perhaps you could take one of the others for your *friend*,' the young woman replied with a sneer. 'Or better still, why don't you buy one, you tight old git!' Adding 'weirdo' not quite under her breath.

Clive was undeterred. It was as though once he had

taken the initial plunge, his commitment to the mission, whatever it might be, was unconditional.

'I'm afraid you don't understand. It is that magazine in particular that I need for my friend. There is something in it that she would very much like to see, and it's an old magazine so I can't buy another copy.'

'That's really not my problem is it, mate?'

'No, love. Your problem seems to be a complete lack of good manners and a mother who didn't know how to raise her kids right.'

The receptionist, barely older than the patient she was addressing but in possession of an air of authority that belied her youth, got up from behind her desk and approached the young woman with unmistakable intent. She held out her hand.

'That magazine belongs to the dental practice.'

The young woman tossed it onto the table.

'The dentist will see you now,' the receptionist told her. 'And here's hoping you need several fillings and extensive root canal work.'

Once they were alone, the receptionist handed the magazine to Clive. He was touched and slightly flustered by her unexpected kindness. He studied her name badge whilst gathering appropriate words to express his gratitude.

'Thank you so much – Chloe. I'll bring you a replacement straight away. There's a newsagent just around the corner . . .'

'Don't be daft! It's just an old magazine. It would have only ended up in the recycling bin.'

'Well, thank you for persuading the young lady to part with it.'

'Huh! She's no lady, she's just a stroppy little cow. That's why she's got a ring in her nose. And anyway, it's my pleasure. I hope your friend likes it.'

Clive left the surgery with the magazine tucked safely inside his bag and a mental note to take Chloe some flowers next time he was passing.

Billie sat in The Tea Leaf staring at the magazine that lay open on the table in front of her. An elegant woman in a well-tailored suit with several strands of pearls around her neck stared back at her from the photographs taken in various rooms of the grand country mansion that she shared with her husband, Lord Longhorn, and their two Siamese cats, Tang and Ming.

'And you're absolutely sure that this is the woman who left me outside Madame Burova's booth?'

Clive sat opposite her, stirring several spoonfuls of sugar into his tea. He nodded earnestly.

'But it was such a long time ago. How can you be so certain?'

Clive seemed unperturbed by her scepticism.

'Because I never forget a face.' He sipped his tea and replaced his cup carefully in its saucer. 'I used to work for the police, you know.' He tapped the side of his nose conspiratorially. 'Undercover, of course.'

By the time Billie returned to the booth, Imelda had already gone home. It was a dreary afternoon and a sky smutted with fat, grubby clouds threatened imminent rain. The promenade was very quiet and there were no prospective customers in sight. Billie opened the magazine again and flipped through the pages. She had thanked Clive but hadn't really known what else to say to him. It was clearly ridiculous to think that there was any truth in what he had told her. But that wasn't to say that he was deliberately lying. If anything, judging by her previous conversations with him, he seemed incapable of artifice. But she could see that he had developed a fondness for her, and she wondered if that might have led him to invent something that might please her. She slapped the magazine shut angrily. Now she was being patronising. Clive might be unusual, but he certainly wasn't stupid. He wouldn't just choose some random woman from a magazine and pretend that he recognised her as being Billie's mother simply because he had a crush on her. No, the most likely explanation was that Lady Longhorn bore a passing resemblance to the woman that Clive had seen outside the booth over four decades ago. It was simply his memory playing tricks on him.

Billie tossed the magazine onto a pile of paperwork waiting to go in the recycling bin, and then pulled on her coat, ready to go home.

54

1974

Jeanie stroked the fluff of blonde hair that crowned the baby girl's head and marvelled as the tiny fingers gripped her thumb.

'She's beautiful,' she whispered.

Vivienne smiled. She was sitting beside her daughter's cot in the private maternity home where she had spent the final weeks of her pregnancy hiding from the world and planning her next move.

'Have you given her a name yet?' Jeanie asked.

Vivienne shook her head. She stood up and wandered over to the window that looked out over a well-kept lawn. At its centre stood a sundial mounted on an ornate stone plinth. Its brass plate and gnomon glinted in the spring sunshine; a relentless reminder that time was ticking away.

'I'm not sure I should if she's going to be adopted.'

Jeanie gazed down at the cherubic little girl who wriggled contentedly in her arms, snuggled in a soft pink blanket. She wondered how Vivienne could even consider parting with her.

'Are you sure that's what you want to do?'

Vivienne kept her back to Jeanie. 'I'm not sure I have a choice. I couldn't possibly manage on my own and I can hardly take her home. Can you imagine it? Hello, Mummy and Daddy, and welcome back. While you were gone, I qualified as a secretary, almost finished finishing school – oh, and gave birth to an illegitimate child.'

'Don't you ever think about her father?' Jeanie asked.

Vivienne turned to face her.

'It was one night. A stupid fling, best forgotten.'

'But . . .'

'No buts.' Vivienne's stony expression made it clear that there was to be no further discussion.

'When do you leave for London?' she asked, deliberately changing the subject.

Jeanie had been offered a job as a singer in a club through a contact of Charlie's, and after numerous arguments with her dad and the eventual intervention and support of her Aunt Ruby, she had been permitted to accept.

'Tomorrow. I can't wait! I'll miss Larkins but this is my big chance! It's . . . well, it's London!' Her excitement crackled.

'I'll miss you. You've been a good friend.'

'I'll miss you too,' Jeanie replied, but she wasn't so sure it was true. Her world was now bright with endless possibilities and their friendship was one that she had almost outgrown. She was a songbird about to fly the nest, while Vivienne would consent to have her wings clipped and return to her gilded cage.

Jeanie handed the baby back to Vivienne, who gently kissed her daughter's cheek and laid her in the cot.

'I bought her a present.' Jeanie took a small package wrapped in tissue paper from her bag. It contained a silver christening bracelet.

'I thought that maybe we could call her Billie, just for now. After Billie Holiday.'

Jeanie had been afraid that Vivienne wouldn't want to give her baby a name, but she couldn't bear the thought of the little girl being given up without anything to say that someone had cared about her. Vivienne took the bracelet from her and ran her fingers over the letters engraved on its surface.

'Billie. It suits her.' She slipped the bracelet onto her daughter's deliciously pudgy wrist and angrily wiped away the traitorous tears that she was unable to contain.

'Yes, of course we should call her Billie. But on one condition.' Vivienne took Jeanie's hands in her own and squeezed them tightly.

'Promise me that you'll never breathe a word about any of this to anyone. Ever.'

55

Now

Sparrow and Mabel were chasing one another up and down the beach, skittering pebbles in their wake. Billie was walking behind them, listening to Treasure tell her something that brought a flush of shame to her cheeks and tears of frustration to her eyes.

'You're sure?' she spluttered. 'You're absolutely positive?'

Treasure smiled. 'Cross my heart and hope to die.'

Sparrow and Mabel had found a huge swathe of smelly seaweed and were now playing tug-of-war. Mabel won and rushed back to Billie and Treasure to proclaim her victory and parade her prize, which she shook vigorously, slapping them both on the legs.

'Bugger! Bugger! Bugger!' Billie yanked her bowler hat down over her eyes and stuck out her bottom lip like a toddler having a tantrum.

'"Bugger" because you just got whipped with wet seaweed or "bugger" because of what I said?' asked Treasure, grinning.

'Bugger because I'm a complete and utter dimwit. And partly because of the seaweed,' she added, rubbing the damp calves of her jeans.

'So, Clive really did used to work for the police?'

Treasure pulled a tennis ball from his pocket and threw it for Sparrow to fetch.

'In a manner of speaking, yes. It wasn't anything official – he wasn't on the payroll – but according to an old colleague of mine they would let him know if they were looking for someone in particular to "help with their enquiries" and he would keep a look-out and give them a shout if he spotted anyone of interest.'

'But why Clive?'

A soggy tennis ball was deposited at Treasure's feet. He lobbed it into the air and then wiped his hands on his jeans. 'Because Clive is a super recogniser.'

'A what?'

'A super recogniser. It means he's one of a tiny percentage of the population who have an extraordinary ability to memorise and recall faces.'

'And he could do that even if he'd only seen someone once or twice?'

'Yes.'

'Even if it was years ago?'

Treasure nodded.

'Bugger!'

'So, that woman Clive showed you in the magazine was very probably the same woman he saw leave you outside Imelda's booth.'

Billie shook her head in disbelief. 'That's right, rub it in!'

'Where's the magazine now?'

Billie looked suitably shamefaced. 'I put it out for recycling,' she admitted. 'But it's not just that. Clive tried to help me. He did something kind and I dismissed it. I judged him because he's not like everyone else, and I decided that made him less ... what? I don't even know. But it made it easy for me to discount what he said – to trivialise it and him. And now it turns out that the fact that he's not like everyone else is the very reason why I should have listened to him and believed him. I'm thoroughly ashamed of myself.'

'You should be.' Treasure was serious. 'But at least you've realised your mistake, and now you can make it up to him.'

'How?'

'I've no idea. But I'm sure you'll think of something.'

Sparrow and Mabel were tiring now and trotted along in front of them, their tails high and their pink tongues lolling from the sides of their mouths.

'Can't you at least remember the name of the woman in the magazine?'

Billie frowned in concentration. 'It was a Lady something beginning with L. Lady Longhorn!'

Treasure laughed. 'Well at least it gives us something to Google. And I do have some good news for you too.'

'Well, praise the Lord! What is it?'

'My cousin, Jeanie – the one who used to work at Larkins when Imelda was there – she's coming over from France in a couple of weeks. She's singing at Twinwood Festival but she's stopping off here for a few days first. Maybe she'll be able to tell you more about the people in that photograph Imelda gave you.'

Billie managed a half-smile.

'Come on, trouble,' Treasure teased. 'I'll buy you a drink.'

56

1995

Beaumont Hall was approached through an enormous pair of black and gold wrought-iron gates, and thereafter along a pristine gravel drive bordered by dark, shadowy woodland underplanted with purple and pink rhododendrons. The drive was long; no doubt intended to heighten the anticipation of the visitor to the splendour that lay ahead. Imelda had been driving for twenty minutes and there was still no sign of the house. She had been invited by a Lady Longhorn to give readings for her weekend guests at her country pile. The men had clay shooting and trout fishing to keep them occupied but their wives expected to be entertained and Lady Longhorn had thought that 'tarot readings and the like' might be just the thing. This type of booking was becoming increasingly popular and Imelda had done several to date. They were lucrative and gave her the opportunity to see inside some of the country's finest homes, even if she didn't always enjoy meeting their residents. Imelda didn't know Lady Longhorn but assumed that she had been given her name by one of her friends or acquaintances who had already had a reading.

When she turned the final bend, the woods fell away to reveal acres of gently undulating grassland grazed by a herd of fallow deer. The house itself was an elegant and impressive stone edifice of crisp architectural symmetry with mullion windows that winked in the sunlight and a balcony than ran almost the entire length of the first floor. On the roof, battalions of tall chimneys stood to attention behind a balustrade. The front elevation looked out over a lake where several swans drifted languorously through water that mirrored the blue sky above. Imelda was disappointed. There was no question that Beaumont Hall was magnificent, but the architect's rigid adherence to the strictures of good taste had rendered the overall effect rather bland. Imelda had hoped for rebellious gothic turrets, mysterious attic rooms, perhaps a clock tower and certainly a tangle of wisteria clinging to the wall and framing the doors and windows. She followed the drive round to the side of the house where a dozen or so cars were already parked, and left her 'vintage' Jaguar next to a considerably newer model. She was welcomed at the front door (Imelda refused to use the servants' entrance as she had been instructed) by the housekeeper, who showed her through to a bright, sunny room overlooking the lake where a round table and two chairs had been set out for her to use.

'Would you like some tea while you wait?' the housekeeper asked.

'That would be lovely. Earl Grey with lemon, please.'

The housekeeper nodded and left Imelda to unpack her velvet cloth, crystal ball and tarot cards. When she returned with the tea tray, the housekeeper glanced at the tools of Imelda's trade. A tiny sneer curled her upper lip.

'You do know that these la-di-da ladies don't believe a word of any of this? It's just something to keep them quiet until cocktails are served before dinner.'

Imelda smiled. 'Well, perhaps I can change their minds. Would you like me to do a reading for you?'

The housekeeper started as though she'd been scalded. 'Certainly not! Lady Longhorn would have a fit! And besides,' she added, remembering her scepticism just in time, 'it's a load of nonsense.'

That afternoon, Imelda read for a steady stream of well-heeled women who padded across the Persian carpet in their Jimmy Choos, pressed their Wolford-clad legs together and folded them primly to one side as they sat in the chair opposite her. Their questions were familiar and predictable. Money and sex, marriage and divorce, birthrights and betrayals featured heavily. The sole exceptions were a woman who wanted to know how she could prevent sawfly destroying her gooseberry crop (Imelda referred her to *Gardeners' Question Time*) and another needing help to dissuade her husband (who was 'in trade', she had whispered) from holding his knife like a pen when he was eating. Imelda didn't need the cards for that one either.

'Lay a pen and a fork at his place setting for meals,' she advised. 'I think he'll get the message.'

At just past five o'clock, Imelda stood up, stretched and wandered over to the window. The surface of the lake was now mottled by the reflection of glowering storm clouds and the swans bobbed on the water, their feathers ruffled by a gathering breeze. There was no knock to announce the entrance of Lady Longhorn.

'Good afternoon, Madame Burova. We spoke on the telephone. I'm Lady Longhorn.'

She offered Imelda her hand. As the skin of their palms met, Imelda felt an ominous prickle of recognition, not of the woman herself but of her cold nature.

'Would you read my cards for me?'

'Do you believe in tarot, Lady Longhorn?'

'I'll answer that after you've read my cards,' Lady Longhorn replied.

Imelda handed her the pack to shuffle and then laid the cards in a spread known as the Gateway of Fate that she used to give a general reading rather than to answer specific questions.

'You've always had plenty of money, but it hasn't always been good for you. It hasn't always made you happy.'

'I could hardly be poor and living in a place like this,' Lady Longhorn replied.

'You have a solid relationship with your husband, but you've never been in love with him. He's not your soulmate. In fact, you lead largely separate lives.'

'In a house this size, that's not terribly difficult. And I don't believe in soulmates. They're the stuff of Mills and Boon, not real men and women.'

Imelda worked through the cards, revealing that Lady Longhorn had two sons. 'An heir and a spare,' she confirmed wryly, and had a privileged but rather empty life that looked set to continue, uninterrupted by anything of interest or excitement. But there was one card that intrigued Imelda.

'You have a daughter,' she said, pointing at the moon on the table. 'But she's a secret in your past. You never speak about her, do you – Vivienne?'

Imelda couldn't pinpoint the exact moment that she had recognised her. But the more she spoke, and the more Imelda looked into those grey eyes, the more certain she became that this was the woman she had despised for more than twenty years. Vivienne met her gaze defiantly.

'Am I right in believing that you can never repeat what passes between you and a client during a reading?'

Imelda nodded.

'Well then, it seems I must acknowledge that perhaps the cards have some validity. If, indeed, that is how you found out about the girl.'

'How else could I possibly know?'

'Perhaps you saw me leave her in the doorway of your booth.'

It took Imelda a moment to register what she was saying.

'You? It was you?'

Vivienne leaned back in her chair and sighed. 'Yes, Madame Burova, it was me. And spare me any sancti-monious outrage. I was young and spoilt and made some very bad decisions' – she looked directly at Imelda – 'which I regret. But I can't change the past.' She sounded recalcitrant rather than remorseful.

'But why did you abandon her? Why have her at all if you didn't want her?'

'You mean why didn't I have an abortion? Honestly, I'm not sure. I made an appointment – even got as far as the clinic, but I couldn't do it. Perhaps I'm not made out of stone after all,' she added sardonically.

'Then why didn't you have her adopted?'

'Because I didn't want to leave a trail. I wanted to go back to my old life and pretend that she had never existed – a clean slate. I couldn't have my entire future jeopardised by one stupid mistake. I booked into the maternity home under a false name. It was expensive, and money can smooth out any number of creases and silence awkward questions. When I checked out, I simply told them that I was going home.'

'So why did you leave her outside my booth?'

Vivienne shrugged. 'It was an impulse. I knew she'd be quickly found there. And Cillian thought very highly of you,' she added pointedly.

Imelda had been wondering how long Vivienne would be able to resist mentioning his name.

'Who was the father?'

'I'm sure you have your suspicions, but *he* never knew.'

Imelda was tired. She wanted to go home. 'Is that why you brought me here, to taunt me? It certainly wasn't to entertain your lady guests, was it?'

'You're right. Although it seems you were quite a hit with them. No, I invited you here because I want to ask you a favour.'

Imelda could hardly believe what she was hearing, but she was curious to learn whatever it was that Vivienne had the audacity to ask.

'This year will be the girl's twenty-first birthday. I have no wish ever to meet her or have any part in her life, but I do feel some sense of responsibility and I have some things that I would like you to pass on to her,' Vivienne said, handing Imelda two envelopes. 'Perhaps not now, but at some point in the future. I'll leave it to your discretion as to when you think she might benefit from them most.'

'What are they?' asked Imelda, turning the envelopes over in her hands.

'One is a contribution towards her financial security and the other is a photograph of her father.'

Now Imelda understood. The photograph was the bait to ensure that she was hooked.

'Why not get a solicitor to handle it for you? I thought you said that money could smooth out any creases and silence any questions?'

Vivienne smiled coldly. 'It can also buy loyalty. My husband is a very powerful man. His currency has a far better exchange rate than mine. If I were to do this officially, there's a risk that he would find out, and that's not a risk that I'm prepared to take.'

'And exactly how do you expect me to find your daughter?'

Vivienne flinched at Imelda's choice of words. 'You're a very resourceful woman, Madame Burova. I'm sure you'll find a way.'

'But how do you know you can trust me? I could just leave with the envelopes and do what I like with them.'

'You could, but you won't. You're far too honourable. And besides, you wouldn't want to deprive the innocent party.'

Imelda packed up her things and shoved the envelopes into her bag. 'You know nothing about me.

Whether I'll keep your secret and do what you ask is a question you'll have to ask yourself every day. Goodbye Lady Longhorn.' And with a smile, Imelda closed the door quietly behind her.

As she climbed into her car, the first drops of rain splattered onto the windscreen. She slammed the door shut and jammed the key into the ignition. She resisted the temptation to rev the engine to vent her rising temper but made sure that the Jag's wheels span on the gravel as she sped away, showering the neighbouring car with stony shrapnel and leaving ugly grooves on the surface of the car park. Imelda was desperate to open the envelope containing the photograph, but not until she had left that abominable woman's property. A sob caught in her throat and she swallowed it down, furious that Vivienne could still get to her after all these years. The only person that Vivienne had ever cared about was herself, and Imelda could see that neither marriage, motherhood nor maturity had changed that. Vivienne's instinct for self-preservation above all else was visceral. *This year will be the girl's twenty-first birthday*, the same age Cillian's child would have been had she lived. The baby girl that Imelda had cherished but her body had been unable to keep safe long enough for her to be born alive. And then she had found *the girl*, outside the booth, just days after her own baby should have been born – a beautiful, healthy but unwanted baby girl, and a knife to her heart. It had been heartbreaking to hand her over and now she knew that it had been Vivienne's doing. But she promised herself that she wouldn't let her own feelings prevent her from doing what was right for Vivienne's daughter. She would make sure that one day the envelopes were delivered.

She reached for the chain around her neck and squeezed the points of a star hard between her finger and thumb, using the pain to help her focus on the road ahead. Eventually she saw the gates through the driving rain. As soon as she found a safe spot she pulled over and switched off the engine. The rain drummed on the car roof and Imelda sat very still and listened for a moment, before reaching into her bag and retrieving the envelope. She ripped it open, sick with fear that she would see the face of the man whom she would always love. And there he was, smiling. But he wasn't alone, and Imelda knew now that she'd been played.

57

Now

Imelda had retrieved the magazine from a pile waiting to go into the recycling bin. She was curious as to how it had got there. It didn't look like Billie's type of reading material and it certainly wasn't hers. She had flicked idly through the pages with little interest until she had come across the feature on Beaumont Hall. The house and its mistress were a perfect match; both elegant bastions of upper-class smugness and cold convention. This morning when they had arrived at the booth, Imelda had finally asked Billie about the magazine and Billie had told her all about Clive and his undercover work for the police and how he was absolutely sure that Lady Longhorn was Billie's mother.

'It's a good thing that I rescued it from the bin, then,' was Imelda's only reply. Billie had gone off with Mabel to see if she could find Clive and buy him a morning coffee and a pastry as part of her mission to recompense him for the fact that she had doubted his word.

'But he doesn't even know that you did,' Imelda had reminded her with a smile.

'Maybe not, but I do,' Billie had replied.

Imelda sat in the doorway of the booth watching the promenade slowly come to life like an emerging colony of ants under the canopy of a perfect blue summer sky.

'Good morning, Madame Burova. It's wonderful to see you again.'

Imelda shielded her eyes from the sun. The woman standing in front of her looked as though she had just walked off a film set. Her dark hair was styled into perfect curls pulled back on one side and fastened behind her ear with a silk rose. Her dress had a fitted bodice and a nipped-in waist with a generously flared skirt, and her shoes were sling-back kitten heels with scarlet bows. But for all this, it was her voice that truly caught Imelda's attention; rich and smoky like a fine malt whiskey. It was familiar too, but a memory from long ago that took a while to surface. As the woman waited patiently, her smile grew broader.

'Jeanie! Jeanie Rogers! Well, look at you!'

Imelda stood up and held her at arm's length, staring at her in disbelief before pulling her in close for a hug.

'Treasure told me that a woman called Billie wants to talk to me about Larkins and that I would probably find her here,' Jeanie said when Imelda had finally released her.

'That's right. She's gone out with Mabel, my dog, but I doubt she'll be long. Why don't you come in and sit down for a bit?'

Jeanie followed Imelda inside the booth. 'Treasure said that Billie had a little shop inside the booth, but surely you haven't stopped giving readings, have you?'

Imelda shook her head. 'I tried to retire, but I missed it too much.'

'I never forgot the reading you gave me at Larkins. You told me that singing would bring me happiness and great success.'

'And the cards were right, weren't they?'

'Yes. But that reading gave me the guts to try – to follow my dream.'

'With a voice like yours, you were never going to fail.'

'Do you have any idea what Billie wants to talk to me about? I asked Treasure, but all he would say was that it wasn't his story to tell.'

'I have a pretty good idea. And I don't mind telling you, because it's partly my story too.'

Jeanie sat up very straight in her chair as though bracing herself for what was to come.

'A few days after you left Larkins all those years ago to work in London, a baby was abandoned in the doorway of my booth. A baby girl, and I found her.' Imelda watched Jeanie's face, trying to gauge her reaction, but so far, she had only registered surprise.

'The child was adopted but knew nothing about it until both her adoptive parents had died. That child was Billie and she's trying to find out who her birth parents are.

'Her birth mother found a way of passing some things on to Billie without revealing her own identity, including a photograph of her father. But it's a group photograph and Billie has no idea which of the men is her father.'

Jeanie remained very still and said nothing.

'It's a photograph of the entertainment staff at Larkins at the time when you and I both worked there. I think that Billie just wants to ask you what you remember about the people in the photograph.'

'Billie's quite an unusual name, isn't it?' Imelda could see the disquiet beginning to cloud Jeanie's face.

'Yes. She was wearing a silver bracelet engraved with her name when I found her.'

This detail clearly unsettled Jeanie.

'And does Billie have any idea who her birth mother might be?'

Imelda handed Jeanie the magazine, which was open at the appropriate page.

'A witness believes that he saw that woman abandon Billie as a baby.'

Jeanie stared at the pictures, clearly trying to make sense of what she had just heard and what she was seeing. Eventually she shook her head.

'Oh God, Imelda. What did she do?'

'Did you know about the baby?'

'Of course I did. I ran around helping her while she was pregnant, doing her shopping and keeping it a secret. She made me promise never to tell a soul. I felt sorry for her. Despite her cockiness, she seemed so lost and I was the only friend she had. But I wonder now how much of it was just an act to get what she wanted. I visited her in the maternity home the day before I went to London and she seemed fine – too fine, actually, for someone who was about to give up their child. But then maybe that was an act too – a self-preservation thing.' Jeanie shrugged. 'I took the bracelet as a present. I wanted the baby at least to have a name even if it was only temporary. Vivienne told me that she was handing her over for adoption and then she was going home so that her mother could find her a suitable husband.'

'Well, it certainly seems as though she succeeded in that,' Imelda replied ruefully.

'I couldn't understand why she would settle for such an empty life.' Jeanie glanced at her watch. 'I'm really sorry, Imelda, but I've got to get going. I promised Auntie Diamond I'd pop in and see her at the care home.'

'Well, give her my love. Look, I'm having a bit of a party at mine tomorrow afternoon. It's my birthday. Why don't you come along and bring your husband, too. You can chat to Billie there.'

'I'd love to!'

'Good. Treasure's coming so he can show you where it is.'

Jeanie got up to leave, but Imelda couldn't let her go without asking.

'Did Vivienne tell you who the father was?'

Jeanie looked a little sheepish. 'She did. But it was just a one-off. That night when there was the big fight in the entertainment lounge and everything got smashed up. She was drunk, he was drunk. To be honest, I think she did it to bolster her bruised ego and he was flattered that she finally paid him some attention.'

Jeanie saw the confusion in Imelda's face and suddenly the awful realisation dawned.

'Oh, Jesus, Imelda! You surely never thought, never believed for one moment that it was Cillian?'

'Happy birthday to you!'

The assembled party raised their glasses and toasted Imelda's health and happiness. They were sitting outside in the jasmine-scented garden drinking champagne and eating birthday cake. Imelda sat down for a moment on the steps of the vardo with Mabel, who had been allowed a tiny piece of cake, promptly spat it out and was now sulking until someone gave her a palate-cleansing sausage. She was also displeased with Sparrow, who was sitting at Treasure's feet having not only eaten his own piece of cake but also the piece that she had spat out. Imelda reached for the chain around her neck and the precious memories of a birthday long ago, washed clean and bright by a simple truth. Her friends all seemed to be enjoying themselves. Treasure and Billie were chatting to Jeanie's husband. Jeanie, who had arrived just in time for the toast, was thrilled to be reunited with Henry but kept calling him Charlie, and Esther was regaling MI5 Clive with salacious tales from her salon. Imelda had been extremely surprised and delighted when Clive had accepted her invitation on the proviso that 'I might not stay long', and whilst she couldn't swear that he was exactly enjoying himself, at least he'd stopped looking desperately in the direction of the door. Imelda got up and wandered over to join the others.

'I told Billie about our chat yesterday. She was over the moon. Have you met her yet?' she asked Jeanie.

'Not yet. I've been too busy chatting to this gorgeous man,' Jeanie replied, squeezing Henry's hand. 'Come on, Charlie, let's top up everyone's glasses and then we can reminisce about Larkins.'

They strolled off arm in arm towards the kitchen to collect refill bottles of bubbly.

They were gone some time.

'I think those two have got lost,' complained Esther, waving her empty glass at Imelda.

'I'm sure they're just gossiping about the good old days,' Imelda replied, knowing exactly what they were talking about. At that moment, Jeanie and Henry reappeared.

'What on earth kept you?' chided Esther. 'I'm parched.' And then she noticed Henry's pale face and slightly deranged grin.

'Are you all right? You look a bit peculiar.'

Henry glanced around until he caught sight of Billie and then he laughed, and his eyes filled with tears. 'I'm fine,' he said, 'but I'd like you all to know that I've just given birth to a daughter!'

Billie lay in bed talking to her mum and dad. Imelda's party had gone on longer than anyone had anticipated. Following Henry's revelation there had been astonishment, congratulations, explanations, tears, laughter and hours of storytelling about their time at Larkins. Imelda had broken the news to Billie the night before, but they had agreed that Jeanie should be the one to tell Henry. It was now a little after 2 a.m. and Henry was asleep in the guest room having drunk far too much champagne to be trusted to get home safe and sound.

'Remember what happened last time you were this drunk?' Jeanie had teased him. 'We need to put you to bed – alone – and lock the door for your own safety!'

'You'd really like him,' Billie said. 'He's kind and funny. He plays the piano at St Pancras and he's a John Betjeman enthusiast. He didn't know anything about me! He only slept with Lady L once, back when she was plain old Vivienne. It sounds as though he was really drunk and she seduced him – he was younger than her.'

Billie paused for a moment, realising that this probably wasn't creating the impression of her birth father that she was aiming for. 'He's got three rescue chickens called Hilda Ogden, Minnie Caldwell and Ena Sharples,' she added, hoping to redress the balance in Henry's favour. 'And yes, Dad, I know he was married to a man and that's probably a bit tricky for you to understand but trust me, you two would have got on like a house on fire.' And then the thought suddenly struck her that the three of them could all have been in St Pancras at the same time. She could have been there with one dad whilst the other was playing the piano. They may have even stopped to listen to him for a while. Billie gazed out through the open curtains at the moon. Imelda had told her that its meaning in the tarot pack was a daughter or someone a little crazy. Billie felt like both of those right now. But in a good way. She had been horrified to discover that Imelda and Cillian had been so in love and about the baby they had lost, but only because she had been so insensitive about wanting Cillian to be her father, and she now realised how much that must have hurt Imelda. She considered herself very lucky to have Henry – who was not only a complete sweetheart, but also still alive! And as for Lady L – that damn magazine had been ceremoniously dumped in the bin once and for all.

58

Now

Sunlight sparkled on the water in the harbour like handfuls of strewn stars, and little boats gently bobbed up and down, their masts chinking in the breeze. Imelda, Esther and Henry sat outside the pub in Baltimore, County Cork, admiring the view. The trip to Cillian's hometown had been a birthday present from Imelda's friends, and Esther and Henry had volunteered to accompany her while Mabel stayed at home and kept an eye on Star, Treasure and Billie. Imelda had never been to Baltimore. She had always planned to, but her plans had never come to fruition. Until now. She had never met any of Cillian's family or even visited his grave. She had written to his mother shortly after his death and had received a polite but brief reply. She worried that she had been presumptuous; that their relationship had been too short-lived to justify any claim of grief or kinship on her part. But now, finally, she was here in the place where Cillian had been born and raised. She could see the beacon that he had told her about up on the headland. Lot's Wife, the locals called it, after the biblical woman who turned into a pillar of salt. It looked like a fat, white skittle.

'Are you ready?' Henry asked her. 'Or would you like another drink first? Dutch courage,' he teased.

Imelda drained her glass and stood up. 'I'm as ready as I'll ever be.'

Esther and Henry walked her the short distance from the pub to the gate of a terraced house with a green door that overlooked the entrance to the harbour. Its tiny front garden was full of pots brimming with daisies and geraniums. Henry and Esther ushered her through the gate and then waited while she rang the doorbell. As soon as the door opened, they turned and walked away. Imelda felt sick with excitement and sick with fear that she had travelled all this way and might be met with bewilderment or worse still, hostility. The woman at the door was in her late sixties and Imelda knew from her Facebook profile that she had been christened Fionnuala after her great-granny, but everyone called her Nuala. She was married to James O'Riley, had four children, nine grandchildren and two wire-haired daschunds. She enjoyed gardening, cooking, and music by The Pogues and was a massive *Peaky Blinders* fan. She was also Cillian Byrne's baby sister. She had his eyes. She smiled at Imelda expectantly.

'I'm sorry to just turn up like this, but I'm visiting the area with friends and I just wanted to say "hello" while I was here . . .' Imelda's words trailed away uncertainly.

'Right,' said the woman, still smiling. 'And will you be saying hello to everyone in Baltimore?'

Imelda realised her crucial omission and laughed. 'Oh God no, I'm sorry. I meant to say I used to know your brother – my name's Imelda Burova – but it was a long time ago.'

The woman shook her head. 'I can't believe it! I bloody knew it! James!' she called back into the house. 'Get your-self down here at once and see who's come.' She took Imelda by the arm and led her inside the house where she almost squeezed the life out of her in an emotional hug.

'I always said you'd come. I knew you would. Mind you, you've kept us waiting long enough!'

'I'm sorry. I meant to come sooner, but things were – complicated. I didn't even know if Cillian had mentioned me at all.'

'Mentioned you? Sure, you were all he talked about that weekend. We were sick of hearing about you! No, just kidding! He said that he'd found his perfect woman and that next time he came home you'd be coming with him. We couldn't wait to meet you.'

Over the next couple of hours Nuala shared stories of Cillian that spanned the years from a cheeky little boy to a handsome young daredevil. She showed Imelda photographs and when it was time for her to leave, Nuala gave her several to take with her.

'Be sure to come again tomorrow and I'll give you and your friends a guided tour of Baltimore and then you can all come back here for your tea.'

Imelda promised that she would.

'And one more thing before you go. Thank you. Because of you, when Cillian died, he was the happiest man alive. I can't tell you how much of a comfort that has been to me for all these years.'

Imelda decided to walk for a little before she joined Esther and Henry back at the hotel. She wanted to bask in the happiness of knowing that Cillian had shared his feelings for her with his family. She set off along the clifftop towards the beacon. The colours of the sea, the sky, the grass and the rocks were as bright and fresh as the wind that whipped her dress around her calves and her hair across her face. She paused for a moment to catch her breath and looked up at the beacon that dazzled white in the sunlight. In the distance, a figure stood on the headland – a lone sentinel staring out to sea and by his side a loping, long-legged dog. He seemed oblivious to everything except the infinite expanse of sky and water before him. But then he turned towards Imelda and raised his hand in greeting. She raised her hand to her lips and blew a kiss in return.

'I love you,' she whispered. 'I always have.' Tears blurred her eyes and by the time they had fallen, the man and the dog had gone.

A few thoughts and more than a few thanks

There were times when I thought I would never finish this book. Mum and Dad both died while I was writing it and I miss them more than I can say. But even in their final days they would always ask 'How's the book coming?'. Well, you guys, I got there in the end. Thank you for everything you sacrificed to make sure that my life was easier than yours and that I would have the opportunity and belief to follow my dreams. It took me a while, but I am so grateful that you lived long enough to share it with me.

Although I write fiction, I believe that for my stories to read authentically some elements must have their foundations in fact. Parts of this novel are based in the UK in the early 1970s, in a place and time where I grew up, and I have portrayed society as I remember it rather than how I would wish it to have been. The first legislation protecting individuals from discrimination on the grounds of race, gender and marital status had yet to come into force and I experienced first-hand the cultural, social and political climate that prevailed on the streets, in the playground, on the TV and radio and in the press. Society was openly racist and sexist, and attitudes and actions that were commonplace then, are painfully unpalatable and rightly condemned today. Motivated by the injustice I witnessed and experienced, I spent ten years of my previous career as a senior race and gender equality advisor, and then as Head of Diversity In Employment for a large local authority that provided a range of public services to a racially diverse community. We have come a long way since then, but we still have a long way to go.

As always, I am indebted to the many people who support me. Thank you to Laura Macdougall, my brilliant agent and friend, for her wisdom and unstinting support. She is simply the best and I am lucky to have her. Thanks also to the whole team at United Agents for all their hard work and to Laura's other authors (affectionately known as Team Laura) for their friendship and encouragement.

Once again, the lovely Lisa Highton has polished my words with her sensitive and skilful editing, and I thank her for her patience, humour, and kindly tolerance of my foibles. She's an absolute brick (in the nicest, most elegant way). Thanks also to all the good people at Two Roads, particularly Alice Herbert, Jess Kim, and Emma Petfield, and to Cari Rosen for doing a splendid job of copyediting, and Amber Burlinson for proofreading. A special thank you to Sarah Christie who has designed my beautiful covers since the beginning and who worked with the amazing Jordan Bolton on our new look.

A massive thank you to all the book bloggers, reviewers, booksellers and librarians who help readers to find my books and heartfelt thanks, as always, to my wonderful readers for all their messages, for sharing their lives with me (and photos of their dogs) and for buying and reading my books.

In preparation for this novel, I spent many weeks learning to read Tarot cards. My teacher is a wonderful woman called Sue Peppiatt who has been performing mediumship, reading palms, crystal ball and Tarot cards for over thirty years. At my request, Sue was the first person to read this book, because I wanted to ensure that, as far as possible, I had written knowledgably and respectfully about Imelda and Shunty-Mae; their culture, gifts and profession. I am hugely grateful to Sue for her generosity in sharing her extensive knowledge and experience, for her patient teaching and for her advice and guidance regarding *Madame Burova*. I couldn't have done it without her.

I should also mention Eva Petulengro, whose life story was the inspiration for *Madame Burova*. She was born into a traditional Romany family and lived and worked in Brighton reading palms and Tarot cards from the age of twenty. She became a famous clairvoyant and fortune teller and her booth can still be seen on the sea front. Her autobiographical books, *Caravans and Wedding Bands* and *The Girl in the Painted Caravan*, were an essential part of my research.

I must also thank Dr Katya Burova – an incredible woman and a true force of nature – for her friendship and the loan of her name.

Howard Travis is an officer and a gentleman, and I owe him several pints. He facilitated my research on prisons in the UK and various police related matters. He escorted me on my mission to discover the truth about 'super recognisers' and introduced me to Dave Graney whose help was invaluable – thank you, Dave.

Thank you to the England Cricket Team for your stunning performances in 2019 and to the BBC 5 Live commentary team who kept me sane through a tough summer.

Thank you to Paloma Faith for her gut-wrenchingly beautiful song, 'Only Love Can Hurt Like This', which I played endlessly while writing about Imelda and Cillian.

And finally – thank you to Paul, Squadron Leader Timothy Bear, Zachariah Popov and Moo Moo for being my safe harbour in stormy seas.

Ruth Hogan

About the Author

Ruth Hogan was brought up in a house full of books and grew up with a passion for reading and writing. She loved dogs and ponies, seaside piers, snow globes and cemeteries. As a child she considered becoming a vet, show jumper, Eskimo, gravedigger, and once, very briefly, a nun.

She studied English and Drama at Goldsmiths College, University of London where she hennaed her hair, wore dungarees and aspired to be the fourth member of Bananarama. After graduating she foolishly got a proper job, and for ten years had a successful if uninspiring career in local government before a car accident left her unable to work full-time and was the kick up the butt she needed to start writing seriously.

It was all going well, but then in 2012 she got cancer, which was bloody inconvenient but precipitated an exciting hair journey from bald to a peroxide blonde Annie Lennox crop. When chemo kept her up all night, she passed the time writing and the eventual result was her debut novel *The Keeper of Lost Things*. Since then she has published two further novels, *The Wisdom of Sally Red Shoes* and *Queenie Malone's Paradise Hotel*, and for her fourth, *Madame Burova*, she learnt to read Tarot cards and developed a hankering for a traditional vardo and pony.

She is now living the dream (and occasionally nightmare!) as a full-time writer in a chaotic Victorian house with an assortment of rescue dogs and her long-suffering husband. She describes herself as a magpie; always collecting treasures (or 'junk' depending on your point of view) and a huge John Betjeman fan. She still loves seaside piers, particularly The Palace Pier at Brighton and would very much like a full-size galloping horses carousel in her back garden.

A Word About Our Covers

When we first published *The Keeper of Lost Things* in 2017, we created what would become an iconic jacket design. One million copies later, and with Ruth on her fourth book, we thought it was a good opportunity to look at relaunching with a brand new cover approach. It was very important to us that this new vision reflected the marvellously rich world of Ruth Hogan's stories and her larger-than-life characters. Acting on a recommendation from fellow designer Sara Marafini, our Design Manager for all Ruth's books, Sarah Christie, approached designer Jordan Bolton whose work in miniature seemed to be the perfect marriage of concept and content. We hope you agree that we have produced beautiful jewel like covers which really complement Ruth's writing. – *Lisa Highton, Publisher, Two Roads*

'Charming', 'uplifting' and 'joyful' was the brief I was given, and Jordan excelled. With painstaking care, he made these book jackets come to life, successfully creating the wonderfully unique experience of starting an adventure with Ruth . . . – *Sarah Christie*

I started by making a miniature shop window from foamboard and finding the most evocative objects mentioned in each book. Ruth's world has a particular vintage aesthetic, which meant recreating many of the items from scratch with moulding clay, which I then painted, or by finding pieces and adapting them to fit our vision. To add a personal touch, some of the items actually belonged to Ruth, such as her pink Doc Martens on *Madame Burova*. All objects were life-sized and photographed individually. I then printed them off as miniature cardboard versions, placed them in the shop window, and photographed them. Once I uploaded these photographs to my computer, I overlaid the original photo of the objects on top so they would have the detail of the life-size objects and give the final cover the impression of being the size of an actual shop window.

Reading fiction is such a unique experience. More so than any other art form, it asks readers to bring your lives and memories to fill in the blanks, to create that little movie playing in your head as you read. It asks you not only to read but to create. The book you are holding was created by the author, by the publishing company, by the cover designer, and by the manufacturer, but it is not finished until it has been read by you, and the story you read will not be the same as any other.

– *Jordan Bolton*

A longer version of this article can be found at www.ruthhogan.co.uk
Follow Jordan Bolton 📷 @jordanboltondesign

PILL 05-05-21.

PILLGWENLLY.